SHADOW OVER CEDAR KEY

by the same author

The first Brandy O'Bannon mystery:

Trace Their Shadows

SHADOW OVER CEDAR KEY

A Brandy O'Bannon Mystery

Ann Turner Cook

To Betty, an attentive listener at my Luty book talk,

Ann Turner Cook
(the Gerber baby)

Mystery and Suspense Press

New York Lincoln Shanghai

SHADOW OVER CEDAR KEY
A Brandy O'Bannon Mystery

Mystery and Suspense Press
an imprint of iUniverse, Inc.

For information address:
iUniverse, Inc.
2021 Pine Lake Road, Suite 100
Lincoln, NE 68512
www.iuniverse.com

ISBN: 0-595-27843-4

Printed in the United States of America

*To my husband, Jim, who is always
patiently supportive,*

*and to our four children, Jan, Carol, Cliff, and
Kathy, who daily honor the bond between mother
and child*

Foreword

Once the center of commerce on the Gulf coast of Florida, the hamlet of Cedar Key still thrives—as it has since 1859—at the end of its isolated road, about 130 miles north of Tampa and St. Petersburg. Most of the time it goes about its quiet business of crab and oyster fishing, except for a lively seafood festival in October and another for art in April. Visitors have been tip-toeing in and out of this laid-back nineteenth century village for years, fearful that it might succumb to the tourist trade like most of old Florida.

But this pioneer community of about one thousand has survived almost intact. The Cedar Key Historical Society featured in the novel still maintains its museum, the walking tour, and its authentic old homes. The centerpiece and Grande Dame of the town remains the 145 year old Island Hotel.

A few miles to the north lies Shell Mound, brooding above the waters of the Gulf as it has for perhaps twenty-five centuries. According to reports in the local newspaper, the site is still haunted by a woman with a round light, the ghost story that intrigues our reporter. The best account of this specter appears in an October 31, 1982, *St. Petersburg Times* Halloween story by Mark Allan Ralls. Historic details about the Island Hotel come from "Island Hotel: Cedar Key's Old Gray Lady," *North Florida Living*, April 1986.

As depicted, Cedar Key was pummeled by the well-documented hurricanes of 1950 and 1972, the rogue Easy with much more deadly force than the later Agnes, although neither actually cost lives.

The plundering of the forests and the oyster beds during the nineteenth and early twentieth centuries were true disasters, which contemporary environmentalists now work to correct.

The characters, however, are all fictional. The hotel has never been owned by a Scotsman. Five generation families do exist in Cedar Key, but none to my knowledge by the names of Waters and Thompson. The golden retriever Meg, however, was real. She lay at my feet while many of these chapters were written and seemed gratified to have a key role.

Because the novel has a 1992 setting, the research was conducted then and reflects that time period. For example, the telephone company has plucked the quaint phone booth from the hotel lobby, a victim of the ubiquitous cell phone. Still, the hotel retains its historic charm.

I owe a special debt to Molly Brown, once a member of the Island Hotel staff, who first told me of the hotel basement and later gave me a tour of its dusty compartments. I also want to thank Harriet Smith, a local naturalist, for information about the area, and my newspaper friend Lenora Lake Guidry for her insights.

I am especially grateful for the cooperation of the Levy County Sheriff's Office of Florida and the Cedar Key Police Department.

Sheriff Walter C. Heinrich, Retired, of Hillsborough County, advised me on the crime scene and the potential of laser fingerprinting. I also need to thank literary agent Lettie Lee of the Ann Elmo Agency in New York, who believed my books should be published, and most important, editor and Life Enrichment Center writing instructor Staci Backauskas, whose editorial assistance was invaluable.

The Island Hotel abounds in legends—some ghostly. The current owner will probably be glad to draw up a chair in the lobby, turn through the album of the hotel's historic photographs, and explain to guests its sometimes eerie and always impressive past.

PROLOGUE

▼

Allison did not think about death when she arrived in Cedar Key, only about the approaching storm. Tense and shaking, she carried her little girl from the car through the wind and rain and up the cabin steps. But the hurricane was not what she feared most.

The downpour stung the toddler's cheeks and she whimpered. Allison made a shushing sound, immediately lost in the creak of tree trunks and the rush of water along the shore. Wind shrilled through the cabbage palms beside the road, where three other resort cottages stood dark and silent.

Behind her the car trunk slammed shut. Allison could see the sturdy stranger in a raincoat, her suitcase in one hand, splashing around beside the driver's side. She pushed open the unlocked door and stepped into the bleak front room. Without this good Samaritan, they would still be stranded at the café near the bus stop, twenty-three miles from Cedar Key. She could find no taxi cab, no local bus service, only this friendly driver on the way home before the storm.

Her heavy bag landed with a thud beside a tattered day bed. "If the hurricane hits at all," her rescuer said, "it'll come ashore in the next two, three hours. If it gets bad, I'll come back. Take you to the school house. Be ready in case."

Allison had heard from her aunt about these occasional hurricanes. Cedar Key, linked by bridges to the Florida mainland, made a vulnerable target. Through a back window above the kitchen table she could see curling white spray, could hear the pounding of surf. The sky boiled with mammoth black shapes.

The stranger dropped the sodden newspaper she had bought on the table, snapped on a gas heater in one dim corner, and handed her a heavy flashlight from a shelf over the stove. "Electricity's gone off. It'll be dark soon." From the musty smell, she knew no one had recently stayed here.

Allison remembered her aunt's instructions when she left New York. "I should make a local call."

"You'll have to wait until tomorrow. Phones are out." The door opened again to a blast of cold air, closed, and she could hear her benefactor sloshing back down the few steps.

Allison unwrapped the damp blanket from around her two-year old and carried her little girl down a short hall and into the only bedroom. She'd been able to buy milk and hamburgers at the café, but the child was tired. Her tiny arm drooped, fingers still clutching her blue terry cloth teddy bear. She'd had three days of smelly strangers, unfamiliar bus stations, her mother's constant tension, then the last long drive in the fading light.

Allison pulled down the spread and laid her on the double bed. Brushing back her silky hair, she bent to kiss the pinched little face. "We're finally here, Bee." She pulled off the child's slip-on shoes, decided to leave her in the pink bib overalls, and tucked a quilt around her. Rain beat against the window. "We may move again tonight. Right now you and bear have a nice sleep."

For a minute Allison sat on the bed, hands clenched, a slim young figure in the shadowy room. She felt sure she had more than enough money to last until she found a job. She planned to hold a comfortable amount in reserve. When Allison had opened her thick billfold in the café, the cashier warned her about carrying so much cash, but she had no choice. Now she wouldn't have the hotel bill she'd expected. Until the weather cleared, the helpful stranger said she could use the cottage rent free.

After the storm, she would telephone her aunt's friend and open a bank account. The woman did not anticipate her call, but when she saw Allison's letter of introduction, she would surely help her get settled. Allison had planned with care. She would wait tables, work in a gift shop, clean at the one hotel, anything. She would stay in Cedar Key, miles from the nearest highway, in an old town the rest of the world had forgotten. When the window pane rattled, she glanced up, dark hair glistening, olive skin almost white against the shadows. Rain drummed above her. At least her aunt would know they had arrived safely. She had mailed a postcard from the café at Otter Creek.

Rising, she looked again at the child snuggled against her blue bear, dark eyes closed. It was because of little Bee that she was here. She pulled the door partly closed behind her, and to the whine of the rising wind, the little girl slept.

In the chill of the front room, Allison tested the flashlight by sweeping a beam of light across the wooden floor before setting it on an end table. Then she opened the suitcase, pulled out a dry pair of jeans and a fresh shirt, and stepped into the cramped bathroom to strip off her wet blouse and slacks. After laying her rain slicker on a chair, she sank down on the day bed opposite the bedroom door, draped the chenille cover over her legs, and scanned the soggy newspaper. Below stories on the bombing in Viet Nam and the campaign of Senator McGovern, she found a bulletin about Hurricane Agnes. It was plowing up the west coast with winds of ninety-five miles an hour.

She could hear water lap against the pilings under the cottage and wind tear at the roof. Through threadbare curtains at the front window, she watched headlights flicker past through the heavy rain, moving away from the shore. While she wondered whether to dress, bundle Bee in blankets, and find her own way to the school, a car ground to a stop in the driveway and someone ran up the steps, rapped sharply at the door, and shouted, "Open the door! I've come for you. Hurry!"

With relief she leapt up and flung open the door.

*   *   *   *

Loud sounds roused the sleeping child. Angry voices in the next room. A door slammed. Her eyes snapped open. Bee pushed the covers aside and drew the cloth bear closer. She heard her mother's voice, first calm and insistent, then suddenly high and shrill. "No! No!" Something heavy fell with a creak and a grating of metal springs.

Then a scream swelled beyond the wall, and a terrible thumping began. The child's heart jumped. Kicking off the sheet, she struggled with her bear to the edge of the bed, clung to the covers, slipped over the mattress edge to the floor, and crawled under the bed. In the other room she heard a gasp.

Trembling, Bee peered through the half open doorway. She could see the back of a dripping figure lean across the day bed, a long arm raised. For a split second the big flashlight gleamed, then fell again with a thud. Bee no longer heard her mother's voice. Instead the figure turned. The feet strode across the floor toward the bedroom. As the door swung open wider, Bee shrank farther back against the wall. The shoes halted, paused for a minute, then retreated. Again the front door opened. For a moment she thought the person had gone. Then the figure hurried back. It pulled the hood closer around its head, bent, and shuffled backward, dragging a limp form in jeans to the outer door.

The red trail from the day bed to the door meant nothing to the little girl, but paralyzed with fear, she saw her mother's matted hair moving across the threshold, saw her still, pale face. In a flash, the arms reached down from outside and lifted up her mother's body. A car trunk banged shut. Bee crept out from under the bed. She heard splashing outside and an engine started up in the growing darkness. With a sob she tottered into the room.

Her mother was gone, everything she had carried into the room—her suitcase, her purse—was gone. Even the day bed cover. Rain splattered in through the open door, smearing the scarlet puddles on the floor.

She screamed, "Mama!" No answer. The car gone, too. Water swirled at the foot of the cement steps, giant shapes swayed up and down, and the air roared around her. She put one small foot down on the cold step and drew it back. Whimpering, she trotted back into the bedroom, dropped to the floor, and pushed her feet into her slip-ons, the way her mother had taught her. Beneath her, water washed against the planks of the floor.

She struggled to her feet and trudged back toward the outside door. Here she picked up the bear, clung to him, turned around, and backed down the cement steps into the wind, her only thought to find her mother. Behind her the door slammed shut.

Her legs stung with cold. Soon her pink coveralls were plastered against her small body. Her soaked hair flew around her head. She righted herself at the foot of the steps, wavered, and plunged forward, still screaming, "Mama!" The only answer was the bellowing of the wind, a sharp salty smell, and frigid water pelting her face. Waves thundered nearby on big rocks, poured around them, crept near her feet. Wind gusts knocked her over next to a tree, drove her down in the flood up to her knees. She pulled herself up, clutching the trunk, beyond crying. Her eyelids would scarcely open. Where was her mother?

Far, far away she could see a thin glow. Leaving the tree behind, she pushed on through the spinning water toward the distant light, but was caught by a fierce blast and blown into a mass of shrubbery. Gripping the soggy bear, she closed the numb fingers of the other hand around a root and held on.

CHAPTER I

▼

The road ran west under the clear Florida sunlight. As her husband drove over the final bridge into Cedar Key, Brandy O'Bannon opened an untidy notebook and studied the classified ad clipped to a page:

> <u>Wanted</u>: Woman, daughter, 2, moved to Cedar Key June 18, 1972. Urgent message. Contact immediately. Privacy assured. Emergency. Leave phone number for Anthony Rossi, Island Hotel.

This ad had intrigued her. On a slow day at the Gainesville bureau, reporters often flipped through the regional classifieds, searching for story ideas. Who was this woman who had disappeared for twenty years? And in a tiny Florida town of artists and fishermen and aging docks?

As a potential feature, the missing woman ad was a long shot, but Brandy needed this working holiday with John. She smiled up at him. "I read that a cat can sleep undisturbed in the street here. My woman and child should be easy to spot." Only now, she thought, the child would be about twenty-two.

Fifty miles of pines and back roads separated the busy university city of Gainesville from nineteenth century Cedar Key, as exposed on its Gulf coast island as a shell washed ashore. They passed a shallow bay, bristling at low tide with oyster beds and a cluster of crab traps, then a fish processing company. Brandy jotted down a few descriptive notes, then glanced again at John. Since they left the main highway thirty minutes ago, he had hardly looked at the cabbage palm hammocks, the pines, the soaring hawks and turkey buzzards, the isolation. Usually he gloried in escaping the city, in taking their pontoon boat far down the Florida rivers, in camping out in the wildlife refuges and the state parks.

"Near here there's a wonderful out-of-the-way fish camp on the Suwannee," she said. "It's at Fowler's Bluff. We could rent a boat there. Meg would love it." On cue, the golden retriever sleeping on the back seat raised her creamy-gold head and peered out the window.

Today John probably didn't want to be here. He wanted to be in Gainesville. She watched his profile in the strong October light—deep-set eyes, a straight nose, if a bit sharp, an assertive chin. Now his lips turned up in a rare half-smile. "The main trouble with Cedar Key is that it's always getting slammed by hurricanes. That empty lot we just passed—years ago some vacation cottages were swept away there. You picked some weekend get-a-way."

"Not to worry. The only bad weather now is off Cuba." Brandy tucked a cartoon they had both laughed at back into the notebook and closed it. Her random note-taking offended John's sense of order. Architects were tidy by instinct.

"I should've stayed in town and worked on the bank restoration drawings. We've had some structural problems." His dark eyebrows lifted. "I've been on stories with you before. You going to stash me away in some seedy hotel and forget about us?" He gave her a rueful glance.

"No way, my love." She patted his knee. He would not pour over the bank plans alone. He'd have the help of his intern, Tiffany Moore, a perky blonde with high cheek bones and a sultry voice. Brandy worried about the time John spent with her. Brandy's own face, she thought, was a bit too round, her mouth overly wide. She consoled herself that he had once admired the elegant tilt of her nose.

Of course Brandy wanted him here, but it wasn't easy, working on a story while she tried to tantalize her own husband. She cocked her head toward him. "There's either a story about this missing woman or there's not. You'll like the historic hotel, and we'll have most of the weekend for ourselves. We can check out the fish camp and picnic at Shell Mound Park tomorrow. It'll be romantic. You'll see."

No need to tell him yet that the State News Editor had assigned her an additional story about the Indian midden known as Shell Mound.

The classified ad about the missing woman had first hooked the State News Editor. He had leaned his lanky frame back in his chair, studied it with cheeks puffed out, tapped his pencil once or twice on the desk, and nodded. "Okay, sounds weird enough. Check out this guy Rossi." But one story wasn't enough. Maybe he didn't yet trust her to follow through. Reaching into a drawer, he'd handed her a memo. "Check out this Halloween feature while you're in Cedar Key. A fishing buddy called this morning, said the local paper ran a story today about the Shell Mound spooks, a girl and her dog. Says they're on the prowl again." He'd grinned.

The memo gave no details, only the name of the community paper and a contact there. Apparently the legend was well-known. She'd have to look for a new angle. But her first task was to find Rossi and pry loose his story, if there was one.

With the interview in mind, she had stowed her usual jeans in her suitcase and chosen a tailored navy slack suit with a crisp white blouse for the day. On the telephone yesterday, a clerk at the Island Hotel said a Mr. Rossi was expected. She needed to produce a strong feature, or two, if she was ever to move from the three-person bureau to the news room downtown.

John swung their small sedan left, onto a street of weathered cypress and stucco buildings, their Victorian balconies shading the sidewalk. "The whole town's on the National Register of Historic Places," Brandy said. "No beach. Fewer than a thousand people. That includes some laid back tourists." She hoped this would be another long weekend like the one at Daytona a few months ago, lazy beach reading by day, making love by moonlight.

They passed an art gallery, a small pink museum, a fire department tucked under a balcony railing, and a café. In the next block John pulled up to a square burgundy and cream building with the solid look of a nineteenth century fort. A large *Island Hotel* sign hung from the second floor balcony.

John's interest in the old structure had induced him to come. "One of the oldest hotels in the state," she said. "I'll find out about this guy Rossi while you register. Then I'll take care of Meg. A clerk told me they would recommend a place to board her."

Instantly a thumping began in the back seat. She pushed the golden retriever away from John's charcoal slacks, now sagging from the hook at the back window, and plucked from them a few red-blonde hairs—Meg's, not her own. They were almost the same coppery color. She and her dog had been a pair three years longer than Brandy had known John Able, but he'd never quite accepted Meg, just as he'd never quite accepted the demands of her job. "Meg will love Shell Mound, too," she said.

Under the high ceiling fan, the lobby felt cool. Brandy gazed approvingly at the varnished chairs, the plain bench, the old Victrola beside a pot-bellied stove, the windows trimmed in cypress. From behind the counter on one side of the long room, a man of medium height with curly gray hair and very blue eyes came out of the shadows carrying a book. He glanced at the lap top computer in John's hand, the Nikon around Brandy's neck, and her loose leaf notebook. "Must be the newspaper lass. I'm your proprietor, Angus MacGill. Room's ready, Miss O'Bannon."

"*Gainesville Tribune*," she said. John was accustomed to her professional name, but he hated her to be addressed as "Miss." She took his arm. "My husband, John Able. We're both interested in the hotel. He renovates historic buildings. I write an occasional column about them."

"Hotel dates back to 1859," the Scotsman said.

Brandy peered at the register. Her quarry had already checked in. The name above John's was Anthony Rossi of New York. "The gentleman who registered just before us is the person I came to see. Did you read his ad? He names the hotel." She opened the notebook and handed the clipping to him. "I expect you'll be getting his messages."

MacGill scanned the words, the mouth in his square face clamped tight, then thrust out his lower lip and scowled. A swinging door opened to his left as a young desk clerk with plastic rimmed glasses and French braids trotted in from a nearby passageway. "You were asking about Mr. Rossi?" she chirped. "He signed in yesterday."

Brandy looked at the hotel owner. "Mr. Rossi's trying to locate a woman who hasn't contacted her family for twenty years. Were you in Cedar Key in 1972?"

The Scotsman shoved his book under one arm. "Nosy bugger, that Rossi. Pushy New Yorker. Asking a lot of questions. Not likely to win him friends around here. In Cedar Key we live and let live."

Brandy noticed the title of a volume on a short bookshelf behind him, the collected poems of Robert Burns. "Ah, yes," she said, "but we mustn't hold a man's origins against him. 'A man's a man for a' that.'" Having a degree in literature came in handy, but she was aware that he had not answered her question.

The clerk parked her glasses on the top of her head and leaned forward. "Mr. Rossi said he was going over to the police department a few minutes ago. Said we could reach him there if he had any calls." From a stack of papers on the counter she handed Brandy a map of Cedar Key. "If you want to find him, he'll probably still be there. A block off Second Avenue, behind City Hall."

MacGill's mobile face went still. Then he glanced at the girl, his frown deepening. Behind him rose a print of Edinburgh Castle's stark walls. Its dark parapets gave the lobby a brooding quality that the proprietor would not have intended.

Brandy put a finger on the map and changed the subject. "We need to board our dog. Can you suggest a kennel in the area?"

MacGill ran one stubby hand through his hair and paused. "A lass works here heard me say a newspaper reporter was coming this weekend. Says she'll take care of your dog. She has a bonny fenced garden. She wants to talk to you about newspaper work, mind. We've got no kennel in Cedar Key." He pointed toward the main street. "The lass's not here now, but her mother will still be in her art gallery on Second Avenue. Be closing up in about half an hour. She'll show you to the house. Name's Marcia Waters. A water color artist."

Brandy handed John the camera. "While I'm finding Mr. Rossi and taking care of Meg, you can get us settled and imbibe the ambiance."

John looked out at the silent street, at its fringe of tattered cabbage palms and its cracked sidewalks, and then at the lobby sign that read "Neptune Lounge." He gave her another lop-sided smile. "I plan to imbibe something with considerably more wallop. And soon."

Brandy grinned and started toward the double glass doors. He would enjoy lining up their shoes in the closet, facing all their clothes on hangers in the same direction, and organizing the medicine chest before she could bounce in and create her usual good-natured disorder. He'd set up his small tape player, put on one of his favorite études, and get in the mood to relax.

In the car Meg laid her head with its curious cream-colored mask on the back of the driver's seat and made a small, complaining noise in her throat. Brandy gave her a pat before wheeling back down Second Avenue. On a side street behind the white wooden city hall, she spotted a Police Department sign. The department shared a modest annex with the library, each marked by a bright blue door. Opening her bulging notebook, she removed a memo pad, tucked it into her purse, and swung out of the car.

Inside the reception room, a swarthy man in an open-necked sport shirt was leaning over the counter, talking to a tall officer in a black uniform. Brandy moved up behind the petitioner. With one blunt finger the man tapped a large black and white photograph on the counter. "Back in June of 1972 somebody in Cedar Key saw this woman. I need to talk to the chief. Is he back yet?"

Brandy's blue eyes widened. Thanks to the chatty hotel clerk, her timing was perfect.

"Hadda little kid with her, a girl two-years old. The woman meant to live here."

The officer ran a hand across his expanding forehead and into its bristly rim of hair and shook his head. "Never seen her. But I wasn't here then. Sorry." His melancholy eyes lent the last word credibility. "The chief gets back from vacation tomorrow. I'll give him your card." He glanced at a clipboard. "Anthony Rossi, right?"

"You got it." The New Yorker removed a pair of rimless glasses and rubbed his eyes. "I'll leave a copy of the picture. Checked with a data base before I came down, and the Bureau of Vital Statistics in Jacksonville, driver's licenses, everything. She gotta be using an alias. That don't surprise me."

He replaced the glasses and tipped his head back, a stocky figure with an angular face and a prominent nose. "Somebody in a place this size oughta remember her. We know my client's niece got here okay. The aunt got a post card from her niece. She mailed it from a café a few miles up the road, and she knew where to go for help." He leaned on one elbow and stared at the portrait, as if willing the subject to appear. "Had plenty of scratch. Sold some bonds and cleaned out her checking account. My client didn't figure on hearing from her niece again, unless she had trouble."

He looked up, pushing his face closer to the officer. "I checked the date. A hurricane hit the town early the next morning, but the record shows no one got hurt. The niece was to let my client know if she left Cedar Key." He dropped his gaze. "The kid, she'd be grown now. My client don't want me to give out the real names yet. Not 'til we find her and get her okay."

Above his St. Bernard eyes, the officer raised his brows, but he nodded. "Right."

For the first time there was an appeal in the investigator's voice. "It's kinda urgent. My client's in the hospital. Finding her niece, that's her last wish. So far I got zippo. I'll check with the chief when he gets back tomorrow. Until then, I still got one lead."

Brandy sidled closer and peered down at the eight by ten. It showed a slim young woman with delicate bone structure seated on a white bench, dark hair to her shoulders, dark, solemn eyes, arms crossed, a faint lift to her lips. She wore a white, lacy dress—maybe a bridal gown, Brandy thought—and on her left hand a large diamond with brilliant smaller ones descending on each side.

The officer scooped up the photograph and slipped it into a manila folder. "We'll check it out."

As the investigator turned away from the counter, Brandy stepped between him and the door. "Mr. Rossi, I'm from the *Gainesville Tribune*. We're interested in your search. Cedar Key's in our region."

Rossi scowled. "News sure gets around, don't it? I got no information for reporters."

Brandy was surprised. He had, after all, placed the ad. She had expected him to welcome the paper's help. Still, she smiled agreeably. "We could publicize your search. Lots of readers don't look at the classifieds."

"We don't want publicity, M'am."

Behind her the door opened. A secretary hurried in with two Styrofoam cups of coffee. As Brandy moved aside, Rossi stalked out onto the porch. He stopped on the steps and when she caught up with him, he was pulling a pack of cigarettes out of his breast pocket. He was not much taller than she, but his body was solid and his posture confident. He bent down and a light flickered under his cigarette. Then he straightened up, inhaled, and gazed at the quiet street under its haphazard clumps of cabbage palms. "Thought this was some kinda beach resort."

Brandy shook her head. "It's not. That's its charm." Later, she would remember how he looked at that moment—the cheap sports coat and polyester pants, the creased forehead and alert stare—a wary alien on a quest, bewildered by the muted rhythm of Cedar Key.

From her purse she took a card with her name, bureau address, and phone number. "I'm staying at the same hotel. Call me if you change your mind."

Although he shook his head, he thrust the card into his pocket before climbing into a two door blue Chevrolet with a Gainesville airport sticker. In her car a few minutes later she noted its description in her notebook, along with the facts she'd learned about the missing woman, and poked a few loose papers back into the binder. Brandy remembered how methodical, brief, and neatly printed John's lists were, but she wrote down everything—books to read, people to talk to, ideas for feature stories, phrases that struck her fancy, facts from interviews.

Rossi was hiding a good deal, she decided, as she rounded the corner of Second Avenue. That meant there must be a dramatic angle to the story. She would question anyone she could find who was in Cedar Key in 1972.

The art gallery was the only tenant in a green frame building across the street from the Cedar Key Historical Museum. As she parked she could see through high windows into a shadowy room hung with watercolors. A bell jangled when she stepped inside and stood before somber splashes of browns and pale greens.

In a frame on one wall a cormorant clung to a piece of driftwood, a black shape against an ashen sky. Next to it cabbage palms leaned above a dark river as an osprey plunged for the kill. On an easel in the foreground a horned owl soared above a tall mound pocked with moonlit shells. While Brandy absorbed Marcia Waters' predatory vision, the artist herself emerged from a back room. She was pulling on a nubby black sweater—a rawboned woman, quite tall, with a thin, sun-browned face. She tucked a wisp of white hair into the bun at the nape of her neck and faced Brandy, eyebrows lifted.

Brandy smiled. "Mr. MacGill at the Island Hotel sent me. I'm Brandy O'Bannon from the *Gainesville Tribune*. I'm working on a couple of Cedar Key stories. He said you could board our golden retriever."

Marcia Waters opened the door onto the sidewalk. "I believe my daughter promised Mr. MacGill. She charges ten dollars a night. The fact is, we have quite a menagerie already. I keep a private bird sanctuary."

Brandy picked up a handout about the artist from a wall stand and followed her outside. "Do you always work on nature studies?" she asked as Mrs. Waters locked the door.

The artist glanced back, her face somber. "It's my way of preserving what's left of old Florida."

Brandy looked at the brochure. "You've lived in Cedar Key since the 1940's. Maybe you could help me with my two local stories."

Mrs. Waters snapped her head up. "That depends. We respect people's privacy here." She strode to a battered van at the curb. "Follow me. The house isn't far."

As Brandy nosed her car out behind the van, she thought again of John waiting for her at the hotel, and felt like a gymnast on a balance beam, teetering between job and marriage. A working weekend had seemed like a brilliant strategy: she would ferret out a difficult story, maybe two, while keeping her husband safely at her side.

These past few weeks, while she spent days on a color story in Ocala, two more in Tallahassee, and grueling overtime at the bureau, had she lost her husband to his intern? When he felt neglected, Tiffany Moore always found time for him. Even after hours, even on weekends. And this was only the first year of her three-year apprenticeship.

Frowning, Brandy drove past white frame houses, turned northwest beside a tall Victorian home with a filigreed porch railing, and rounded a bay labeled Goose Cove on the map. She did not want to think now about Tiffany Moore, her mini skirts, her tight curls, or her low voice when she asked for John on the telephone. This weekend Brandy would focus all the charm she could muster on John. She had brought a snug dress that flattered her curves and seductively high heels.

Through the windshield she watched late afternoon shadows settle over the hushed street and its canopy of Spanish moss. She couldn't concentrate only on John. She had to interview someone about the Shell Mound ghost and locate, with or without the investigator's help, the mother and daughter who came to Cedar Key twenty years ago, and then vanished.

CHAPTER 2

▼

Mrs. Waters drew up before a one story cottage flanked by cabbage palms, a narrow porch, and a bamboo fence. While the artist held open the gate, the retriever pulled Brandy in a red-gold blur across the front lawn, under the limb of a live oak into the back yard, and stopped on a gravel path between beds of black-eyed Susans, elderberry, and wax myrtle. In the corner of the garden a small fountain splashed in a tiny pond beside a wire enclosure.

While Meg stood wagging her cream-colored plume of a tail, the artist stopped, and gave her a business-like pat. "My daughter's probably finished feeding the birds. I expect she'll take care of your dog next."

For a moment Brandy knelt and put her arms around Meg's golden ruff. "You'd sniff out the missing woman if you had the chance," she murmured. "Never mind. At Shell Mound I hear there's a doggy spirit, too."

Rising, she followed the older woman through a back door into a studio lined with wooden cabinets, some slotted for pictures, and shelves stacked with tubes of paint. Brandy stopped at a drawing board under a bank of windows to study a completed water color of a horned owl. From a gnarled branch it stared into the moonlight, a huge bird with ear tufts like demon horns and hooked claws. Brandy was struck by the round eyes in the flattened face, by the hypnotic effect of the stale yellow irises and the stony pupils.

The artist looked at the picture with a slight smile. "A killing machine. Sometimes nature's like that. People, too. Cara and I took some excellent night photographs of the owl. We even managed to make a tape of the owl's hooting. It nests near Shell Mound." She slipped into a paint-splattered smock and rolled up the sleeves, revealing sinewy arms and wrists.

Brandy welcomed the opening. "I'm researching the legend of Shell Mound for a Halloween feature. You must've heard of a round light that's supposed to appear there. Sometimes a girl with a dog."

Mrs. Waters snorted. "Poppycock, of course. Something in the local paper about it yesterday. Fact is, the round light's probably illegal hunters, knocking around the woods at night."

Beside the door the artist picked up three framed watercolors, all storm scenes that had been turned to the wall, and led Brandy through a pair of French doors into a simply furnished living room with a fireplace in one corner and watercolors on every wall—Gulf scenes, crimson sumac, white ibis with curved beaks.

Brandy paused before the mantel. On it two small, oval portraits, one faded with age, faced each other in connecting silver frames, photographs of dark-haired little girls. Across the room on a small table a studio portrait of a young woman in a graduation gown gazed back with brown, liquid eyes, hands on a camera in her lap.

The stiffness in the artist's face softened as she followed Brandy's gaze. "My daughter, Cara. She plans to carry on my work with the bird sanctuary. I'm an old woman, and it's a big job. She's also a help with nature photos. Familiar with the whole area. She'd know more about the Shell Mound tale."

Brandy turned to see a slim young woman emerge from the hall in jeans and a canvas apron. Along her high cheekbones and slender neck, dark hair fell like a curtain. Large eyes and a height on no more than five feet gave her an elfin look.

"I managed to cut all the monofilament line off the pelican you brought in yesterday," she said to her mother, and then gave Brandy a shy glance.

The artist nodded, pleased. "We left Brandy O'Bannon's dog Meg in the yard." She turned to Brandy. "My daughter, Cara. You'll see her again in the hotel dining room tonight."

Cara spoke up. "I love dogs. I'll take good care of her." She held out a hand to Brandy, her expression a little anxious. "You're the newspaper woman from Gainesville? I asked Mr. MacGill to recommend me for dog sitting. I wanted to talk to you."

Brandy smiled as they shook hands. "I'm on my way back to the hotel. I'd be glad to give you a lift."

Cara whirled toward the hall, calling over her shoulder to Marcia, "Truck will bring me home. I'll put out some dog food and be changed in a minute."

Mrs. Waters set a watercolor of a hurricane scene she had carried from the studio beside the front door. Brandy was startled at the ferocity of the image. A mammoth black wave rose from seething waters, its crest deathly white. Below it crouched the frail buildings of a town.

"The storm surge of 1896," the artist said.

Brandy sensed an opening for her other story. "This reminds be of another question. A private investigator in town is looking for a woman and child who dropped out of sight here in June of 1972, just before a hurricane. He says it's important to find them, but the woman must be using another name. Any idea who that might be?"

For a fraction of a second Mrs. Waters hesitated, then looked down and shook her head. "There were no strangers who stayed in Cedar Key after Hurricane Agnes, and no fatalities. The man's mistaken."

Brandy had heard about the protectiveness of small town natives, and this woman would be stubborn. As they stepped outside and stood on the cleanly swept porch, Brandy smiled. "I hope nature doesn't take another swipe at Cedar Key while we're here. October's still the hurricane season."

The other woman did not smile back. Instead her tall, spare figure turned to face the island's jagged western shore. "Nature has reason to punish this town," she said. "The cedars, gone. The oyster beds pillaged. Still, sometimes nature rewards those who pay her back."

"The environmentalists?"

"And perhaps the painters." Mrs. Waters looked at Brandy, her gray eyes troubled. "Fact is, if the tropical storm near Cuba heads this way, we'll evacuate. You'd need to find another place for your dog."

Behind them the door opened. Cara appeared in a white uniform and burgundy apron and glided after Brandy down the front steps.

"I'd like to ask some questions about the Shell Mound ghost," Brandy said when they reached her car. Cara tucked her skirt beneath her and slid into the passenger seat. "Your mother told me about your nature photographs there, and your work in the bird sanctuary."

As Brandy pulled into the street, Cara turned toward her, a pained glint in her eyes. Brandy was conscious of the fragile bones in her face, the sensitive mouth. "Mother told you I plan to carry on her work. The truth is, I don't want to spend my life in Cedar Key. I want to be a professional photographer. I've learned all I can from books and magazines. I need college courses. Mother doesn't understand that."

The yearning in Cara's voice sent Brandy's memories reeling into the past. She was seventeen again and with her own mother at the dining room table, surrounded by her mother's literature and grammar texts, her tidy stack of term papers, her red pen, her precise lesson plans. She listened to her mother repeat in a voice that could slice meat, *"Get your degree in English, get certified to teach. You'll have security."*

And her own argument. *"I don't want to teach about language. I want to use it."* Brandy gave Cara a quick, sympathetic look.

"Maybe I could be a newspaper photographer," Cara was saying. "I'm pretty good and I learn fast."

Brandy swung the car past the concrete block high school. Beyond it, she could see mud flats barbed with oyster beds. "Start with a job that's less ambitious. Maybe an apprenticeship at a photography studio in Gainesville. Then you could take some university courses, work your way up. Have you told your mother how you feel?"

Cara's young face clouded. "I don't want to hurt her feelings, but the truth is, Marcia's not my real mother. She just likes me to call her that. She's my foster mother. My foster dad might've listened, but he died five years ago. Without me, Marcia would be alone. She won't hear of my leaving. I've had to respect that."

For a moment Brandy again was a high school senior, sitting in her father's littered study among his history and social studies books, his current events clippings and maps. *"You'd be a great reporter,"* he was saying, his round face aglow. *"You care about words and about people. Go for it. Do your own thing, Bran."*

She had tried to please them both, taken an English degree along with communications courses with an emphasis on print journalism, and then found a job at a small newspaper. Although her father died the year she graduated, she was still trying to prove he'd been right.

"I think people should do work they enjoy," Brandy said.

Cara stared into the growing dusk. "My foster mother doesn't listen, and I can't disappoint her. I owe her too much." She lifted slender shoulders in a helpless gesture. "Truck keeps begging me to stay, too. I'm twenty-two. If I don't get away soon, I never will."

"Is Truck someone special? You said he was bringing you home tonight."

Cara shrugged. "A guy I've known all my life." With a slight frown, she looked away. "A friend who'd like to be a lot more. Has an oyster fishing business here. Marcia thinks he's wonderful, mainly because he wants to keep me here, too."

Brandy raised her eyebrows. John said she got too involved in people's problems. He was probably right. "Maybe you should take charge of your own destiny," she said anyway.

Cara was quiet for a few seconds. Then she straightened her shoulders and her voice dropped. "I'm not even the real Cara Waters, you know. Cara Waters is dead."

Startled, Brandy slowed the car.

"The real Cara Waters drowned in a freak hurricane. Marcia found me like a stray kitten years later during another storm." A sudden sharpness spiked her words. "No one knows who I am, least of all me."

Brandy gaped at her, astonished. Had she found the lost child, if not the missing mother? Cara would be about the right age. She floundered for a response. "But you have a fine home here. Is it important to know?"

Cara's voice sunk almost to a whisper. "Of course it is. Somewhere I might have a father, brothers or sisters."

Brandy noticed she did not mention a mother.

"Marcia doesn't understand. All that matters to her is her precious pictures and her bird sanctuary. She has some kookie idea that we owe Cedar Key and nature something."

"For what?"

"For delivering me from the hurricane. So I've been enlisted in her fight."

Warnings signals were going off in Brandy's head. Don't jump into this problem. It's too personal. Think of John's advice. Marcia didn't want to talk about the missing woman. She would certainly resent Brandy's questions if she probed further. Better marshal a few facts first. She drove on for a few minutes in silence, casting about for another subject. Ahead she could see the dark waters of the Gulf and a tiny beach.

"I do need to ask you about a story I'm researching. Your mother said you're familiar with Shell Mound. Tell me about the recent reports of the unexplained light. If there's anything new, I could use it for a Halloween feature."

Cara looked away again, perhaps let down by the shift in topics. "I guess you know Shell Mound's a place the original Indians piled oyster and clam shells. The mounds are common along the coast. A friend told me about a story in yesterday's *Beacon*. I don't know what people see, but it must be something." A sudden smile flitted across her heart-shaped face. "The paper said a fisherman's wife took some kids out to Shell Mound for a picnic and stayed late. They all say they saw the round light. They piled into the car and drove home, totally psyched out."

"You didn't see the story yourself?"

"Marcia took the paper to the gallery. It was gone when I got there." Brandy tried to recall the clippings in her notebook. "I believe there's an eighteenth century woman and a dog."

"It gets written up a lot. People claim they've seen a girl in a long white dress. But the main thing is the light, a bright light in place of the woman's head." Cara made a spreading gesture with one hand. "She's supposed to appear for miles around the island and the Suwannee River, but they say she always comes back to Shell Mound."

"There's a wolfhound, I believe."

Cara shrugged her narrow shoulders. "The story is, more than a hundred years ago the girl saw pirates hiding a treasure. She was caught and murdered and buried with the treasure, along with her dog. Now they're supposed to guard the site."

"The map shows a swamp near there," Brandy said. "Probably the light is swamp gas, or hunters with head lamps." She considered the subject. How could she give an old story a new slant? She shot Cara a quick, inspired glance. "Has anybody ever tried to photograph this figure or this light?"

Cara shook her head. "Not that I know of." Her voice took on a sudden eagerness. "Maybe I could help with your story, prove what I can do. I have the equipment for night photography." The words tumbled out. "Let's try. The sightings usually come in a series. We'd have to stake out the place pretty late at night. I'll take pictures and you write the story."

"How safe would we be?"

"Safer than on the street or in a mall parking lot. Marcia sometimes carries her gun in case of rattlers. She can shoot, but I can't. Anyway, we've never needed one."

Cara's daring surprised Brandy. Maybe the daughter had grown accustomed to tramping through the woods at night with Marcia. Brandy bit her lip. "It would be a good angle for a Halloween story, all right."

"Tonight's the best chance. A storm may come up later this week. I wouldn't go then."

Brandy sighed. "My husband's the practical type, and cautious, but maybe I can persuade him to go with us."

Cara looked at her watch. "Coming to dinner at the hotel? I'll be serving in the dining room. You could let me know then."

Her slim jaw tightened. "I won't tell Mother. She's never ready for me to do anything on my own. But if I could take a picture good enough for the Gainesville paper, somebody might offer me a job." Her brown eyes shone again. "Maybe I could even do some research, begin to find out who I am."

Brandy swung the car away from the Gulf onto Second Avenue, past white frame houses with fretwork balconies, some with side halls and open porches, all nineteenth century, all now dark.

"The *St. Petersburg Times* ran a story about the Shell Mound ghost about ten years ago," she said. "A reporter found some wooden slats and old coins at the burial site and, oddly enough, the bones of a large dog."

As they pulled up to the curb, Cara nodded and gave Brandy a searching look. She hesitated a few seconds, and then said in her soft voice, "That's not the only unidentified skeleton around here." She slipped out of the car, then turned back. "I've got to get to work now. I'll tell you later about a really mysterious skeleton. It's in the Cedar Key cemetery now. No one knows whose it is, but I have a theory."

While Brandy stared after her, Cara sailed through the double doors, long hair floating behind her.

CHAPTER 3

▼

In the lobby Brandy glanced at her watch. Five o'clock. She didn't see Rossi or his car. She would wait until she had more facts before talking to him about Cara. Besides, the investigator hadn't been willing to help her. From the counter she scooped up a copy of the local newspaper, scanned the Shell Mound story about the previous night's ghostly sighting, and jotted down a staff phone number from the masthead. Because she knew the hotel did not furnish telephones in guest rooms, she stepped into a booth in the corner near the dining room and emerged a few minutes later disappointed on two counts.

The managing editor knew nothing about a missing woman and child, although he admitted the paper dated back only nine years. Also the latest witnesses to the apparition come from nearby Chiefland and rejected any further interviews. For that story, Cara's idea for stalking the specter held the most promise.

Brandy advanced on the counter. MacGill should know if John had gone out. The hotel owner stood beside the clerk, talking to a lanky customer in a navy blazer, a blond ducktail curling over his collar. "My boat's tied up at the Dock Street marina," the young man was saying. "Plan to get an early start on the flats in the morning."

The sports fisherman turned a slickly handsome face toward the clerk and grinned as she handed him a key. Behind her plastic rimmed glasses her eyes were alight. He shifted his appraising glance to Brandy, smiled, tossed the key up, caught it, and crossed to the rear of the lobby. The proprietor watched him run lightly up the stairs. "He's from Miami Beach, he says. Came into the lounge a year ago." MacGill thrust out his lower lip. "Lad surprised me. It's the first time he's stayed at the hotel."

Brandy opened her battered notebook. "I told you I sometimes write about historic preservation. At a another time, I'd like to talk to you about the hotel." She laid a clipping with her photograph on the counter. "My husband still around?"

He nodded toward the staircase. "Have a look on the second floor balcony. It runs along the front of the building."

Upstairs the door to their room stood open and the soothing strains of Chopin wafted through the hall. She found John, stretched out on a bamboo sofa overlooking the inlet, absorbed in Peterson's *The Role of the Architect in Historical Restorations.* A gulf breeze brushed through the cabbage palms across Second Avenue and ruffled his hair.

"About time you got back." He looked up and caught her wrist, pulling her toward him. Maybe with Tiffany Moore out of the picture, she thought, her stock was going up. Perhaps John would even take an interest in her Cedar Key assignments.

Bending down, she kissed his forehead. "I missed you." Gently she detached herself and looked over the railing. From the balcony she could see fishing boats moored in the inlet, and beyond, a fringe of wooden restaurants along Dock Street. In the Gulf above Atsena Otie Key, the sky was tinged blood red.

"Rossi's not cooperating," she said, "and I haven't talked to anyone who says they know about the missing woman. But lots of odd things go on in this little town. The young woman taking care of Meg says no one knows who she really is. She just turned up here during a storm when she was little. Doesn't seem likely that two women her age— both unidentified as children—would live in a town this size. Cara wants to talk to me about an unidentified skeleton buried here, too. Maybe she thinks there's a connection."

John sat up, lines forking between his eyes. "Look, Bran. You get too involved in people's lives. In the past your snooping almost got you killed."

"But I helped solve a murder."

He rubbed his forehead, a signal of frustration. "Promise you'll stick to writing your assigned stories. Don't go poking into this girl's business."

Brandy plumped down beside him, "Maybe you'd prefer the mystery of Shell Mound. According to the local paper, the ghost walked last night." She tilted her face up to his. "We could explore that mystery together tonight."

"I don't think so." He gave her a sly smile. "That's not the kind of exploring I had in mind."

Her plan for John was working fine, she thought, but at the expense of her stories. She never quite achieved a balance.

By the time Brandy had changed into her snug black and white crepe, and they had taken their seats in the dining room, darkness had descended on Cedar Key. The dry seed pods of a mimosa tree rattled against the empty verandah screen, and along the floor a clump of palmettos cast a long shadow. Because she found the town charming, she was puzzled by a sudden twinge of dread. Maybe it was the ghost talk.

Against a cypress panel wall, under one of Marcia Waters' scenes of a prowling Florida panther, the fisherman from Miami Beach toyed with his cocktail glass. While John studied the menu, the other man raised one eyebrow and grinned at her. She looked away. Maybe tonight her dress was hooking the wrong fish.

The New York private eye sat a small table by the lobby door. As he picked up his menu, Brandy wondered if a New Yorker would have a taste for Florida's fresh heart of palm salad. When he reached into his shirt pocket for his glasses, she nodded but he ignored her. She hoped he had kept her card. Maybe they could collaborate. Her lead was better than his.

Remembering Cara's suggestion they try to photograph the Shell Mound ghost tonight, she smiled at John. "I would really like your help on the Shell Mound story," she said. He hadn't forgotten her earlier suggestion and frowned across the mauve tablecloth. "Be practical. Tramping through the swamps at night isn't my idea of quality time. And, of course, we'd see nothing. Some female let her imagination run away with her. Are you going to believe a car load of scared kids?"

"People keep seeing something. I'm not saying it's a ghost."

He leaned forward, over the crystal wine and water glasses. "Don't even think you two women could go out there alone. No telling what kind of scumbags hang around the area at night. I don't care how well your new friend knows her way around. It isn't safe." He settled back and unfolded his napkin. "I thought we'd spend most of the weekend together. If you're too busy, I could go back home and check on the bank plans."

Brandy shook her head, re-shuffling her priorities. "We'll see Shell Mound tomorrow, together. In the daylight. I ought to call my editor, though. Let him know I haven't got anything yet on either story."

As she spoke, Angus MacGill came into the dining room and bent over the investigator's shoulder. "Telephone, Mr. Rossi," he said. The New Yorker rose and followed MacGill into the lobby. Brandy was wondering if Rossi had a call about the missing woman, when Cara appeared to take their order. Through the swinging door came the tantalizing smell of the hotel's famous spicy chowder. Brandy looked up, apologetic. "I'm sorry, but my husband says our plan is too dangerous. I guess he's right."

Cara raised her pencil above her pad. "That's okay." Her face remained expressionless. "I totally understand. Of course, with the right equipment one person could do it. Someone who knows the area."

Someone like Cara, Brandy thought.

"The moon should be bright tonight," Cara added. The young woman reminded Brandy of the Pre-Raphaelite women she had seen pictured in English literature books, all lithe necks and pale hands. That image fitted her obsessive fear of storms Marcia Waters had mentioned. Yet Cara had unexpected toughness. She was ready to plunge into the woods alone. Brandy felt a pang of guilt. She had suggested the venture.

After a dinner of Shrimp Island Hotel, they found MacGill in the lobby, posting Brandy's historic preservation column on a bulletin board beside the counter. Behind it, the man with the ducktail was now cozily chatting with the clerk. Fast worker, Brandy thought.

The owner gestured toward the open door of the Neptune Lounge. "Mind you see our famous murals. How about an after-dinner liqueur?"

A crowded lounge makes a ripe source of information, Brandy thought. When she tugged at John's arm, they followed MacGill into a dim, cypress-lined side room. Several patrons had already gathered at the bar. Above tiers of bottles, rose a faded painting of the bearded god Neptune presiding over a bevy of submissive mermaids.

"Painted in 1946 with some locals as models," the hotel owner said. "Some say the mermaid on the left looks a wee bit like our friend Marcia Waters." He winked one bright blue eye at Brandy. "As she was about forty years ago." MacGill moved past a pale mural of a coastal river and selected a table. "Marcia's a fine artist, but a bit daft. Has a lovely daughter, mind." John and Brandy sat down in canvas chairs opposite MacGill, while he softened his last remark with an infectious grin. Through the back window Brandy could see a full moon above the bayou and a fisherman's skiff in the black water.

MacGill signaled a plump cocktail waitress behind the bar. "Cara's a wee slip of a thing, but smart. More's the pity she's not at a university."

Brandy shook her head. "Looks like Mama wants to keep her 'a violet by a mossy stone, Half-hidden from the eye.' I understand Cara has a boyfriend here."

MacGill lifted his head at the Wordsworth quotation, then nodded toward a heavy set man in jeans and rubber boots at the bar. "Truck Thompson." He dropped his voice. "He's wanted to marry Cara for years, before she ever got out of high school. Marcia's dead keen on the idea."

Brandy swiveled about to get a better look. Thompson was leaning on his elbows, his back to the bar, talking to someone at a table by the door. She saw a wide face, sun-reddened, a bristly mustache, a thick neck and body. She frowned. "He's a bit old for our Cara, isn't he?"

"Truck's about fifteen years older, but Marcia says he's well established. Bottom line is, if she marries him, she'll stay in Cedar Key. Marcia hasn't any family. Cara's all she has. It's not been easy for Marcia, or for Cara either, after Mr. Waters died. I've given Cara what work I could at the hotel."

When the middle-aged waitress with the chubby face appeared, MacGill ordered Drambuies for the three of them. Then he tilted his head back, his words deliberate. "Mind, Truck fits Marcia's scheme of things. Inherited a fleet of fishing boats from his father and made a go of it. Has a fish and oyster house on the street behind the hotel." When the waitress returned with their drinks, MacGill sipped from the delicate glass and rolled his eyes in appreciation.

"And what about Cara's feelings?"

The corners of his eyes crinkled. "Oh, Cara? I don't think the lass fancies him much. I think she wants to get away."

Brandy decided to probe a bit further. "Cara was saying some pretty strange things to me this afternoon about not being the real Cara Waters."

The muscles in MacGill's jaw stiffened. "Gets her knickers in a twist now and then, does our Cara. Goes dramatic about being a foster kid. I'd take no notice."

A movement in the doorway caught Brandy's attention. She looked across the packed lounge where the private investigator had paused, adjusting his eyes to the shadows. Something in the curve of his shoulders and the set of his head suggested defeat. He glanced around, then crossed the room and took a seat behind them.

MacGill leaned toward him. "It's your first time with us, lad. I'll stand you to a drink. What'll it be?"

Rossi ran one hand through his thin, dark hair, weighing the offer. "Scotch on the rocks," he said at last. "And thanks."

MacGill beckoned to the cocktail waitress again, gave the order, and turned again to Rossi. "All the locals know by now you're on the look-out for some woman's gone missing. Find out anything?"

A lull fell over the voices at the bar. Truck Thompson turned toward their table. By his blond ducktail, Brandy recognized the Miami Beach tourist in fashionable polo shirt and corduroys, a foot on the rail, half facing them.

"Mind, I hope the phone call at dinner was good news," the Scots-man added.

Rossi sat back while the cocktail waitress set down his drink. "My client was a cancer patient. Wanted to see her niece before she died. The aunt had news for her, but she didn't make it." He sighed and wiped his rimless glasses with a handkerchief.

"So you're giving up the search then?"

"I got an agreement for my fee. I'll collect the rest of it, okay. And I know someone else who'll be interested, but it's too bad about the old lady."

Rossi thought a minute, then settled his glasses on his nose, pulled a small manila envelope out of a breast pocket, removed a black and white photograph, and placed on the table a smaller copy of the picture Brandy had seen at the police station. Once again she gazed at the poised set of the woman's head, the long straight hair, the dainty features.

"Take a gander," the investigator said to MacGill. "See if it jars loose any kinda recollection."

"A pretty little thing," John said.

MacGill glanced down and away. "Never saw the lass."

"You here in '72?" It was the second time MacGill had been asked that question. Brandy was conscious of the waitress's moon face looking over her shoulder as the proprietor nodded, his shrewd bright gaze on Rossi. He ordered a Stoli on the rocks along with another Scotch whiskey for the private detective. Truck Thompson had followed the waitress to the table, a beer in one beefy hand. He stared down at the picture, pale eyes close together in a broad face.

"She come here June 19, 1972," Rossi said, his voice a little loud. "The picture's twenty years old. Would look a lot different now, probably. Had a kid with her about two and a half, a girl."

Truck's head jerked up, a startled look in his colorless eyes. Rossi studied the oyster man. For a minute no one spoke. Then Truck fingered his heavy mustache. "Don't remember her," he said, backing away. "Hey, never seen anyone like that around here."

The Miami tourist now left the bar and edged into the group next to Brandy. His eyes swept her coppery hair and the smooth curves of her breasts with a look that left her feeling undressed. Close up, he reminded her of those sullen male models in *Gentleman's Quarterly.* She recognized the Armani jacket and the Gucci watch. Probably a man in his early thirties.

"This lad's Nathan Hunt," MacGill said, eyebrows twitching upward. "Mr. and Mrs. Able. Care to join us?"

"Couldn't help hearing the gentleman here," Hunt said easily, setting a highball glass on the investigator's table. When he shook hands around, Truck stepped farther back, maybe, Brandy thought, because of the professional fisherman's disdain for the amateur. Hunt pulled a chair between Brandy and Rossi. "I've spent a lot of time in Cedar Key," he added. "Not as far back as '72, of course, but I have friends who have." He took a quick look as Rossi slid the photograph back into its folder. "I could make a few phone calls, ask some questions. I might turn up something."

Rossi took a long swallow, removed his glasses again, and tapped the rim against the envelope. "Might jog somebody's memory if I said there's a lotta money involved, for the kid, anyways. If the woman, or her daughter, don't wanna be found, that's okay. I'll collect the rest of my fee and fade."

His dark eyes locked first with MacGill's, then with Thompson's. "A life of luxury's out there for that girl, if she wants it." He sat back and thrust the envelope into his breast pocket.

MacGill turned his squat glass in a circle on the table, Truck's silent bulk still behind him. Hunt leaned back and laid one ankle across the opposite knee. Brandy was surprised to see on his socks, above his costly Italian shoe, the finely stitched monogram, "B.B." His half grin showed perfect teeth. "What do the local gendarmes say?"

"Not much—yet." Rossi was making quick work of the second Scotch. Next to the elegant Hunt, his rumpled sport shirt, perma press pants, and cheap walking shoes looked shabby.

John yawned, rubbed Brandy's sleeve, and nodded toward the door, but she was studying the faces around her. In the low light MacGill might be the subject of an Old Master's portrait. He had the calculating eyes and the strong chin of a prosperous burgher. Truck would've been a muscular peasant, toiling in the corner of the canvas.

"I like to finish my jobs." Rossi was looser now. A touch of alcohol, Brandy thought, does wonders to oil the flow of language.

"Maybe the woman and child never came to Cedar Key," Hunt said.

"She come here all right." The private detective paused and lifted his glass. "Maybe even to this hotel. She was supposed to stay here, but she changed her plans. Mailed a postcard from the Greyhound bus stop at Otter Creek. It gave the new address."

There was a pregnant pause. Truck's gravelly voice broke the silence. "That date. That's the day before Hurricane Agnes struck. Wouldn't nobody come to Cedar Key then."

Rossi drained his glass. "You gotta good memory for dates." He tilted his gaze up at Truck. "She did come, though. We know that much. Somebody drove her here."

Truck's heavy shoulders lifted, a disbelieving shrug.

"The woman couldn't of left town right after the hurricane, either," Rossi said. "I've done some checking. For a coupla days the only road out was flooded." He gave them all a level look. "She never wrote again. That means she's still gotta be here. That was the agreement with her aunt, that she'd write again if she left."

Brandy realized many of the customers had deserted the lounge, and once again it grew quiet. "Let's split," John whispered, running one hand down her back, his lips against her ear.

Her dress had done its job and Brandy patted his arm, her eyes still on Rossi. He removed his glasses again and folded them into a case, his hands now a trifle unsteady. "I checked out that local address this afternoon. The lot's empty now, but the deed records oughta show what used to be there. And who owned the place. Whoever that was, must've seen her and the driver." His face darkened. "Could be the same person."

He stood and rifled through his billfold for a tip. "Tomorrow's Saturday, but the clerk at the court house promised to look it up and give me a call."

He started for the door, then turned. "I got an appointment with the police chief tomorrow. He was here then. He'll check his records. I expect the woman and her daughter are walking around Cedar Key right now, using different names. Anyone think of something, I'll be in Room 27."

MacGill began pushing back his own chair. "I do need to see someone before it gets any later." For a minute the waitress lingered beside MacGill's table, settling the bills, full lips twisted in an odd smile, as if they shared an in-house joke. "Do you think," she murmured as she pocketed her tips, "that private eye showed up at the hotel nineteen years too late?"

MacGill paused. Brandy noticed his eyebrows lower and his mouth contract into a thin line as he glowered at the waitress without answering.

CHAPTER 4

▼

In the dim upstairs lobby Brandy followed John past murals of a savannah and into the rear corridor. A light burned under the private detective's door, #27, one of the smaller rooms that had a private bath across the hall. She noticed a second bedroom off the passage, still dark, beside the back door where a staircase descended from a metal landing to the yard and garage. On the screen door a note reminded hotel guests to lock up if they came in through the rear entrance after the hotel closed at eleven.

"How small town quaint," John remarked.

Beyond the narrow road behind the yard, Brandy could see a pier and in the unfenced area between the garage and the street, a rake and spade where someone had started a garden. Mosquito netting draped their bed, an anachronism, given the screens and air conditioner. On the bed lay two books she had packed, the latest P. D. James mystery and another more slender volume, John Ciardi's translation of Dante's *Inferno*. She'd expected to catch up on leisure reading and continue a review of classics she'd enjoyed in college, but she'd have little chance this weekend, after all. Brandy crossed to the window and peered below the rolled bamboo blind. A bushy southern red cedar crowded against the pane. Beyond Third Street lay Back Bayou, its black waters rising with the tide. Truck Thompson's fish and oyster house, she remembered, was down that road. She released the blind.

"Did you notice that everyone in the lounge except us, and maybe the fisherman from Miami Beach, had something to hide? Even the cocktail waitress. Did you hear her last remark?" She watched John remove his shoes. Without answering, he pulled back the mosquito net canopy over the bed, while she crossed to the old-fashioned dresser with its framed mirror and removed her earrings. "There's an unidentified skeleton in the cemetery, too. Cara wants to tell me about it. Maybe these things are all somehow connected."

As he unbuttoned his shirt, John shook his head. "If Rossi won't tell you who he's looking for, I don't see how you can cover that story. I'd keep quiet about your suspicions." Brandy thought she was good at a lot of things, but not at keeping quiet. He stepped out of his slacks and folded them over a hanger. "And I didn't care for the way the guy from Miami Beach was giving you the eye."

Brandy smiled. "Keeps you on your toes." But she didn't feel light-hearted. Through the window a bright moon outlined the ragged pines and oaks rimming the island. Several dark miles to the north lay Shell Mound. She thought of Cara Waters and her camera. If Cara went out there tonight on the Halloween assignment, Brandy would feel responsible. Unfastening her gold belt, she leaned forward and pulled her dress and slip over her head. "Cara feels abandoned by one mother and trapped by the other." She tossed the two on a chair. "She needs help. Besides, I hate to go home without either story."

John came toward her, a slight edge to his voice. "I don't want to hear any more about missing women or unnamed skeletons." He encircled her in his arms. "You weren't very eager to leave the lounge. Tonight's supposed to be ours."

"I know," She laid her head for a moment against his chest. Remember your priorities, idiot, she told herself.

Deftly he unhooked her bra. "Forget your job tonight."

"That's not hard." But even as she tilted her chin upward and gave him a deep kiss, she thought how dark the woods at Shell Mound must be.

*   *   *   *

During the night Brandy awoke to the muffled closing of a nearby door and the creak of a floor board. The old hotel seemed alive with the gathered energy of the years—Federal and rebel officers from the Civil War era, long-ago merchants from its general store days, dead owners from the past. When footsteps shuffled past their door, her heart jumped. Only some guest going to a bathroom off the hall, she reasoned, while taking a measured breath. She glanced at her travel alarm clock—twelve-thirty, surely too early for a fisherman to leave. Voices murmured in the hall, then quieted. Perhaps a late visitor answering the private detective's invitation. She would check with Rossi in the morning. The back door of the hotel squeaked open and then closed. Her curiosity almost drove her to the window, but she remembered the chill blackness of the Cedar Key night and snuggled instead against John, feeling reassured by his warmth. He was breathing deeply, but he moved his arm across her back. In spite of Tiffany Moore, they'd been close tonight. At least that part of her scheme was working.

She thought over the conversation in the lounge and the cocktail waitress's final comment, that Rossi had come to Cedar Key nineteen years too late. She would rise early, before John, and record in her notebook everything she'd heard, in case Rossi did want her help. Otherwise, she'd call the State News Editor or his assistant and explain she'd drawn a blank. In the afternoon she and John would drive to the Suwannee River, take Meg for a run at Shell Mound, and savor another cozy evening together. She'd spend some time refreshing her memory of Dante's *Inferno,* plunge through the depths of his hell and relish his escape at the end, and then they'd enjoy a relaxed trip home on Sunday.

But before dawn Brandy jerked awake, shaking. She'd been fleeing some monstrous overhead shadow, battling wind and rain through a swamp, when her feet sunk, trapping her in muck. For a second she lay still, calming herself and recalling Marcia Water's talk about a hurricane. Still shaking off the nightmare, she heard footsteps come up the back stairs. Someone unlocked the door, slipped into the rear hall, and a few minutes later, ran down again. A distant car door slammed. This hotel's a regular Grand Central Station, she thought, and then remembered that Nathan Hunt, the Miami tourist, planned an early fishing expedition. Putting the nightmare and the hall noises out of her mind, she rolled over once more and slept.

*   *   *   *

That same night about eleven Cara Waters climbed down from the cab of Truck's pick-up to find Angus MacGill standing with her mother on their porch. With a preoccupied smile, he nodded to Cara, but she noticed that his eyes looked troubled.

"Don't let me interrupt," she said. She wanted time to prepare.

Marcia stood very straight and crossed her lean arms over her chest, looking defiant, her voice strained. "Angus is just leaving."

After his car drew away from the curb, Cara expected her mother to speak to her about MacGill's visit. But in the living room the older woman sank into a chair, her long fingers twisting a handkerchief. Then she rubbed her forehead, complained of a headache, and started toward her bedroom. Cara felt relieved. Her mind was filled with her own scheme. She had thought of little else since she talked to the reporter.

In the hallway she quietly opened the closet door, reached into a corner, and drew out the lightweight tripod. Carrying it into her own room, she sat on the bed and listened to the older woman leave the bathroom, go into her bedroom, and shut the door. Cara would have to wait for her foster mother to settle down for the night.

Lifting from a bookshelf her large volume of James Valentine's *Florida: Images of the Landscape,* a prize she found in the Cedar Key bookstore, she studied the dazzling color photographs, all composed as skillfully as paintings. In a few minutes she set it back beside a book of black and white photographs made with a large format view camera. Instead of the career she dreamed of, perhaps as a free lance photographer or a professional employed by an important studio or publication, she was supposed to be content with the bird sanctuary, the art gallery, and waitress and cleaning jobs at the hotel. Yet she did not want to hurt her foster mother, not ever.

At a window she knelt and peered into a dark sky lit by the full moon, enough light for her task. She picked up her canvas backpack, took the tripod, and fastened it to the metal frame. Next came her 35 mm. camera, already loaded with fast panchromatic film. She checked. Two exposures left. Her cramped darkroom in the kitchen pantry was not equipped to develop color film, and Cedar Key had no place to leave it. But later tonight she could drive to Chiefland and drop the roll at an all night drug store. It would only take an extra hour. That is, if she got a picture.

Better not risk a flash. If she caught illegal hunters, they would see the light. With the fast film she could take a long exposure from a distance of perhaps forty feet. She wanted to be as far from her subject as possible. She grinned at the thought of exposing the so-called specter, but as long as she was alone and unarmed, she'd better be careful.

Behind the bamboo fence the reporter's dog woofed, probably at a possum. Perhaps the O'Bannon woman would help her. A reporter would have useful contacts. In the pockets of her backpack Cara placed a short telephoto lens, a zoom lens, and the cable release, then made sure she had an extra roll of film, batteries, and a small flashlight.

Her lips were set, her eyes bright. If she could get a picture of the intruder, it would be in every newspaper in Central Florida. Just for making the attempt, she would be interviewed by the reporter, might even escape Cedar Key, might even get a job offer Marcia couldn't ask her to refuse. She had studied every book on photography she could find. Now was the time to prove her ability, to earn the money for the Communication and Arts program at the University in Gainesville.

For a moment Cara's face clouded. Of course, she owed a greater debt to her foster parent than most daughters did to their true mothers. She could never forget that, but here was a chance to accomplish something on her own, something no one else had tried. She might catch in her lens the Ghost of Shell Mound. And if it was a hunter with a miner's light on his cap or a ball of gas, so much the better. Marcia would then be proud of her.

Cara had read fishermen's accounts of the phantom for years—unsatisfactory descriptions of a white light that bounced among the trees, skittered across whole islands in a matter of minutes, and disappeared; of the school children frightened away from Shell Mound by a perfectly round light on a willowy body that vanished into the hole on Shell Mound. But she never saw any real evidence.

Things were buried at Shell Mound, of course. That's what such a midden was for. Once pottery shards, shell necklaces, perhaps the bones of early native Americans had lain there, but they were plundered long ago. Now it was illegal to dig at the site.

She felt in the pockets of her jeans for her car keys. She would take the old station wagon and leave the panel truck. Marcia needed it for hauling injured birds and large pictures. She had thought of telling Truck about her plan after they stopped at the café on Second Street for coffee. But he seemed agitated about something he had heard in the lounge, something he would not discuss. Anyway, Truck's main concern tonight was protecting his oyster beds from thieves. He would've made fun of her for trying to photograph a phantom. And he would certainly not help her escape Cedar Key.

When she and Marcia worked the Shell Mound area at night, they had permission to leave their car in the safety of the campground. If the caretaker asked, she would say she was trying for another shot of the Great Horned owl that nested there, an excuse she knew she owed to Marcia.

Adjusting the backpack comfortably on her shoulders, she bent down and lifted her plastic hiking boots out of the closet, tucked them under one arm, and opened her bedroom door. The space under Marcia's door was dark. In her tennis shoes, Cara tiptoed across the hall, through the living room and dining areas, and out the kitchen door into the carport. Marcia would be more alarmed than Truck at the notion of Cara going out alone, even though they had squatted with a tripod together for hours among the moonlit pines and palmettos, hoping for a flash shot of the owl or a night-feeding heron.

Cara stowed the backpack with her boots in the passenger seat of the station wagon, and putting the gears in neutral, pushed the car out of the driveway and into the silent street. As she finally started the engine, she checked her watch: twelve-fifteen.

After rattling over the four bridges, she swung onto Route 347, past the pine tree farms to Shell Mound Road. No other cars passed her on that straight stretch of asphalt. She skirted Black Point Swamp, pulled around a chain barrier into the campground, and parked at a distance from the caretaker's trailer.

Once out of the station wagon, she opened the passenger door, hoisted the backpack again onto her shoulders, settled the wide, padded shoulder straps, and thrust her feet into her boots. An orange moon now rose high above the tattered scrub oaks of the park. The air felt moist and fresh, but she could smell damp grasses and exposed soil. She locked the car, crossed the road, and found the narrow trail where the pavement ended. It forked off from a dirt road that ran under giant oaks toward the mound. Flicking on her flashlight, she peered again at her watch: one thirty-five.

She set out on the woodland trail, over pine needles and leaves, between twisted oaks and stubby palmettos, around the swamp's edge, breathing in the heavy odor of wet soil and decaying plants. Occasionally, the sandy ground gave way to saw grass and bare cypress trees. She thought of bobcats and rattlesnakes, but she counted on her footsteps to frighten them off. Her trek was not silent. Night insects twittered and whirred. From the marsh came the croak of frogs. Once an alligator bellowed.

At last the trail inclined upward. She could make out the cluster of huge oaks that stood to the east of the mound, could feel the crunch of shells beneath her boots. She hiked up a rise. Before her lay a wide expanse of marsh grass, and beyond the tidal flats, the black waters of the Gulf. Heart knocking against her chest, she crept between two gnarled oaks and knelt beneath their twisted branches. Here she would wait, several feet above the road that curved around the hilltop. The mound was in full view, perhaps forty feet away, its half-buried shells white in the moonlight. She slipped behind a myrtle leaf holly, unfastened the tripod, and hid its slender legs among the prickly leaves. With shaky fingers, she mounted the camera, affixed the zoom lens, and screwed the six foot flexible cable release wire into the shutter release button.

Then Cara dropped down on a bed of leaves. She felt safe. She could relax, hidden by saw palmettos and a veil of Spanish moss. Leaning her back against the rough tree trunk, she realized how tired she felt. A spot between her shoulder blades ached. Before her the Gulf lay still, the tropical storm hundreds of miles away. Far in the distance she heard the sound of a car's engine. Just for a minute she would close her eyes and rest. Her head dropped, the woods around her faded away, and she dozed.

In a rush she was alone again in the shadowy room she had visited so often in nightmares. Wind screamed outside, rattling the window. Rain pelted the glass. While she lay paralyzed with fear in the bed, she heard a shriek, heard something heavy fall, then a soft rhythmical thudding, again and again. She would be torn by the wind, helpless again in a huge, wet blackness, deserted, grieving for something irretrievably lost.

Her head jerked, she trembled, and her eyes opened wide. Again she was under the tree. How much time had passed? The moon was lower in the western sky, but the soft, staccato thuds in her dream had not stopped. In a hollow beside the mound, next to a large cedar, she could see a dark figure bend and rise, a spade scooping, lifting, the sand falling with a soft rattle again and again. For a moment she panicked. People said that pirates had buried a chest here, had murdered the girl who saw them, and threw her body into the same pit. She stifled a cry, feeling a sudden affinity for that long ago, maybe mythical, girl.

But this figure looked too solid; the noise of the shovel sounded too real. She steadied herself. Illegal treasure or artifact hunters, probably, she thought, modern pirates. She caught up the shutter release, with a trembling finger pushed the button, and counted thirty-five seconds. The film advanced with a quiet hum. Bracing one hand against the ground, she pushed herself into a crouch. Dry leaves rustled under her. The figure stopped, turned. She froze. She prayed she would be mistaken for a night animal.

Her sight was partly blocked by shrubs and Spanish moss. She could not see the figure's face, but the camera lens had a clear view, and above sailed a bright full moon. The head lifted, stared in her direction. She clicked the button again. That was what she'd come to do.

CHAPTER 5

▼

When Brandy and John descended to the dining room for breakfast at eight, two other tables were occupied. Nathan Hunt's slim figure bent over a plate of melon and eggs. He had either gone out in his boat very early, Brandy thought, or was starting late. Truck Thompson, still in black jacket and boots, had also come in for breakfast. He held a steaming cup of coffee level with his mustache, his face flushed and the corners of his mouth grim. In the lobby doorway stood Angus MacGill. The only missing member of last night's group was Rossi.

As Brandy and John took a table, Cara came swinging around the black screen from the kitchen, a tray of eggs and bacon shoulder high. As she set it down before Truck, she gave Brandy a knowing look. She wasn't groomed with the care of yesterday, and the color in her dainty cheeks was pinker. "I was just telling Truck and Mr. MacGill about my excursion last night," she said.

Brandy laid down her menu and sighed. At least Cara seemed all right. "You didn't go out to Shell Mound alone?"

"Yes I did." Cara's glance swept over the others. "Brandy here's a reporter. She says her paper would like a picture of the Shell Mound ghost." Her brown eyes focused on Brandy, her eager voice rising. "I did get a shot of someone. It wasn't a girl in a flowing gown. It sure wasn't a hunter, either, unless he goes after game with a spade."

Truck glowered. "Had no damn luck myself. In my boat most of the night for nothing."

"Actually, then, I had better luck."

Brandy spoke up. "Did the person digging see you?"

"Don't think so. Heard me, I think, but probably thought I was a possum or a deer. I snapped two shots in good moonlight. At least one ought to get the face."

MacGill picked up his coffee from the side board and slid into a small table by the door. "A dig there's illegal, mind. It's a dicey business, taking a picture. Did Marcia approve?"

Cara pulled her pad and pencil out of an apron pocket. "I didn't tell her last night. I had to this morning, though. She heard me change clothes."

John and Brandy both ordered fruit and eggs. "And the photographs?" Brandy asked. "When will they be developed?" Maybe she could at least cobble together the Shell Mound story.

"Dropped the film off in Chiefland. That's why I was out so late. No place here to handle it." She indicated Cedar Key's backwardness with a shrug. "I can't do color in my darkroom. The pictures will be ready Tuesday morning, right after I finish serving breakfast." She picked up Nathan Hunt's empty plate.

"No mysterious round light?" Brandy asked, hopeful.

"Sorry. But maybe I can prove who was digging at the mound. Might be a story in that."

John gave Brandy a righteous look. "I said the stunt would be dangerous. No telling who was fooling around the mound. You know we'll be back in Gainesville by Tuesday."

Brandy glanced at him across the table. "I'd make a trip back to see a really interesting picture."

Hunt rose, picked up his Windbreaker, and looked at MacGill, who was cutting into a hard-boiled egg blanketed in sausage. "Sounds like we've all been out last night. I went after croakers and grunts early this morning myself. No luck. Going to try around the mouth of the Suwannee."

He had gone and John and Brandy were finishing breakfast when the breathless young desk clerk bobbed through the door. "It's Mr. Rossi, sir," she said to MacGill. "I can't locate him anywhere. He's just gone!"

MacGill's square face darkened. "Without checking out?"

She retreated a step. "Must've left, really early. His car's not here and his door's partly open." Brandy remembered the footsteps on the back stairs and said a quiet, "Damn." If Rossi was gone, her chance of covering the missing woman assignment was gone, too, as well as the ghost story, unless Cara's picture exposed a hoax.

Brandy and John followed MacGill upstairs. While John disappeared into their room to brush his teeth and collect the camera, Brandy stood at a discreet distance and watched MacGill open the investigator's door. When he entered, she edged forward and peered inside. The closet door stood open, its hangers bare.

The bed covers were turned back and disheveled, although she could see no indentation in the pillow. On the bedside table MacGill discovered the room key. Under a water glass beside it lay several bills.

The Scotsman pocketed the cash. "At least, he didn't try to do the dirty. He got no calls before we closed up. None except the one at dinner."

Brandy stepped into the room. "I heard someone in the hall after twelve. Then someone came in and left by the back stairs very early this morning. Maybe Rossi got news of the woman he's looking for."

"How?" MacGill stooped over the waste basket, shook his head, and lifted out an empty Scotch bottle. "Looks like your man had one over the top before he left. He showed a taste for the stuff in the lounge. He'd hardly be fit to drive."

Cara, once more in jeans, slipped past John as he descended the stairs and appeared in the doorway. "I'll clean the room. They don't need me in the kitchen." She favored Brandy with a warm smile.

John would be waiting. "I hoped Mr. Rossi would contact me before he left town," Brandy said to MacGill, then turned to Cara. "Before we pick up our dog for the day, we're taking the historic driving tour. It includes the old cemetery. I'd like to see the grave you mentioned." Maybe she could still make sense of all these fragments of information.

Cara brushed her hair back with fingers that trembled a little, her voice low. "Mr. MacGill lets me have the flowers from the dining room. I'm taking some out there in about half an hour. Meet me there. I've got an old newspaper clipping to show you."

Brandy had started across the downstairs lobby when the desk clerk called to her. Reaching behind her, the woman lifted a message from a mail slot. "With Mr. Rossi gone and all, I forgot. I took a phone call for you early this morning, about seven-thirty." She handed Brandy the paper. Brandy scanned the clerk's neat hand. "Forget the classified ad story," the note read. "A more important one's breaking here. Come back to the bureau as soon as you can."

"Can I call back?"

"The person said they couldn't be reached today or tomorrow."

It didn't sound like the State News Editor or his assistant. No specifics. "Did the caller leave a name?"

The clerk shook her head. "Said he was calling for your boss. I couldn't even tell for sure if it was a man. There was a lot of noise and the person spoke real soft."

Brandy asked John to wait, stalked to the phone booth, and called the bureau. The sports editor answered. No one else was in the office. He didn't know of a change in anyone's story budget. Or about any sudden big news. Both the State News Editor and his assistant would be at the city desk today as usual. Brandy asked if he would verify the early morning message and call her back if it were genuine. She hung up, a bit rattled. Was Rossi that concerned about her questions? Who else would want her off the story?

About a half an hour later Brandy and John located the old graveyard on Cemetery Point, bounded on three sides by marsh land and
shallow inlets. It lay on a gentle rise, its graves covered with pine needles, a few of the oldest with oyster shells. At one side of the circular
drive sat an unkempt station wagon.

While John stayed behind the wheel, reading a leaflet about historic
homes, Brandy stepped out into the sharp smell of salt air. A cool
breeze made her thankful for her long-sleeved white shirt. The only
sound came from traffic on the other side of a shallow bay, the only
motion from Cara at the edge of the graveyard, laying a centerpiece of
white and gold chrysanthemums before a small headstone.

"Give me a few minutes," Brandy said to John.

He looked at his watch. "It's nine-forty. If you're set on taking Meg,
we'd better pick her up soon. We ought to get to the Suwannee fish
camp around noon."

Brandy nodded and began picking her way among tombstones.
When she was quite close, Cara sat back on her heels and squinted up
at her. "Someone was in the cemetery last night," she said. "There's no
real protection, not even a fence. Kids come in to party." She pointed
to tire tracks over a grassy area and a few pieces of broken glass beside
the ruts.

"It's a shame," Brandy agreed. She peered at the modest gray stone.
She could read "Rest in Peace, Ye known but to God," and below that,
"Female, 1973."

Cara settled down on the grass. "Got a minute?"

Brandy lowered herself beside Cara, while an osprey wheeled up
from a nest in a tall marsh pine and dived toward the water.

"Marcia doesn't like me to come here. I don't tell her anymore."
Cara gestured toward Brandy, palms up. "After all, she hasn't told me
much. She found me during the hurricane of 1972. She was on her
way to the school house for shelter. My foster dad was already there,
but Marcia had been helping a friend on First Street board up her windows." Cara glanced down. "I'm sure she saved my life. I can never for-

get that. She says I must've been left by migrants. Some came here several days earlier, she said, looking for work at the fish houses. The Health and Rehabilitation Service office finally let Marcia and my foster dad keep me. They'd been foster parents before."

"And the woman buried here?"

Cara's large eyes met hers. "More than a year after the 1972 hurricane, a skeleton of a young woman was found in the old cistern in the hotel basement. No one knows how it got there." Her voice quivered. "But the day I was found, a woman and a little girl about my age left Otter Creek for Cedar Key. The woman was educated, well-dressed. I read about them in an old newspaper at the Historical Society Museum. I brought you a copy of the story. No one knows what happened to them."

She made an effort to steady her voice. "I think the woman buried here was my mother."

Carefully Cara lifted a Xerox copy of a clipping from a plastic bag and handed it to Brandy. Then she looked away. "I think I must be that girl, and if I am, my mother was not some migrant worker that can't be located."

Brandy folded the paper and slipped it into her pocket to read later. "You said there was another Cara Waters."

"Long before I was born, Marcia had a little girl about my age. Looked a lot like me. She was lost." Cara drew her knees up and locked her slender arms around them.

"Lost?"

"Like I told you, her name was Cara, too. She drowned in the hurricane of 1950. They had a house on the Gulf then, and it got swept away, the little girl with it. Marcia thinks her death was part of some awful retribution. The whole fishing fleet was smashed. Oyster men lost everything. They'd been ruining the beds, of course, over-harvesting. My foster dad was the foreman of a timber company. Then, of course, lumbering wasn't controlled. All the old forest was already gone. He was almost killed when the wind ripped the roof off the shack he'd gone to for shelter."

"No wonder you're frightened of hurricanes."

"Mr. MacGill says hurricanes hit here so often because we're stuck in an island in the Gulf. But Marcia thinks nature's programmed to strike back."

A horn honked. Brandy looked at her watch. Five of ten. As she lifted herself up and brushed off her slacks, Cara scrambled up beside her. "After the first little Cara drowned, Marcia worked with environmentalists for twenty years. She thought people had been ruining the natural environment. If they were being punished by nature, Marcia wanted to restore what had been lost." She looked up to see the osprey fly back to its nest, then began again. "Then she found me in another hurricane near the same place. It was like her child had been brought back by the storm. That's why she gave me the same name."

Puzzled, Brandy looked at her as they started back toward the road. "Did she think you were the same child?"

"We looked similar, but I don't think she really confused us, not after a while. But deep down, maybe she always has."

"And when you were found, you couldn't identify yourself?"

Cara shook her head. "Marcia says no one could make out what I was saying. I was too scared. They say I wasn't even three yet."

As John eased the car down the road toward them, Brandy reached the driveway, Cara beside her. "We're going to pick up Meg and go out to Shell Mound this afternoon," Brandy said. "I'll take some pictures of my own."

Cara nodded. "You could stop at the caretakers and report the digging. He doesn't have a phone in the trailer."

Brandy opened the passenger door and paused. John would certainly say that Cara's identity was not Brandy's problem. He had asked her to be quiet about her suspicions. Yet someone should tell Cara about Rossi.

"A private investigator from New York was staying at the hotel," Brandy said. "He was looking for a woman who disappeared in 1972, said she came to Cedar Key with a little girl. He wouldn't tell me the missing woman's name. The investigator was Anthony Rossi. He left this morning early, but he said money was involved for the missing child. You should try to reach him."

Cara's eyes widened. "The hotel should have his address." The quiver returned to her voice. "The newspaper said the woman buried at the hotel was murdered. The case was never solved." She put one hand on Brandy's arm. "You're a reporter. You know how to investigate things. I hope you'll help me find the truth."

Brandy gave a slight nod and slipped into the car seat. "I'll think about it."

When Cara turned away, John gunned the engine and headed for the cemetery entrance. "That girl's not your problem, Bran."

She opened her notebook and scribbled a few lines. "Just curious. Might be a story there. And I do wish I could do something to help her."

He gave her a tight-lipped glance. "You may end by doing the girl more harm than good." She wished John was not so often right. She doodled a gravestone in the margin, then closed the book, unfolded the Cedar Key map, and switched to a topic he would find more agreeable. "Why don't I drop you off on the main street? You could pick up a picnic lunch at the café while I collect Meg."

Neither MacGill nor Truck had told Rossi about the skeleton in the hotel cistern, a reservoir for storing water long ago abandoned. Why? She hoped Rossi had not left town without keeping his appointment with the police chief. Surely the chief would mention the unsolved murder. Brandy gripped her notebook, eager to jot down the thought that had taken form. She wondered if the cocktail waitress was referring to the skeleton in the basement when she said Rossi came to the hotel nineteen years too late. Brandy would have to bounce that idea off Rossi when she saw him again—if she saw him again.

CHAPTER 6

▼

John stepped out of the car at the café. "Next stop, the Suwannee River." Brandy was pleased to see his rare half-smile. Before she drove to Cara's house for Meg, she pulled the folded newspaper clipping from her pocket. It was from the regional edition of the Gainesville paper, dated June 25, 1972. Below items about George McGovern's campaign aides and the bombing in Viet Nam, Brandy read:

MYSTERY CHILD STILL UNCLAIMED

Officials in Cedar Key are still unable to locate the parents of the little girl found wandering along a Gulf-side street the night of June 18, as Hurricane Agnes began moving into the area. Charlotte Wilson, H.R.S. spokesman who now has custody of the child, estimated her to be two years of age. No one is reported missing in the area and inquiries nationwide have produced no response.

During a search of Levy County for the girl's parents, local police officers interviewed a cashier at the Otter Creek Cafe who said a young woman and small child arrived there on a Greyhound bus and ate at the restaurant late the afternoon before the storm struck. The cashier, Betsy Mae Terry, said the woman inquired about a bus to Cedar Key.

About thirty minutes later the woman told the cashier she had found a ride and drove away in a car. Mrs. Terry did not see the driver, however, and said she did not get a good look at the child. She was unable to identify the little girl later found in Cedar Key. She gave the police a detailed description of the woman, and they are attempting to locate her.

Police Chief Wiley Saunders suggested that the girl might have been abandoned by migrant workers who were seen in town prior to the hurricane and whose whereabouts are unknown.

The child is in good condition, but disoriented, and unable to help with her identification. She was rescued from the storm by artist Marcia Waters, 46, of Cedar Key and taken to the school house for safety. Mrs. Waters and her husband, prominent local citizens and approved foster parents, have asked to care for the little girl until her parents can be found.

Brandy tucked the newspaper article with care into her notebook—another piece of the puzzle. She would fax a copy to Rossi's office. Swinging the car around, she drove back up Second Avenue to collect her golden retriever. Marcia's station wagon already stood in her driveway.

The artist met Brandy on the porch in a white shirt, long denim skirt, and sandals instead of her smock, probably a concession to meeting customers in the gallery. She folded her arms across her chest. "I understand you encouraged Cara to take a foolish risk last night," she said.

As Brandy edged into the living room, a door in the hallway opened. Uncomfortable, Brandy shifted her focus to Cara's slight figure coming out of the hall. Since their meeting in the cemetery, Cara had changed into a blue and pink paisley print dress with a Peter Pan collar. Brandy wondered if the immature style had been Marcia's selection.

"I had no idea Cara would go to Shell Mound alone," Marcia said.

Cara hesitated in the doorway, but she spoke up. "Catching whoever was digging near the mound was a real service to the parks department, even if I didn't get the picture I went for." She straightened her shoulders, as if remembering something else, even more important. "This morning Brandy told me something no one else would."

Brandy dropped her gaze while Cara stared at Marcia. "An investigator's been in town. He had information about a woman who might be my mother. I'm sure that's what Mr. MacGill came here to tell you last night. You know how much I've wanted to find out about my birth parents! Now the man's gone."

Marcia flushed, Brandy did not know if from anger or hurt. "I suppose she told you money might be involved. Is that what really interests you?"

Cara's eyes clouded and she sank into a chair before the fireplace. Confronting her foster mother, Brandy thought, was not what she did best. Marcia turned to Brandy. "We have to leave now. Cara's helping in the gallery today. Your dog's leash is on a peg at the back door."

Brandy glanced at the photographs on the mantel. In the faded one, the child's eyes and hair were lighter than Cara's, the oval of her face a bit fuller, but they had a similar delicacy. Marcia Waters had lost one daughter, Brandy reminded herself. She did not intend to lose another. Brandy moved toward the door. "Is there a description of the child who came here with her mother? Anything that would connect her with Cara?"

"The cashier at the Otter Creek café was the only person who talked to the woman," Cara said. "You've seen her account. Useless."

Brandy looked at the artist, but Marcia shook her head. "A hurricane was coming. I'm sure the woman simply changed her mind about coming to Cedar Key. Quite sensible." She arched her neck and seemed to look down at Cara from a great height. "Cara persists in this fiction. Her attitude's common among adopted children. She wants to glamorize her birth parents. The fact is, she was most likely abandoned by workers trying to escape the storm. We're not likely to learn anymore at this late date." Marcia picked up her black sweater from the back of a chair. "We've got to go. The gallery should be open now. The weekend's our best time."

Cara helped lift Brandy's bouncing retriever onto the rear seat and gave her a quick nuzzle. "You're a sweet dog," she said. "I'll see you tonight." But the life had gone out of her voice.

Cara's trapped, Brandy thought, as she pulled away from the curb. Unless she had help, Marcia Waters would never let her break free. She'd never go away to study, or find her original family or be herself. She looked again at her watch. She was fifteen minutes late for meeting John.

She was almost to Second Avenue when she slowed at an intersection and noticed a commotion at a tiny Gulf beach a block to her right. Several men in jeans and coveralls were standing around or leaning on pick-ups, a fish and oyster panel truck was parked to one side, and what appeared to be a wrecking truck was backing toward the water. A white police car with red and blue stripes zipped past.

A few minutes later Brandy found John beside the salmon-colored museum, his camera aimed at a flock of yellow-breasted birds feeding on the berries of a Red Cedar. He held up a white café bag, proof that he had kept his part of the bargain, and opened the driver's door. "I can't wait to check the width of the boat slips at Fowler's Bluff." He grinned. "I'll see if our boat would fit. Then on to your Shell Mound picnic among the haunts."

Brandy slid over into the passenger seat. "One short detour," she said, her smile apologetic. "Something's going on at the end of E Street, just a couple of blocks from here." She loved the unadorned labeling of Cedar Key's downtown streets. No developer's Sunset Lanes and Rolling Gulf Avenues. Just plain numbers and letters in proper sequence. "Let's duck down and take a look."

Above Atsena Otie Key the sky threatened rain, and the morning's breeze had become keener. "The paper says the storm's going to hit Key West," John said, turning left at the next block. "At the rate it's moving, it won't get near here 'til the middle of the week."

Brandy reached back to open a window for Meg, letting in a pungent whiff of rotting seaweed. "We'll be long gone then."

By now the wrecker had backed across a band of flattened sandbags and a few feet of beach, littered with Gulf sea grasses. A cable was slowly reeling in a car. She could see the shiny black suit of a diver in the water. A small crowd in jackets and jeans had collected along the concrete abutment left of the narrow strip of sand. A pick-up truck stood to one side, a Marine Service Divers sign on the cab.

Near a clump of cabbage palms at the corner stood the tall officer Brandy had seen with Rossi at the police department, and with him Angus MacGill in a knitted cap and sweater. When the policeman waved their car away, John turned at the bottom of the slight hill and parked down the block on First Street. As Brandy climbed out of the car, she could see shrimpers watching from a trawler that lay off shore, and a sports fishing boat with a covered command console drifting toward them.

"Tide's about out," MacGill said as they joined him. "It was high about four this morning. No one copped onto the car until ten." He gestured toward a frame house on the other side of an adjoining vacant lot. "Then someone over there rang these lads."

John looked across the street at a white frame house with concrete steps leading up a hill to a screen porch. "Didn't anyone hear a car go into the water?"

The officer was now sketching a diagram of the scene on a small pad. He glanced up at the nearest house, his eyes, shielded by the black cap, even more melancholy than the day before. "Family there's on vacation. So far no one heard anything definite. Would've been about seven feet of water here early this morning."

"Officer Doggett, Brandy O'Bannon…" MacGill began, noticed John and added, "…Able. A reporter from Gainesville."

"Don't know as folks there'd be interested in this accident, Ma'am." Doggett turned and looked up the rise of E Street, past the Fish and Oyster panel truck. "Looks like the poor devil came down the street much too fast, couldn't make the sharp right hand turn at the corner of

First, and plowed off into the water, right? Would've sunk out of sight pretty fast at high tide."

Beside the wrecker Brandy recognized the powerful figure of Truck Thompson in his fisherman's cap and black jacket. He had taken his big hands out of his pockets and was helping the wrecker crew re-secure the cable. "Thompson could save them some trouble," Brandy said. "Looks like he has the muscle to lift the car straight out of the water."

MacGill nodded. "Truck's a strong lad, right enough. Before this shellfish farming came in, a man had to stand six, seven hours a day with a pair of heavy tongs, raking up oysters and lifting them into the boat. Learned the trade from his dad, and nobody better at it.

"Had quite a reputation for fighting in high school. They say even the girls he dated were afraid of him. It still takes a cheeky lad to cross him." MacGill's lower lip protruded. "Someone did once, mind, about two years ago when Truck got his Project Ocean Oyster lease. Truck caught the lad helping himself to Truck's bed. The poor bugger was lucky to get away with a few bones still intact."

Brandy took a second look at the oysterman's solid physique. "Was he charged with assault?"

MacGill grinned. "Truck's family's been in the oyster business here for five generations. For a few days it was sticky wicket. But in the end, no charges were filed. He's not so nervy since he got serious about Cara."

A diver lifted his mask and came sloshing across the beach toward Officer Doggett. "No luck, man," he called. "Door's open on the driver's side, like I said, but I can't see a body. Might be blood on the front seat." The diver's craggy young face looked distressed. "Maybe the driver got out, but he didn't make it to shore. The tide would've started running out pretty fast about four." Before he turned toward the truck, he handed Doggett a small packet. "Found these broken glasses on the floor. They might get lost." He gazed across the calm

Gulf waters. "We'll need to get a boat and search for the body off shore."

The officer's heavy face seem to sag even more. He lifted his cap and scratched his high forehead. "No footprints. Just skid marks at the corner. Hard to see why a guy would come down the hill that fast. Maybe he didn't know about the turn, right?"

The wrecker crew had now pulled the car onto the beach and began hoisting it up with their crane. Doggett stepped across the street. "Got to move your panel truck, Mr. Thompson," he called. "The wrecker needs more room."

Truck's round head swiveled in his direction. "Got plenty damn room," he snorted.

The officer gave him a bland look. "Move it now, Mr. Thompson."

Truck stamped across the bed of seaweed, small eyes aflame, growling, "Got one too many damn cops in this town."

"Right," said Doggett, unperturbed.

Brandy shook her head. "He's still got a temper. Does it bother Cara?"

MacGill settled his cap more firmly over his ears. "I expect she knows if she ever leaves Cedar Key, he'll be in a wax, that's for sure." They walked across to the beach and stared at the dripping car, a blue Chevrolet coupe. MacGill cocked his head. "Sounded like luggage banging around in the boot."

"Divers brought out a briefcase," Doggett said. "Recognize the car?"

Brandy bit her lip and nodded. The Gainesville airport decal was clear on the rear bumper. She had written a description of it the day before.

"Rossi," she said.

MacGill spoke up. "Makes sense. I pulled an empty bottle of Scotch whiskey out of the bin in his room this morning. He must've had a skinful."

Doggett dropped his voice, his St. Bernard eyes doleful. "Happens all the time. Guy gets smashed and racks up another DOA, right?" With long strides, he advanced on the wrecker.

While Doggett and the mechanic opened the door and peered inside, the motorboat moved in closer, its driver standing at the console, binoculars trained on the scene. Brandy could make out "Fisher-man's Fling" on the bow. Nathan Hunt of Miami Beach was satisfying his curiosity. The officer looked toward Hunt, his mouth turned down.

"Something rum about that lad," MacGill said. "Doggett knows it. Sports about in his fancy boat and says he's dead keen on fishing, but no one ever sees him do much. Boat's got a lot of storage, mind. I ask myself what's he carrying, if not fish?"

Brandy stared at him. "Are you suggesting something illegal?"

MacGill lifted his head and chose his words with care. "I'm not say-ing anything, except the narcs staged a drug bust right here at Dock Street a couple of years ago. They didn't bag the whole ring, and my friends tell me they didn't stop the drug trade around here, either."

Brandy looked again at the slim figure of Nathan Hunt in a madras plaid Windbreaker, surveying them all from the under the broad brim of a sun hat.

"Tarted up like a dog's dinner all the time," MacGill added. "Free to come and go. No job that I can make out. I say, where's he get the money?"

"Probably a wealthy man's son," Brandy said. But MacGill had sewn a seed. She remembered the monogram *B.B.* on the fine socks of Mr. Nathan Hunt.

"Odd thing," Doggett said, closing the car door. "Car's on cruise control. Guy wouldn't need that in town."

John took Brandy's arm. "There's nothing we can do here. Let's get on with it. Time's a-wasting." Brandy moved with him toward their car.

"Yeah," she agreed. "I need to be at the museum before it closes at four. I want to see the clippings there about the hurricanes of 1950 and 1972. Those are the years Marcia Waters lost one daughter and found another."

Zipping her jacket against the wind, she turned away from the wrecker and the small car suspended behind it, ready for towing, and sighed. Cara would not now, would not ever, have the chance to talk to private investigator Anthony Rossi.

CHAPTER 7

▼

"That guy's drowning isn't going to ruin our weekend," John said, as he turned off Route 347 toward Fowler's Bluff, nineteen miles from Cedar Key. "If he was dumb enough to stay up drinking, and then leave town before daylight, I'm sorry, but he got what he had coming."

Brandy searched for a fresh page in her notebook. "He wasn't on the road out of town. He was going in the opposite direction. Besides, I think he had important information for Cara."

"There's no question he was drunk."

She looked out into the lonely pine forest. "I just wish I could help Cara," she said in a small voice.

At a wide bend in the Suwannee River they found the fish camp, its store, rickety pier, and boat slips dwarfed by the broad sweep of brown water. Wind ruffled the river's surface and shook the Spanish moss on the oaks along the shore. On the opposite bank stretched miles of undeveloped hardwood swamp that ended in a dense band of cypress and oak at the river's edge.

John parked beside the store, pleased. "This is my idea of a real vacation spot, surrounded by a wildlife refuge. One of the few places in the lower Suwannee that has any houses at all."

Brandy stepped out into the cool, moist air and let Meg jump down and dash to the end of her leash. "Unless you count houseboats." A sizable white one was chugging downstream. By the position of its windows, Brandy judged it had a bedroom, bath, and living area. She could make out fishing rods in a holder on the rear deck and, as it passed by, a large man with bushy black hair at the railing.

John followed her gaze. "Probably out for his last few days of fishing before the storm hits." He pulled a metal tape measure from the glove compartment and stepped over to the nearest boat slip.

Brandy walked the retriever briskly to the pier and stood with her hands in her jacket pockets, thoroughly chilled.

A few minutes later John strode up the wooden steps of the one room store and disappeared through a door plastered with ads for cold drinks, bait, and fishing lures. Brandy bent down to pat Meg, then looked around. The camp had a row of small frame cottages beside the dock, as well as a boat ramp and slips. A skiff with a kicker rocked in the closest one.

"Good fishing," John announced, trotting back down the steps with a brochure. "Catfish, bream, even trophy-sized, large mouth bass. A great place to stay. The slips are plenty wide enough for our pontoon boat."

Except for this one store, the riverbanks looked completely isolated. "Alligators?"

"Well, of course."

"Water moccasins?"

"We wouldn't be swimming." He glanced around at the lonely vista. "Very reasonable price, too. I told the woman we'd be back soon."

Brandy tried to muster enthusiasm as she gazed across the murky water. Yet she was seized by the same dread she'd felt the night before when they were seated in the shadowy Island Hotel dining room. Meg flopped at her feet, whining. "Any marinas nearby?"

"One about fifteen miles down river near the Gulf. At the little town of Suwannee." A crooked smile again lit his face. "This is real Florida. No neighbors knocking around the hall. No restaurants. No lounges

and art galleries. Just trees and river and fish." He gave her a meaning-
ful look that told her he wanted them to be alone, with no distractions.

"It's quiet, all right." Brandy watched the houseboat slip out of
slight around the bend, then turned her back on the dark river and
huddled into the car. Something was wrong, but she did not know
what.

Shell Mound Road ran straight as a shot to the county camp
ground, then ended in a gravel drive that wound under twisted
branches toward the Indian midden itself. John parked next to a single
strand of cable that protected the mound. Across it a dim trail led
upward. Outside the car again with Meg on her leash, Brandy looked
up at the shroud of Spanish moss draping the oaks, then across the bay
to her right, and at the Gulf before them. The wind was still sharp and
she pulled her jacket tighter.

John picked up the paper bag of sandwiches and stepped over the
wire. "Took prehistoric Indians hundreds of years to build this mound
up with oyster shells and all kinds of refuse. It took Americans only a
few years to start plundering it."

"At least it's against the law to disturb it now."

Brandy followed him up the rise, carrying the cooler in one hand
and restraining the excited retriever with the other. "We've got to tell
the caretaker about the vandalism Cara saw."

A thick growth of oaks, cedars, and palmettos crowded the trail, and
beneath the carpet of leaves she could feel the crunch of shells. Meg ran
beside her, nose to the ground. At a hollow to the left she whined and
pulled, but Brandy brought her to heel and labored up toward the
broad summit. Here John stood, breathing in the scent of cedar, and
smiling down at the silent flats of saw grass and needlerush. Beyond
them the Gulf, dotted with tiny islands, stretched to the horizon.
Brandy clamored up beside him, coppery hair blowing in her eyes. Yesterday's brilliant blue sky had been replaced with a flat gray.

"There's a bench," she said, leading the way to the bottom of the
trail on the other side. "A place to picnic."

"My kind of Florida again." John snapped the pop top on a cold drink can, lifted out ham sandwiches, and rustled around in the bag for chips while Brandy pulled out a dog biscuit.

"A treat for a sweet girl. Cara's taken good care of her." She fed the biscuit into Meg's moist mouth. "No one's around. I'm going to let her run a bit."

John gave a short laugh. "Maybe find the ghostly wolfhound, I suppose, a canine spirit companion?"

Brandy smiled as the retriever leapt up the trail, nose to the ground, and disappeared beyond the summit. They could hear her tearing about in the underbrush. "Can't think what Meg is so excited about." Brandy gazed around the thicket. "Wonder where Cara was last night?"

More scratching on the other side of the midden, a low growl. Brandy stood up.

"Better call her back," John said. "Digging here's illegal, remember?"

But Meg saved her the trouble. She came loping over the mound, tail wagging, eyes in the creamy mask alight. In her mouth she carried something dark, something with a strange shape. Brandy shivered when the retriever dropped it, panting, at her feet. A man's soiled shoe.

Brandy picked it up, holding it at arm's length. Where had she seen one like it? "That's odd. It's a perfectly good shoe. No holes in the sole. Why would anyone leave one shoe?"

John rose and stretched. "All kinds of crazies in the world. I told you that when you wanted to come here last night. Watch my sandwich. I'd better take a look." Meg ignored the tantalizing ham and trotted before him, eager tail high. Brandy took another meditative bite, scanning the marshes. They were quite alone.

When John reappeared a few minutes later, his face was tense and had a sudden sallow hue. "I'll stay here and you go for help. The man didn't leave his shoe. The man was still in it."

Within twenty minutes of Brandy's call from a farmhouse on Route 347, a white cruiser with a green stripe and gold star screeched to a stop beside the cable. Deputy Snapp, a thin, blond young man in a dark green uniform, stood several yards from the rough grave and studied the foot, clad in a sandy sock, protruding toe-up from the mulch. At one side Meg had scraped up a pile of dirt and leaves, as she unearthed the part of the victim closest to the surface. Only a portion of the lower leg in dirt-stained, tan pants was visible. Yet they knew that several feet below must be a face.

"Very recent." Snapp's voice sounded strained. "No dang odor."

Brandy suspected he had not processed a murder scene before. He was careful not to walk closer, either from fear of contaminating the crime scene or from distaste, and his hands shook as he tapped in the stakes and strung yellow evidence tape around the mound. After he ducked back into his cruiser and made a call, he advanced toward the bench where John and Brandy had taken refuge.

In a dog-eared spiral notebook, the deputy wrote down each of their statements in a slow scrawl, and then ordered them to wait for the homicide detective. Under a lowering sky they sat side by side on the bench, the forgotten picnic beside them. Brandy lifted a note pad out of her canvas bag and began making a list.

John sighed. "I guess we've shot the rest of our day." He glanced at Brandy's pad. "You might write down everything we won't be able to do."

"That poor guy won't be doing much, either." Brandy looked at the depression next to the trail and went on writing. "I was jotting down the list of questions I want answered at the historical museum."

Meg, on a tight leash at Brandy's feet, let out a bewildered "woof" and dropped her head between her paws. Her delightful find had brought no joy. As for the shoe itself, Snapp left it on the ground where Brandy had dropped it.

"Captain's sending Detective Jeremiah Strong," he said at last. "He's a plumb stickler for collecting and labeling. A lay preacher, too." His tone sounded apprehensive.

In half an hour the homicide detective pulled up in a gray and maroon Ford Taurus. When the door of the sedan opened, a tall, solidly built black man stepped out. A unique specimen, Brandy thought, especially in rural, mostly white Levy County. He skirted the tape, stood for a few seconds, hands behind him, surveying the scene. In a few minutes the Mobile Crime Scene van tore around the curves of the gravel road and parked behind his car. Two technicians waited in the Florida Department of Law Enforcement van, while the detective came toward them with the confident, slightly pigeon-toed stride of an athlete.

"Sergeant Jeremiah Strong, Homicide" he said. "Levy County Sheriff's Office." He was pulling a notebook and pen out of the inside pocket of his gray sports coat when he noticed the shoe. "Get a bag out of the kit in the trunk," he called to Snapp, who had lagged behind.

In a few minutes the young deputy had advanced with a brown paper bag, stooped over the potential exhibit, and hesitated. "Pick it up with your fingertips, by the edge of the sole," Strong said. "Put your name on the bag, the location, and the date." He glanced at his watch. "It's two-thirty."

He then turned a solemn expression toward John and Brandy. The effect was intimidating. Jeremiah Strong was six feet four of taut muscle. He had closely cropped hair, a high forehead, widely spaced eyes, and teeth that looked very white below his neat mustache. Brandy thought the detective probably had no difficulty persuading witnesses to cooperate.

But the tone of his first words surprised her. Nodding at his nervous assistant, he said softly, "The Good Book do say, 'Be patient toward all men.'"

Again they identified themselves and gave their statements. "I'd be much obliged if you'd stay awhile longer." Strong closed his note pad, his voice polite but firm. "Let's see what we got here. Then you can go along."

He took slow steps around the scene, hands clasped behind his back, occasionally stopping to make a brief note. At one point he seemed to be sketching a diagram.

"No footprints over here," he announced, "but some dragging over the leaves. Someone had a mind to cover up the signs." He knelt and peered at the ground. "Over here, Deputy. Reckon we got ourselves a few drops of dried blood. Better save them before we start digging. Hand me the camera and two envelopes from the kit."

When Snapp gave Strong the envelopes, he scooped soil samples from the site with care. "This isn't the murder scene." He shook his head. "We still got to find that."

He circled the entire area with the camera, shooting it from every direction and angle. Then he knelt again beside the cable and drew a line in the dirt. "Access to the scene's here. We all stay on this path."

Finally he stood and started back toward the dark blue van, signaling to the technicians. A stout man and a slimmer colleague came forward with short-handled shovels and began the tedious process of sifting through the soil and uncovering the body.

Brandy turned to John on the bench. "I'm sure I've seen that cheap walking shoe before." She tried not to look at the dark shapes circling high above the marsh—turkey buzzards. "I need to tell the detective that Cara was here last night, that she saw someone digging and may even have gotten a picture."

He frowned. "Hearsay. He'll question everyone. You let Cara tell him herself."

Suddenly the stout crime scene technician sat back on his heels and gave a shout to Strong. The detective hung the camera around his neck, strode to the edge of the rough grave, and bent down. "The guy's not local. Never saw him before."

Tucking her pad back into her bag, Brandy stood, walked a few steps and called to Strong. "Could my husband or I take a look? A man was missing from a car accident in Cedar Key this morning. He'd been staying where we are, at the Island Hotel." She moved closer, thinking of that familiar shoe. "His rental car went into the Gulf, but divers couldn't find a body. A Cedar Key policeman named Doggett was the officer on the scene."

Strong raised his eyebrows. "Maybe the gentleman would see if he can I.D. this body." He squinted at the dimensions of the grave. "Looks like our perp got careless at the end of his job. Buried the head and torso pretty deep, but he wasn't so particular about the feet and legs. Maybe got scared off."

Cara, Brandy thought. He heard Cara and left sooner than he meant to. Lucky thing, Meg's nose.

The technicians scraped the last of the earth away from what Brandy supposed was the head. Strong straightened up and motioned to John. 'We'll check his pockets for an I.D. after the medical examiner's been here. Have a look."

For added security, Brandy wrapped Meg's leash around her wrist. "Does the man have glasses?" She remembered that the diver had found a broken pair in the sunken car.

Strong shook his head again. "Not that I can see. He's face up, though. Makes it easier." By then John had threaded his way up the path to the edge of the hollow and looked down. "It's Rossi, all right," he said to Brandy in a tight voice, then looked at Strong. "His name was Anthony Rossi. Came from New York City."

"New York, you say?" Jeremiah Strong favored them with a grim smile. "Been looking for a New York connection."

Brandy edged nearer up the trail. She could see the bulge of the waxy, soil-splotched forehead, the prominent nose. On Rossi's chest a black, encrusted cloth had been wadded against his body. "He was a private investigator," she added. "Said he was looking for a missing woman and her daughter."

"Yeah." Strong gave her a quick glance. "He'd have a cover."

"I don't know what you're talking about. He said the client he worked for died while he was in Cedar Key, but he was still on the case."

Once more Strong raised his eyebrows. "That sound likely to you?" He frowned. "You're a newspaper lady, right?"

Brandy nodded and, feeling defensive, crossed her arms over her chest.

"The most important thing is, you don't write anything until I say. You going to cooperate, Ma'am?"

"I plan to call my editor, but I'll tell him I'm waiting for a Sheriff's Office briefing."

The white teeth gleamed again. "Soon's we get the hands bagged and the body off to the medical examiner's lab in Gainesville, I'll be to Cedar Key. Get a more detailed statement. Both of you, stay available." He tugged a worn spiral note pad from his pocket and jotted a few lines. "I want to talk to all the folks who saw Mr. Rossi as the Island Hotel. Don't you be telling them about this before I get a chance to talk to them, see how they act." He leaned forward. "Three-quarters of all the crime along this coast is drug crime, ma'am. We been after a Levy County-New York connection for two years. Could be this guy."

John glared at the untidy pile of leaves, sticks, and dirt thrown up by the retriever and rubbed his forehead. "I suppose our dog destroyed most of the evidence."

"That's one way to look at it, I reckon." Strong put his large hands on his hips. "Come down to it, though, without this dog, the perp sure might have got away with murder." He glanced down at the still face in the depression beside the trail. "Like the Bible say 'Look to it; for evil is before you.'"

Brandy did not know if he referred to Rossi's death or his suspected deeds.

They went single-file down to the road where Strong paused at the cable. "Some place there's a spade with dirt on it from Shell Mound." He crossed to the road and pointed. "A separate set of tire tracks." He summoned Snapp. "Better be starting with the casts."

Brandy asked herself where she had seen other tire tracks today. From the van a technician took a camera on a frame that pointed directly down and made a photograph. Then he placed a portable frame above the tracks and started for the bay with a pail. As John and Brandy climbed into their car, the detective and Snapp were holding the ends of a measuring tape and noting the distances of the grave from two widely spaced trees.

On the gloomy drive back to the hotel Brandy opened her notebook and doodled a thick-soled oxford in the margin of a blank page. "Detective Jeremiah Strong's a bright and careful guy, but I think he's on the wrong track."

She began noting what she had seen and heard at the mound, then paused to stare at the pine farm slipping by. "Last night Rossi said he would find out today where the missing woman meant to stay. Said the cottage is gone now, but he would find out who had owned it. Why would he be concerned, if he was here on a drug buy?"

CHAPTER 8

▼

Brandy reached between the seats to pat the golden-red retriever as John parked by the artist's front walk. "One more night with Cara. She'll be good to you," Brandy said. "Don't feel bad. It's not your fault you spoiled our day."

Marcia answered the doorbell, her spare figure draped in her paint-splattered smock. She looked down at Meg, prancing beside Brandy on a short leash, and gave a brusque nod toward the side gate. "Fact is, the gate's already open," she said, spun around, and retreated toward her studio. Meg's not the only one in the dog house here, Brandy thought, guiding the retriever into the back yard and giving her a final pat. She did not see Cara.

But when Brandy opened the lobby doors of the Island Hotel, Cara was slumped in one of the wooden chairs at the round coffee table, leafing through an album of the hotel's history. She looked up, large eyes somber in her heart-shaped face. "Mother and I had another row. We both heard about the private detective's car." She pushed back her veil of long hair. "I think she's glad he may be dead. Now I've got no way to find out if he knew about my real mother."

Brandy pursed her lips and looked at John. "I need to talk to Cara and call my bureau. It may take a little while. Could you wait for me upstairs or in the lounge?"

John rolled his eyes and started up the long white stair case.

She turned to Cara. "Did you ever see the classified ad Mr. Rossi put in the local and Gainesville papers?"

Cara shook her head. "The papers disappeared at the Gallery. Even Mr. MacGill said something happened to theirs. I didn't even hear about it. I doubt I'd have looked at the classifieds, anyway." There it was again—everyone keeping news from Cara.

Before Brandy stepped into the phone booth, she took Cara's old newspaper clipping out of her notebook. When she reached the State News Editor and explained that she'd had a message to drop the Cedar Key stories and come back to the Bureau, he sounded perplexed. "Practical joke, maybe?" He sounded doubtful.

"There's more. John and I found a body today. By accident. The man was murdered. The Levy County Sheriff's Office has to make a positive I.D. before they release the story, but we're sure he's the guy who placed the personal ad. Could be a big story, maybe for a full run." She glanced at the clipping. "Make a note of this name and see if anyone can locate a Betsy Mae Terry. Used to work at the café in Otter Creek years ago. Let me know in the morning. I have a good lead on who the missing child is."

His voice quickened, excited now. "Find out what you can and modem the story tomorrow. Make it before four."

Brandy dropped into a chair next to Cara. "Mr. MacGill must have Anthony Rossi's address. We could try to contact his agency. Maybe someone there knows something." Brandy frowned. She could not break her word to Detective Jeremiah Strong about the body, but at least she could let Cara know the authorities would investigate Rossi. After all, Angus MacGill had mentioned a drug bust in Cedar Key. "I got the impression that the police think Rossi was involved in drug trafficking here. They'll be checking on him."

Cara's lips turned down. "Even if they do, they won't care about me. They won't try to identify the missing woman."

Brandy felt a twinge of guilt. She thought of the tall, lean artist who had saved a tiny child from drowning, and then reared that child as her own. Was Brandy herself responsible for the rift developing between them? John would certainly say so. John said she may be harming Cara, not helping her.

"Marcia's been a wonderful mother to you, hasn't she?" Brandy touched the girl's arm. "She obviously cares about you, and you wouldn't have your interest in photography without her."

Cara glanced down at the open album. "That's true. Of course I'm fond of my foster mother. I don't want to hurt her." Her gaze wandered over a black and white photograph of the hotel interior. It showed the rear of the lobby and a figure in the entry way to the kitchen, holding open the door. "But I've grown up. Marcia refuses to understand that." She tapped the photograph with a slender finger. "I've got to know what happened right here in this hotel twenty years ago."

Brandy sat back, thoughtful. Some questions, she agreed, for Cara's peace of mind should be answered. "We don't know for sure you're the little girl Marcia rescued. But we do know the year and date is right." Besides, Brandy sensed a first rate human interest story.

She ambled across the lobby toward the desk where the young clerk was punching in numbers on a computer screen. John had signed the register right after Rossi. The investigator's address should be there. She rested her elbows on the counter. "I'd like to see if my husband remembered to register yesterday afternoon."

The clerk glanced up, eyes defensive behind her large glasses, reached for a bound volume open on the counter, flipped back a page, and thrust the book toward Brandy. "Your names are here. Mr. MacGill would never, you know, overlook something like that."

The bachelor Scotsman had a loyal following among the staff, Brandy noticed. She peered at Anthony Rossi's now poignant scrawl above John's signature and memorized the New York City address. While the clerk returned to her task with a righteous shrug, Brandy jotted the address and phone number in a note pad and slipped it into her bag, then re-joined Cara.

"Got it," she said, glancing at her watch. Five o'clock already. Too late for the historical museum. "If I write a feature story about Rossi's search, I need background. Like newspaper stories of both hurricanes, the one in 1950 and the one in 1972. But the museum's closed now, and it's not open on Sundays."

Cara shut the album. "I could probably help you there. One of the docents lives right down the street. Maybe she'll meet you at the museum because you're a reporter. The historical society's always looking for publicity."

She stepped into the phone booth beside the lobby doors and in a few minutes came back with a slight smile. "Mrs. Fleur said okay. In about fifteen minutes. I told her you just wanted to see specific newspapers." Cara sat down again and propped her chin in her hands. "She's a sweet old thing, but don't let her fool you. She's still totally sharp. Her family's been in Cedar Key for five generations, like Truck's family, the Thompsons. Before she retired, she was one of my elementary school teachers."

Cara sighed. "I need to get ready to serve dinner by six. When you're through at the museum, come to the kitchen. I'd like to show you the basement. If you write about the skeleton, you ought to see where it was found."

"I need to tell John," Brandy said.

An early October dusk had descended on the balcony when Brandy located him. He sat in the failing light, his historical restoration book in his lap. Chopin had been replaced by the more plaintive Tchaikovsky. Beyond the dockside restaurants and shops, clouds piled in smoky shapes above Atsena Otie Key and a wind blew from the Gulf. "Before we eat dinner," Brandy said, "I want to run over to the museum. One of the docents is going to open up briefly for me."

When Brandy bent to kiss his cheek, he gave her a wry smile. "The weekend's working out like I predicted."

Brandy flushed. There was justice in his complaint. And yet she couldn't turn back now. She had to know more about Cara, about Rossi, about the unidentified woman in the cemetery, and she had to find answers this weekend.

"I won't be long. The docent's already on her way. I'll meet you in the lobby in an hour." As she raced back downstairs, she wondered if she had allowed enough time for a tour of the basement.

Brandy recognized Miss Fleur immediately. She was hurrying down the sidewalk, bulky purse under one arm, a petite, elderly woman in a pale aqua knit dress and sensible oxfords, her white hair in a wispy bun. Brandy waited under the balcony of the salmon-pink museum while Miss Fleur's shaky hand turned the key in the lock.

"Indeed, we're quite pleased to help you." Miss Fleur pushed open the white door. Her voice was soft, like the pouches under her eyes and the folds of skin below her cheeks. "Do come right on in."

She snapped on a light and advanced with dainty steps to a small table where she opened the sign-in book. The long room was lined with wall maps and glass cases on wooden stands. Under the fluorescent lights lay fossil and shell collections, Indian artifacts, antique bottles, eighteenth century dresses and uniforms, impressive layouts on the lost cedar pencil mills, and on the last industry to go, the factory that made palm fiber brooms.

With one fragile, blue-veined hand Miss Fleur waved away Brandy's dollar bill for the collection box.

"It's two hurricanes I'm interested in, 1950 first." The storm, she said to herself, that killed the first little Cara. "Oh, dear, yes. Such a terrible time!" Miss Fleur trotted to a display of newspapers mounted on vertical panels and began turning through them. "I was here, then, of course. Fortunately, the new school had just been built. We used it for shelter. And the new pier just finished a few months before. Gone." She gestured with both hands, thin eyebrows raised, suggesting the enormity of the damage. "You know what that storm was named? Hurricane Easy!"

Brandy paused at a newspaper dated September 6, 1950, with a photograph of President Truman on the front page, and scanned the hurricane story. Easy had begun as a "baby" hurricane—thus its name—and traveled slowly at about thirteen miles an hour up the coast from the Caribbean. For fourteen hours it had remained stationary off shore at Clearwater, eighty miles south. No one expected any real trouble. Almost no one in Cedar Key or elsewhere evacuated.

Then something queer happened. The storm came roaring out of its loop, smashed into Cedar Key early in the morning of September 5th, hovered like a whirling demon all day, its winds clocked at 125 miles an hour before the gauge was blown away. Then it made another loop, moved the eye over the town a second time, and struck again full force. At five that afternoon winds were still estimated at one-hundred miles an hour.

Cedar Key had born the brunt of the hurricane for seventy-two hours, taken twenty-five inches of rain. Half its houses were destroyed by "wind and wave," as well as the newly restored fiber plant and the entire Cedar Key fishing fleet. The hurricane had targeted the town, then bore in twice to demolish it. Nature's vengeance, Marcia would've said, for all the damage to Cedar Key's environment. For her, the "baby" hurricane had a terrible irony. "Was there any loss of life?" Brandy asked.

Behind the table now, Miss Fleur's face crumpled. Her fingers flew to her cheeks. "Oh, indeed, yes. Only one, it turned out, but that one was so dreadfully sad."

"Mrs. Waters' daughter?"

"A baby, really, about two years old. Marcia was a very young woman then. They had a cottage on the Gulf. When the storm hit that morning, Marcia waited for her husband to come home with his pulp-wood crew. Actually, the men couldn't get back to town. Cut off by high water. Had to stay in two little buildings out in the pine woods. Wind tore the roofs off. No one knew how awful the storm would be." Tears trembled in her eyes.

Brandy was aware of darkness now outside. The street was silent except for the rustle of palm fronds against a window and the hollow echo of footsteps on the sidewalk.

"Marcia waited too long," Miss Fleur said at last. "She couldn't get to the school house with the rest of us. She managed to cling to the rafters when the roof went. The house was completely flooded, but the baby—well, the wind tore her out of her mother's arms."

She paused to collect herself, and then her voice became almost a whisper. "I've known Marcia since she came to Cedar Key as a bride. After that day, she was never the same. The child's death was doubly sad because Marcia couldn't have any more children. She needed an operation after the first little Cara was born."

"But she and her husband did become foster parents?"

"Oh, she tried to compensate for the loss." Miss Fleur shook her head. "They took in several children, and she began painting water colors. Both good therapy, we all thought." She clasped her hands together and spread them apart. "But when she found that little girl during Hurricane Agnes, that changed everything for her."

"In June of 1972?"

"I'm sure you've heard the story," Miss Fleur continued in a more cheerful tone. "It was a miracle. That night Marcia was on her way to the school when she found that baby alone. The little thing was almost blown away." Again the expressive hands moved together. "She and Mr. Waters didn't live on the Gulf themselves anymore, but Marcia was helping a friend with her house on the water. Marcia just picked up that child, put her in her car, and brought her to the school house wrapped in an old coat she had on the back seat. Got there before the full hurricane hit. She came running in drenched. I'll never forget. She was half out of her mind. She kept saying over and over, 'The hurricane brought her back!'—like she'd found their lost baby." She glanced over at the newspapers. "That would be late that month."

Brandy flipped to a June 20, 1972, newspaper and scanned it. The Russia-Afghanistan War and Viet Nam were front page news. Early on the twentieth the hurricane raked Cedar Key with winds, flood tides, and tornadoes. Once again the town bore the brunt. High water marooned it by mid-day. The main streets were knee-deep in tides higher than any since 1935. Beach cottages crumbled, their roofs snatched off, their rooms awash in waist-deep water.

"For days afterward the floors of houses along the water were still layered with mud," Miss Fleur said.

"Did most people wait it out again at the school house?"

"Most went to the school house. I did. It's a wonder Marcia made it that time, too. A smaller group stayed at the Island Hotel. It always rides out any storm. Has all these years. But they all had to pitch in and shore up the basement with sandbags."

"Mr. MacGill wasn't here then?"

"He was in town. He'd bought some Gulf side cottages. Those that weren't swept away were so badly damaged, they had to be torn down. He bought the hotel later that year." She rose, joined Brandy at the panel, and pointed with one unsteady finger at the Island Hotel photograph. "A photographer at the hotel took those pictures. Folks couldn't get out of town after the storm for two days. Some were in Cedar Key looking for work. There were oyster and fish buyers here, too. They all took turns with the sandbags."

A tiny light flicked on in Brandy's brain. "So a lot of people went into the basement that night?"

Miss Fleur nodded. "That's what I hear. You can see the owner there, the large woman at the desk, and some of the locals, but there were others we never knew." Brandy counted three disheveled women and six men, standing or sitting in the lobby. They all looked surprised. Obviously, it was a candid shot.

"What was going on along the Gulf that night, before the full hurricane came ashore?"

"Some fellows drove up First Street and around Goose Cove and the bayous, picking up folks that needed to get away from the Gulf. Some fellows you wouldn't expect to help, like Truck Thompson. He was about eighteen then, and wild as a March hare."

"And he came to the school house?"

"Quite late."

"Mr. MacGill. Where was he that night?"

Miss Fleur dimpled. "Such a nice man. He settled here quite broken after his wife passed away, but he's been so good for the community." Her eyes brightened. Angus MacGill had become a popular figure in an insular society. "They say he made a small fortune in shopping centers up north. He'd been here on holiday. When he lost his wife, he sold everything and moved to Cedar Key. That would've been in the early sixties. The night of the storm he came to the school house, too, but late. He lost his own property, but he was out trying to help others."

"And Marcia Waters?"

"She finally found her husband at the school, too. There were hundreds of us. No one recognized the child, not then nor later."

Time was passing. There was John to think of. Brandy moved away from the panels and paused before the door. The lights were out in the art gallery across the street, where on one darkened wall Marcia's drawing of a tiny figure cowered before a giant wave.

"You've been so kind," Brandy said. "One last thing. I heard that a skeleton was found in the hotel cistern a year after Hurricane Agnes. Do you know anything about that?"

A pained look crossed the white brow. "A dreadful mystery, that skeleton. No one had used the cistern for years. I think the water and sewer board required some work on the plumbing, a city inspection, something like that. There'd been talk of another storm on the way, and the workers pulled the sandbags out of the cistern while they were there, to have them ready, you know."

"Mr. MacGill didn't order the work?"

"No. That is, it was mandated by the town. Constantly have to work on maintenance in an old building like that. When they removed the sandbags, they found the bones." She shuddered. "Once in a while people had gone down there for tools and things, and they'd complained of a foul odor. But you know, old basements are likely to smell bad. They'd use poisons to kill rats, and people thought the rats died in crawl spaces and in the walls."

"What happened when the workers found the skeleton?"

"The medical examiner said nasty blows to the head killed the woman. No one in our area was missing, and they never could find out who she was. Folks figured some of the migrants stranded in the storm must've gotten in a fight. A few women were among them. They could've taken the body down the outside steps. Folks parked their cars there to get away from the water on Second Street. The police found the rear door hadn't been locked."

"Cara Waters seems to think the skeleton might be her mother's."

"Oh, dear, I've heard that. So sad. Marcia's been a wonderful mother to her. She's put this town on the map in the art world and with nature lovers, too. The new child was so good for Marcia. I'll tell you the truth. None of us wanted that child identified and taken away." Brandy wondered if that was why MacGill hadn't cooperated with Rossi. Of course, he could have an even more powerful motive.

"With that new baby, Marcia was like a woman resurrected."

Brandy turned the knob. "But Cara wants to leave Cedar Key now. She wants to go to college, to study photography. Surely if she left like that, Marcia wouldn't be losing her."

Miss Fleur drew herself up, her soft features congealed in a teacher's look of disapproval. "That's where you'd be much mistaken. When young people leave Cedar Key, they don't come back."

CHAPTER 9

▼

In the hotel lobby Brandy was relieved to see John and MacGill behind the counter, bending over an architectural rendering of the old hotel, above them the print of Edinburgh castle's bleak walls. She murmured, "Be back soon," and hurried on toward the kitchen.

When she pushed open the door, Cara was waiting, dressed for work in a crisp mauve uniform, her hair bound by a white head band and fastened back with a clip. Yet in those wide eyes Brandy saw apprehension, even fear. Cara led her into a large kitchen, past gleaming metal cabinets and a long wooden table where a cook in a white apron was cutting up garnishes and setting out seasoning.

Cara's slender fingers moved to her face, then flitted back to her waist and locked together. "I want you to see the cistern. It was built to store water. In the fifties people were afraid of an atomic war. Of course, it was never used."

Never used except on one fatal night, Brandy thought. "If you write this story," Cara added, "you'll need to describe it. I won't go down with you. When I went to work here, I learned that I couldn't. I get that feeling, like in nightmares, that I can't breathe."

The stout cook turned to wash carrots and celery at the sink. "Dead right about that." She wagged a plump finger at Cara, a smile on her ruddy face. "Mr. MacGill sent her down for mineral spirits the first night she was here. Found she'd fainted dead away when we finally went to look for her." The large woman shook her head. "We never sent that one down in the basement again."

Cara led Brandy into a small adjoining room with a washer and dryer and halted before the wooden steps that descended into the gloom. "Notice the door from the back parking area," she said, handing Brandy a large flashlight. Brandy remembered that it had been unlocked the night of Hurricane Agnes. "The cistern's in a separate space in the rear. Back in the fifties the owner planned to make it a bomb shelter."

Shining the light before her, Brandy shuffled down the stairs into the stale odor of dank soil. She wasn't sure what she expected to see. After all, the skeleton had been gone for nineteen years. The front of the basement had a cement floor and, she was surprised to discover, was at ground level. Before her a pair of plank doors opened into the back yard. She pushed them apart and noticed a garbage shed to the right. Next to it, a yellow metal fire escape served as a rear exit for the upper floors. In the front section, broken chairs and a ladder leaned against the thick tabby wall of oyster shell, limestone, and sand.

Brandy turned instead toward the back of the staircase and threw the flashlight beam on a narrow passageway that opened into the other room. Stooping, she inched between concrete block partitions into a lower, mustier area with a dirt floor. Against one wall lay old bags of insulation and a broken lamp. Sand bags had been tumbled along another, ready for the next flood. But the most prominent feature was the concrete block cistern, its exterior walls about three feet high, and far below, a fetid pool of greenish water. Beside it lay the scattered boards of what must once have been a lid.

Staring into the silent depths, Brandy felt the full horror of what must have happened here—the rear door banging open, in the darkness outside the mounting roar of rain and wind, a figure stumbling through the back passage, perhaps following the faint beam of a flashlight, a limp woman's body hoisted over a shoulder, or worse, dragged behind, the groan of the cistern lid wrenched aside, the body dumped, the sickening splash as it plunged into the dirty water. Sand bags hauled then in a panic across the damp soil, pitched down into the blackness, the lid shoved in place.

Maybe the murder weapon thrown in the cistern, too, or stuffed in a crevice or covered with dirt. Then the figure groping its way through the darkened basement into the yard, or darting up the kitchen stairs to join the refugees huddled in the hotel lobby and lounge. Who would notice when a hurricane was thrashing its way ashore? Who would miss those sand bags when the others were layered against the rising water?

Brandy found herself shaking, overcome with the closeness, the sour smell, the feel of evil. How easy to pull the lid aside, to push an inert body down into this wet crypt. Within her flickered a current of alarm. How easy, even yet, if the victim probed secret places. Turning, she hurried back through the passage way to the stairs and up into the light.

In the shadows of the cramped kitchen hallway, Brandy met MacGill, motionless as a rock, scowling like a medieval defender of Edinburgh Castle.

*   *   *   *

At six-forty-five John and Brandy selected a dining room table, John once more facing the thicket of palmettos beside the verandah. He fidgeted for a few minutes with his menu, then set it down and leaned across the mauve tablecloth, his eyes searching hers.

"Look, we've made a spotty first half of the weekend, but let's not spoil the rest." He reached for her hand. "I know you're excited about this new story. I should be patient. But let's save tonight and tomorrow for each other."

Brandy nodded and smiled back. "That's a sweet and generous thought." She truly wanted to seize this time with him. Still, over his shoulder she could not help watching Jeremiah Strong stride into the lobby and see MacGill come to meet him. The detective bent forward, shook hands, and motioned toward the hall. Brandy shifted her gaze to John and tried to block out the scene in the lobby, while part of her brain recalled Rossi's sealed room and the deputies who had passed her on the stairs, carrying a kit.

John lifted her fingers to his lips, then signaled Cara, who had finished setting plates on the next table. "Something special from the bar, I think," he said, when Cara stood beside him, pencil poised over her note pad. "Maybe a special wine? or a Margarita?"

Brandy felt warmth in his brown eyes as she settled on Zinfandel and chicken du jour. Perhaps they could recapture the romantic spell of last night. Then, remembering Jeremiah Strong and Cara's Shell Mound photograph, she laid a hand on Cara's arm as she stood by their table. "You need to see the gentleman with Mr. MacGill. He's the detective investigating Mr. Rossi. He was asking questions about Shell Mound." Cara stared at her, uncomprehending. Apparently she hadn't heard about the private detective's body. "You need to let him know you were there, taking photographs."

Cara shrugged delicate shoulders and pocketed her pad. "I'll tell him I was trying for a good print of the horned owl. I'm not telling him I was ghost hunting, and don't you."

John raised his dark eyebrows. "And are you still?"

Cara looked past him at the palmettos, a shapeless mass in the half light. "Not now. The tropical storm's stalled south of Naples. It could move north." She paused before she left their table and added, her voice low, "Although another sighting was reported last night. A fisherman near the mouth of the Suwannee saw the round light."

A half an hour later Brandy had taken the last bite of key lime pie when MacGill appeared in the doorway and gestured to Cara. Behind him loomed the formidable Strong. Brandy had expected him to question everyone who had been in the hotel the night before, but as she and John stepped into the lobby, she was unprepared for Truck Thompson's dramatic entrance. The oyster fisherman barreled into the hotel, broad face flushed and pale eyes bulging, Doggett on his heels. "Lemme talk to the damn detective!"

Doggett steered him to a chair. "Detective Strong will be here in a minute. Wait for the test results, right? It's routine, but it'll take time for the university to check out the soil on the spade."

Truck settled back into the chair, still glowering, and fingered the bristles of his mustache. "Never saw the damn spade at the fish house before. It's not mine."

Doggett shook his long head as if in sorrow and leaned against the wall beside the couch. "That's part of the problem." Brandy stood, intrigued, until John took her elbow and guided her into the lounge. The middle-aged waitress with the plump face had served their Irish creme at a table by the window, and John was lifting his narrow glass to hers, when MacGill came into the room, looked round, and drifted over to join them.

John frowned and rubbed his forehead, but the Scotsman seemed not to notice. He slumped forward, sighing. "I'm whacked out. Don't know what this murder will do to my Seafood Festival trade. Probably get cancellations." Brandy realized he would be concerned about the first of Cedar Key's important tourist events. MacGill lifted his square face, as if he remembered seeing Brandy earlier, his tone suddenly brittle. "Did you find what you were looking for in the basement, now?"

"Just curious. About the skeleton in the cistern, you know." She realized he'd never mentioned it to her.

MacGill's expression in the darkened room was unreadable. He changed the subject. "Truck came raging in here like a bull in a mist. I was the one who identified the spade the police found by his fish house today. It belonged to the hotel. They've taken it away now."

Brandy took a slow slip of the Irish Creme, then fumbled in her purse for a small note pad. She scrawled "spade—Truck?" on one ragged page. "I saw it last night in the back yard, below our bedroom window."

"The question is," MacGill said, "how did it get several blocks away to Truck's place?" He looked at John and sighed again. "Must've been a shock to you, lad, I shouldn't wonder, your man from the sheriff's office turning up poor old Rossi like that. I'm to trot over and identify him, too, mind."

The cocktail waitress set a highball on the table and MacGill took a long drink. "The lads upstairs went through Rossi's room. Haven't found anything. No prints except his and the cleaning staff. We bunkered things up by tossing out the empty Scotch bottle. They think someone maybe planted it, but how was I to know?" He turned the bottom of his glass in circles on the table, then took another modest swallow. "Doggett says the divers haven't found a weapon."

"Rossi was shot, I suppose," Brandy said.

MacGill pursed his lips. "No one's saying to the contrary. The deputies want to check everybody's gun."

Brandy made a mental note to jot the gist of this conversation in her big notebook. At the bar a familiar blond ducktail swiveled in their direction. Nathan Hunt raised a glass toward them and slipped from his bar stool. John's face clouded and he laid a hand on Brandy's arm. Hunt set one of the blue canvas backed chairs between MacGill and Brandy, eased into it, and grinned at MacGill. "Seems like the gendarmes want to see all the weapons in Cedar Key. Luckily, I don't own a gun. Truck Thompson says they'll have to show a warrant before he lets them see his." The smile in his blue eyes was sly, the pupils large and black. "And you, MacGill?"

The Scotsman twisted in his chair and thumped one square fist on the table. "Can't find the blooming thing. Got talked into buying one, in case of robbers or someone cutting up rough. Like a fool, I kept a semi-automatic in a drawer at the desk. Wasn't loaded." He thrust out his lower lip. "Haven't seen it in weeks. Now it's gone."

Hunt leaned toward MacGill. A side lamp lit a profile Brandy thought too white and smooth for anything but an occasional fisherman. "And the bullets?"

"In the drawer, too, damn it," the Scotsman growled. "Gone."

John looked at his watch, slid his chair back, and bent to speak in Brandy's ear. "Let's not get involved again." There was urgency in his hushed voice and she squeezed his hand. While he moved away to find the cocktail waitress, Brandy said good night to MacGill and Hunt and sauntered to the door. In spite of the homicide detective's size, she almost overlooked him in the shadows. Inside the lobby she found herself looking up into the dark face with its widely spaced eyes and tidy mustache. She was quick with a question. "Did Cara Waters talk to you?"

He rocked slightly on the balls of his feet. "Cara Waters may have some important information for us, maybe a picture come Tuesday. She's not sure because of the light. She'll call when she checks the prints." He fixed Brandy with a knowing stare, brows elevated. "Seems the young lady has a particular interest in Mr. Rossi, but she never met the man. Got all her information second hand, and not from Mrs. Waters or her employer."

Brandy knew when she was being gently put down, but she whipped out the tattered note pad anyway. "This is an informal press conference. I called my editor. Are you ready to release any information now?"

"Can't give you much now, Ma'am. The victim is Anthony Rossi of New York City. No suspects yet. We're in the process of double-checking his I.D. and locating his family. The investigation's just started. But you know that already." He smiled. "First time I ever investigated an investigator."

She noticed the fine lines at the corners of his eyes. Laugh lines, someone called them, although a detective didn't see much that was amusing. Perhaps Jeremiah Strong's sense of irony made disinterred corpses more tolerable. "When we got more, I'll get back to you and local newspapers. Come down to it, we'll want a longer interview with you and your husband. Let us know where you'll be for the next few days."

When John returned from the bar and started toward her, she spoke in a hurry. "I was trying to think where I saw tire tracks today, besides Shell Mound. I've remembered. In the Cedar Key cemetery this morning. Tire tracks and small pieces of glass. I believe Rossi's broken glasses were found in the car." She tucked the pad back into her purse. "I suppose you're still trying to find the murder scene." She reached for John's hand as he joined them. "As for me, I'm actually more interested in the first murder here—the woman found nineteen years ago in the hotel basement. Cara Waters and I think there's a connection."

Again Jeremiah Strong's brows went up, and he placed his hands on his hips. "All in good time, Ma'am. We got us a fresh body here and lots to do. How about you and Miss Waters leave this investigation to the Sheriff's Office? Give us a little time to sort things out." The white teeth flashed. "I reckon you take pride in being a mighty good newswoman, Ma'am. But remember what the Good Book say: 'The patient in spirit is better than the proud.'"

Jeremiah Strong, she thought, master of the courteous put down. As the detective disappeared into the lounge, John faced her and put a hand on each shoulder. Anxiety showed in his eyes. "Take his advice. It's good and it's professional. Someone tried to warn you off this morning with that phone call."

Brandy lifted her face and kissed him on the cheek. "Touché." But even as he touched her coppery hair, she was conscious of a suppressed sob coming from the kitchen alcove. She ran her hand down John's arm. "More problems, I'm afraid." She pulled away and crossed the lobby.

Cara, huddled in a chair beside a huge fern, glanced up, eyes glistening in a pinched face. "The detective doesn't care about the skeleton in the basement. He thinks I'm imagining a connection. He won't check what Rossi knew about the missing woman. They think he's just some petty drug dealer." She sniffed and pulled a tissue out of her pocket. "I don't want to go home to Marcia. You're the only one who'll pay attention. You're the only one who can help me find the truth."

Brandy knelt beside her and put one arm around her thin shoulders. "I'll do what I can."

"I've got to talk to you tonight. I've got a plan but you're the best one to carry it out."

Brandy glanced back at John, waiting beside the stairs. "You should go home tonight. We can talk tomorrow, before I leave."

Fresh tears trembled in Cara's eyes. "This has got to be done now. I've saved some money. The station wagon's here at the hotel. I'll leave Cedar Key, go to New York. My God, I may have a father somewhere." She rose shakily. "I know it's not your problem."

Brandy put a hand on her arm. "Wait. Don't do anything rash." She walked quickly over to John. "An emergency. It's Cara. She's talking about taking off to New York to check on Rossi herself. I've got to talk her out of it."

He bowed his head for a moment. "I'm going up."

Back in the alcove Brandy took Cara's hand and drew her onto the deserted lobby couch. She wondered where Truck had gone, but she hadn't time to ask. "Now what's the plan you need me for?"

The pleading look came again in Cara's eyes. "We have Mr. Rossi's address. Someone's got to check out his office, find out who he was searching for. You said someone in his agency must know something. If we don't move fast, all the information will be lost. His client is dead. No one else will care."

Brandy sank back. "Rossi said he knew the woman's name, that he was hired by her aunt."

Cara drew a long breath. "I've got $2,000 saved for college. It's in the bank. I could repay you if you'd go to New York. There'd be a story in it, wouldn't there?" She clasped her hands in her lap, her voice rising. "I wouldn't know what to do. I'd be totally lost. But you'd know."

Brandy bit her lip. "A girlfriend from college shares an apartment in Greenwich Village. We used to room together. She works for a big law firm in mid-town Manhattan. She knows the city like a book."

"Then you'll do it?" Eyes glowing, Cara sat up straight. "I already checked the flights out of Gainesville. The hotel keeps up to date because we have guests who fly in and out. The only regularly scheduled flight out is about eight in the morning."

Brandy gave her a calming pat. "Just a minute. Let me think. In the first place, I couldn't take your money. It would be unethical, and I couldn't leave tomorrow. I've got a perfectly good husband who's been very patient. I promised him the rest of the weekend."

Cara frowned. "Later may be too late."

"Nevertheless, it will have to wait. But I do need to give a quick call to my editor. Strong released a few facts. Maybe I could go later."

While Cara brooded, Brandy dialed the news room. When she reported that the private investigator she'd been assigned to cover had indeed been murdered, she was startled by the editor's reaction. "Things are pretty slow right now, and we're first on the Cedar Key murder." His voice took on an urgency. "I want you to get up to New York as soon as you can. Could be your big break. Find out if this guy Rossi was really onto something. See how he ties in with Cedar Key. Hold on a minute."

He rustled some papers and came back on the line. "We ran down your cashier. Betsy Mae Terry is listed in the Williston phone book. Lives in a retirement trailer park." She jotted down a phone number and address. "It's on the way to the Gainesville airport. Get a flight as soon you can."

Troubled, Brandy stepped out of the phone booth. "Well," she said to Cara, "looks like you get your wish. I only hope John understands. I'll have tomorrow here, anyway."

Cara drew her knees up and hugged them with her slim arms. "Maybe I'll find out who I really am."

Brandy's gaze drifted to the dark castle walls behind the desk and then to the kitchen door that swung open into an almost forgotten horror. Another feeling of dread washed over her, the same squeezing of the heart she'd felt beside the Suwannee. Her voice fell. "We can't be sure the truth will be good news."

But Cara was irrepressible. "Call your old roommate tonight!"

Brandy looked at her watch. Nine o'clock. "I'll have to call for reservations, and I need to reach Betsy Mae Terry."

As she started for the phone booth, the phone rang at the hotel desk. She noticed the clerk write a few lines, then scurry upstairs. Brandy was in the telephone booth making reservations for Monday morning. when John strode into the lobby, carrying his small suitcase. He looked around for a moment, saw her with the phone, pointed up toward their room, waved, and then blew her a kiss. Before she could finish her call, the hotel door opened and closed, and their car squealed away from the curb.

CHAPTER 10

▼

As Brandy shoved open the phone booth door, the hotel clerk gave an embarrassed cough and turned away. Brandy rushed past her and up the stairs, barely noticing the yellow evidence tape still strung across Rossi's door. In their own room John's jogging and dress shoes that had been lined up heel to heel and his tidy row of shorts and slacks were gone from the closet, along with the precisely folded socks from the dresser drawer. Tucked out of sight on a corner shelf, he had left the Nikon for her. She darted into the bathroom. No trim shaving kit sat beside her rumpled bag of make-up. But her blue nightgown had been moved from the back of a chair and laid out on the bed, her slippers collected from the middle of the floor and aligned under the dust ruffle, the bamboo blind drawn against the darkness. On the pillow she spotted a note in John's careful, spiky hand:

I just had a call. More problems with the bank plans. I've got to get back now. You really are too busy with your own story, anyway. Our weekend get-a-away wasn't working out. You're still occupied with Cara Waters.

She felt her eyes grow moist. But there was more. John was always practical.

> *I'm picking up Meg. Your new friend will surely drive you home when you finish here.*
>
> There was a considerable blank space, and then a last thought: *It was sweet while it lasted.*

She slumped on the bed, still holding the paper, and reached for a tissue from a box on the bedside table. Her mother, the English teacher, would call that last *it* an unclear pronoun reference. Did John refer to the weekend, or the marriage? And who made this sudden request? She could guess. What severe problem could develop on a weekend? Tomorrow, while she researched her story and tried to help Cara, he would be with his adoring intern, her blueprints at the ready and all her curves in the right place. She had heard newspaper people say that a journalist should marry only another journalist. No one else could understand the demands of a deadline.

Brandy was blowing her nose when she heard a faint rap on the door. It would be Cara. She lifted her head. She had to call her friend Thea. Maybe she should stay with her. She'd need Thea's help to find her way around New York. She reached into the purse she had flung beside the lap top, eons ago, before dinner, before she slipped on the marriage-work balance beam. John would need more than an hour to drive the sixty miles home. She couldn't phone yet. Giving her eyes a last swipe, she drew out her credit card case.

"Okay, Cara," she said, opening the door. "I'm coming downstairs to make my calls. I'm set for the flight Monday at 8:10." She pulled the door closed behind her and looked at the grave young face waiting in the shadows. "But you'll have to drive me to the Gainesville airport."

In the lobby Brandy leaned over the counter toward the clerk. "My husband had an unexpected emergency. Did you notice who called?"

The clerk took a few seconds to adjust her glasses, then scarcely opened her lips when she spoke, as if reluctant to answer. Yet a glimmer in her eyes revealed a hidden relish. "He did have a call this evening. A young lady."

Somehow, Brandy thought, I've antagonized this woman. Maybe not shone enough deference to her boss. She heard a movement behind her.

"Abandoned? The girl with the perky nose?" The pitying look in Nathan Hunt's icy eyes, the furrows on his well-shaped forehead, seemed to her more calculating than sympathetic.

"An emergency," she mumbled.

The blond eyebrows lifted as he edged nearer and laid a hand beside Brandy on the counter. "Let's commiserate over a drink. The bar's still open." She was aware of his aggressive gaze, of his green onyx ring banded in gold, of his expensive cologne.

"Thanks, but Cara and I have some calls to make." She glanced across at her friend, who had dropped into a lobby chair close to the phone booth.

He grinned. "Maybe later? A man shouldn't desert such a pretty woman. Reeks of over-confidence." He gave her a light touch on the shoulder as the clerk beamed up at him. "I'll be in the lounge if you change your mind. I'm interested in your story, even if your husband isn't."

Why do I keep bumping my shins on you every time I turn around? Brandy thought. Why is such a cosmopolitan playboy hanging out in a backwater town like Cedar Key, claiming to be a fisherman?

Mentally filing Nathan Hunt away for future speculation, she crossed to Cara. "I'll see if I can reach Betsy Mae Terry and then call my New York friend. You ought to go on home."

Cara's eyes showed the strain, but she shook her head. "I'm not eager to see Marcia tonight. You know how she feels."

Brandy sighed. She was partly responsible for the break between them. "You shouldn't blame your foster mother too much. She's afraid she'll lose you if we find your biological family." Brandy remembered John's cautionary warning. "And even if we do, it may not be a happy discovery. There might be a reason why no one has searched for you or your mother."

Opening her purse, she rooted in the bottom for her address book with the Otter Creek cashier's phone number before trudging back into the booth. The phone for Betsy Mae Terry rang six times before the woman picked up. She might already have been in bed. A slow, foggy voice answered, but Mrs. Terry did agree to see Brandy Sunday afternoon.

Next Brandy dialed Thea Ridge in New York. Six years ago, after Thea graduated, Brandy had thrown a farewell dinner party for her suite mate at a Gainesville restaurant. The next day she has seen Thea off for New York, where her friend's well-connected uncle had handed her a word processor's job in his Manhattan law firm, fulfilling Thea's dream of working in Manhattan.

Her old friend's voice boomed in her ear. "Be a treat to see you, Bran, get in some overdue catching up. But it's short notice. I'd be glad to steer you around town. You're welcome to stay here, but you'll have to sleep on the floor, okay?"

Brandy tried to picture Thea in that far off Greenwich Village world. Her figure had the kind of tall boniness that designer clothes craved. On the job her suit would be tailored, her nails manicured, her brown bangs neatly trimmed, and below them, her big eyes outlined in black. They served as beacons for an agile mind. But it was after ten. Now Thea would be in jeans or her long, baggy nightshirt with the University of Florida logo on the front.

"Sure, I'll sleep anywhere. I have two nights, max. It'll save time."

"It's a studio apartment. We're lucky to have it. I wish I could farm my roommate out to friends, but you'll need her here to get in." A nasal tone grated in the background, but Brandy couldn't make out the words. "I would've welcomed the excuse."

Through the glass door Brandy made a thumbs-up sign to Cara. "Two nights, max, Thea. My plane gets into JFK about 12:45 Monday. I'll take a cab, be there by two."

Thea laughed. "Not by New York traffic time, you won't. My roommate should be out of bed by the time you get here. She works nights. I'll leave work and try to be home by 5:30."

Brandy peered at the scribble in her address book under *Rossi*. "Monday afternoon I need to find an address on East Tenth Street."

Thea paused. "You're getting into East Village there, friend. Maybe that area was okay in the past, but this is 1992. Got to be more careful. A lot more druggies there, but my roommate knows the area."

Brandy's only return flight option was Wednesday at eight in the morning. She had a lot of ground to cover in a day and a half, maybe far too much.

As she emerged from the booth, she signaled Cara. "Come on. Let's have a nightcap in the lounge while you tell me anything else you know about the skeleton found here. After that, you've got to go home and face Marcia."

In the darkened lounge, she recognized Hunt's sleek ducktail and his cultivated voice, joking with the cocktail waitress at the bar. At a table under a wall lamp, Brandy dragged her dog-eared note pad from her purse. Once again when the barmaid's round face bobbed toward them, Hunt swiveled around, saw Brandy, and raised his glass level with those flat blue eyes. His lips mouthed "hello."

Brandy ordered a prudent white wine, and Cara did the same, then leaned forward, fingers gripping the edge of the table. "A couple of years ago I read all the 1973 July issues of the local papers. That was the month the skeleton was discovered." Her forehead furrowed. "The reports said the police found fragments of cloth with it. They didn't help identify the victim, but they came from a chenille bedspread."

As the waitress set down their glasses, Brandy reached for her credit card. The woman held up a pudgy hand. "Taken care of."

Hunt stood behind the waitress with an inviting smile. Brandy could ignore his magazine model good looks, his clothes out of *Gentlemen's Quarterly,* a grin that would make other female knees go weak. Still, she had to admit that unlike John, he had shown an interest in her work.

Brandy turned back to Cara, trying to concentrate on her skeleton story. "If she's our woman from Otter Creek, sounds as if she were killed in a bedroom."

Cara nodded and dropped her voice. "Maybe. They didn't find any jewelry, any remnants of a purse, nothing else except a corroded aluminum flashlight, a big one. The police thought it was the murder weapon. The medical examiner said the cracks in the front of the skull and the bad break there matched the flashlight."

Brandy made a quick note. "We'll ask the Otter Creek cashier tomorrow what she remembers about the woman and child who stopped there." Brandy was aware that Hunt was studying Cara, the look in his eyes intense. Cara would be vulnerable to his suave attentions, Brandy thought. She wanted him to ignore her young friend. Fortunately, he had seemed to focus all his attention on Brandy herself. It surprised her. Cara was much more available.

"So here's where you're hiding out!" Startled, they turned as Truck's hulking figure lunged into the doorway and marched over to the table. "I been looking all over for you. Let's go." He still wore black boots, a heavy shirt, and denim pants that smelled faintly of shell fish.

Brandy glanced up, her voice firm. "Cara's having a drink, It's been a tough day."

MacGill followed Truck into the room, and before the younger man noticed him, slid into the bench beside Cara. "Pack it in, Truck," he said. "Have a beer on the house. You worry too much about the girl, lad." Pulling a long face, the proprietor looked around the lounge. "Rossi's death will be in tomorrow's papers. I'll soon seen how many bloody cancellations I get."

Truck's lips tightened under the heavy mustache. "You worry too much about the hotel, friend."

MacGill's misplaced spade apparently still rankled. A lithe Nathan Hunt moved forward and took a chair next to Brandy. "The party gathers." He set his highball on the table. Brandy faced him, hoping to catch him off guard. "Tell us about yourself, Mr. Hunt. We don't know anything about you except that you're from Miami Beach. With a murder investigation going on, looks like you'd want to clear out. Spoils the fishing."

Hunt continued to smile, no humor in his eyes. "I will clear out when I've safely stowed my boat in case the storm hits, and when the detective gives the okay."

"Damn near everyone's a suspect," Truck growled. He had acquired a mug of beer, but he still stood. "Hell, I don't even know the frigging guy. Saw a bunch of deputies across the bay tonight, swarming all over the cemetery. Bunch of comedians. That coon from the Sheriff's Office don't know shit from shinola."

The table went quiet. Brandy broke the silence, even though she knew the futility of reasoning with Truck. "I wouldn't let the good detective hear you say that." What interested her most was that Strong had taken her suggestion about the cemetery.

Cara flushed and stared into her wine glass. "Brandy's investigating, too. She's going to New York Monday morning to find out what Mr. Rossi knew. Maybe he was killed because he stirred up the old Island Hotel murder case."

Brandy frowned at Cara. She had not planned to advertise her trip. "It's true I'm checking out tomorrow, Mr. MacGill," she said. "Since John had to leave early, Cara's taking me to Gainesville."

MacGill raised his hand and signaled to the woman behind the bar. Truck's small eyes fastened on Hunt, who was still gazing at Cara with a frozen smile. The big man shifted his weight and edged closer to Cara. "All this murder talk makes things rough on my girl." He bent toward Cara. "Makes her feel bad about her real folks. Makes her want to get away, be a photographer somewheres else."

He squatted on his heels beside her and looked into her drawn face. "Soon's oyster season's over, I'll take you on a vacation, anywhere you want to go. You can forget all this stuff. When we get spliced, I'll let you spend all your time with a camera, if that's what you want." Brandy sensed Cara stiffen. Truck would *let* her. He doesn't have a clue, she thought. Cara herself scarcely seemed to hear him.

"If I could only remember," she whispered, her mind still on the first murder. "I was *there*. On some level I must know what happened to my real mother."

No one at the table disputed that Cara was, indeed, the child Rossi had been trying to find. But no one had told Rossi.

The plump arm of the barmaid reached down and set a whiskey and water before MacGill. "Why don't you try hypnosis, honey?" she said. "I saw a TV show where a guy put some woman under, took her all the way back to when she was almost a baby. Like two-years old. The woman remembered all kinds of little things. She could describe the house she lived in and what the maid looked like who took care of her. It might work for you."

Cara looked up. "Do you really think so? Maybe I could find someone who practices hypnosis at the university."

The table went quiet again. Brandy was aware that Hunt's arm now lay along the back of her chair. She looked at her watch. Almost eleven. Surely John would be home. She rose.

"I'd drive you to the airport," Hunt said. "Any time at all. Just ask." His grin was back. "I want to hear more about the old murder case. That's a real mystery."

"Cara's taking me, thanks," Brandy said. "We can talk about the case another time, perhaps." She moved away from the table as Truck heaved himself to his feet.

"You didn't give me an answer." He bent toward Cara. "What about we get away?"

She gave Truck an unsmiling glance. "Don't get all riled up. You can drive me home." She might've been addressing a child. "I'll pick up the station wagon in the morning." She faced Brandy. "See you at breakfast."

Truck beamed and followed her out the door. As Brandy turned to leave the lounge, Hunt's limber body leaned uncomfortably close, exuding an undeniable magnetism.

"New York's a big place," he said. "You'll get lost. Better play it safe. Do your investigating where you know your way around, like right here. You could begin with me." She found herself remembering the flimsy latch on her bedroom door.

"Thanks for the advice, but I'll have help. If you'll excuse me," she said, "I need to call my husband and pack." She felt his eyes on her as she left the room.

The phone rang four times before John's impersonal voice came on the answering machine. When she left a message that she would call again tomorrow, she suppressed the alarm in her voice. Where was he at eleven o'clock?

After jotting a few lines in her notebook and carefully dating them October 1992, she crawled into bed, missing John's warmth, his arms around her. His pillow still held the spicy scent of his cologne. She picked up Dante's *Inferno* and flipped through a few cantos. She had loved the quirky savagery of his circles of hell. But the atmosphere in Cedar Key tonight did not put her in the mood for them now. Although the blind was drawn as John left it, she knew beyond the window lay the black waters of the lagoon, and below, the wide doors that led into the basement. A kind of hell had happened there twenty years ago, and the punishment was overdue.

The wind had risen. She could hear cabbage palms and cedars scrape against the old building like forgotten ghosts. Sleep came in fragments, each haunted by a fragile Cara Waters. Once Brandy woke to a shuffling sound in the hall. She heard a soft rap on the door and a rattle of the latch. Nathan Hunt? She sat up and stared. But the chain stayed in place, and she left it there.

CHAPTER 11

▼

In the morning Brandy tapped out on the lap top a brief story about the few facts Detective Strong had released. She would call the department before she left to see if any others had emerged. The Halloween feature could wait until later. Maybe Cara's Shell Mound picture would add bite to the familiar legend.

At breakfast she was relieved to hear that Hunt had left for the marina at the town of Suwannee, and that the tropical storm was still stalled off Naples. She expected Cara to be pleased, yet her friend was zipping among the tables with a tight look around her mouth. After Brandy finished her herbed eggs and muffin, Cara cleared the table with a wan smile. "Marcia wants to see you. She drove me to work this morning, and I'm afraid she's waiting in the lobby to dump a guilt trip on you." Cara lowered her voice. "I'm sorry, but for a long time I've thought she knows more than she's told me. I stepped into her bedroom this morning to tell her I was ready." She sighed. "I'd swear she was hiding something."

This is a time to be assertive, Brandy thought, standing. "I'll talk to her."

When she entered the lobby, Brandy saw Marcia Waters seated beside the coffee table, staring out at the quiet street. Brandy lifted her chin and took a seat across from her. "Cara said you wanted to see me."

Marcia kept her long hands in her lap, her eyes on Brandy. She wore an ankle length denim skirt and a man's white shirt with a paint smear on one pocket. Several strands of gray hair had escaped the firm bun at the nape of her neck.

"I'm here about Cara." She paused to control a slight quiver in her voice. "I know you're trying to find out if that investigator knew who Cara's parents were." Her fingers crept up to the corner of her mouth. "The fact is, you're upsetting Cara, giving her false hopes. All for a newspaper story. The woman the man was looking for probably had no connection to Cara."

Brandy nodded. "Maybe that's what I'll find. Cara just wants the truth, but there's another reason to investigate. Mr. Rossi said the woman's daughter had money coming to her. If we can prove Cara's her daughter, Cara may be able to pay for college herself. Is there anything else, anything at all, you know about Cara's past that would help us?"

A look of anguish flickered for a second in the artist's eyes. "Cara can't find happiness by leaving Cedar Key. She's loved here. She does important work here. She can grow in her chosen profession here." Her hands clasped again "Fact is, you can't know what you'll find. Suppose one of her parents is a criminal?" She stood, her thin body very straight, and it seemed to Brandy, very vulnerable. "They abandoned her, Miss O'Bannon. I'll thank you to leave my family as you found it."

Brandy rose and stretched out her hand to the artist. Behind her she could see the counter clerk, head bent over the morning *Beacon,* listening. A page had not turned since Marcia began talking.

"Please understand," Brandy said. "Cara asked for my help. She's a grown woman. She has a right to make this search, and I have a right to cover the story my editor assigned." When Marcia ignored her hand, Brandy dropped it. "Whatever I find, Cara will always love you as her mother."

Marcia pivoted on her heel, then glanced back. "I understand my daughter's driving you to Gainesville today and picking you up on Wednesday about noon. I hope you don't plan to return to Cedar Key. We don't need more of your kind of help."

With regret Brandy watched her sweep out of the lobby. She admired Marcia Waters, admired her dramatic watercolors, her bird sanctuary, her concern for the environment. But she had lost any expectation of her friendship. She only hoped Marcia's hostility was caused by love for her daughter, not by fear.

As the artist strode down the sidewalk toward the art gallery, Brandy stepped once more into the phone booth. Once more the answering machine clicked on and she listened to John's flat voice inviting her to leave a message. Could he be walking Meg? Unlikely. He would keep her in the fenced yard. If he were outside looking for the Sunday paper, would he think to check the answering machine? Could he have gone to the office on Sunday before nine-thirty?

"I'll be in Manhattan Monday and Tuesday at my old friend Thea Ridge's apartment," she said when the beeps stopped. "I'll call." She left Thea's phone number, but she was thinking not of Thea but of Tiffany—the artful tangle of her hair and her mini-skirt. When John's boss suggested interns should dress more conservatively, John had laughed. "He's so old fashioned," he joked at the table over Brandy's homemade shepherd's pie, while she watched images of Tiffany and her unusually white skin float among the lamb and mashed potatoes. His protégé's saucer-shaped eyes went wide with admiration every time John spoke. Brandy had seen that phenomenon at the office picnic, and once a neighbor had told her, oh, so helpfully, that she sometimes saw John lunching at the mall with Tiffany. If that happened when Brandy was in town, what went on when she was gone?

And Tiffany Moore lived alone.

Brandy slammed down the receiver. Coming out of the booth, she met the clerk's eye. "I'm expecting a call from my husband. If he phones before I check out, please let me know."

The clerk's half-smile, Brandy thought savagely, could be called a smirk. "Check-out time's, you know, at noon," the young woman said.

Upstairs Brandy had begun throwing clothes into her suitcase, when she heard a knock at the door, this time one with authority. She opened to the imposing figure of Detective Jeremiah Strong.

"We need a fuller statement from you, Ma'am," he said, stepping back, "and I need to know how to reach your husband."

Brandy checked her watch. "Fair enough. Then I'm out of here."

While Strong carried her bag downstairs and into a small room between MacGill's apartment and the bar, she followed with her lap top and notebook, glad she had jotted down all the details she could remember. The detective directed her into one of two cane chairs and swung the other around to sit facing her, his spiral note pad braced on the ladder back. As she flipped to her Rossi entry, he raised an eyebrow at the loose pages, the smeary scribble, the doodling in the margins of oak trees and boats and lately, of Marcia Water's predatory owls. But he took notes as she read aloud every remark she had heard from or about Rossi. She ended by giving him John's office number, as well as the one at home.

"Got a positive ID this morning," he said, "and you can give your newspaper the Shell Mound location, say he was staying at the hotel here. But no details about the body or the burial." He looked down, a bit sheepish. "Reckon I ought to thank you for the cemetery tip."

"The murder scene?"

He nodded. "Could be. Metal detector turned up a coupla cartridge casings. Ophthalmologist in Chiefland's gonna check out the glass fragments we found there, see if they match the victim's glasses. Tire tracks look like those at Shell Mound. Don't help us identify the killer, anyhow. The vehicle was the victim's rental car."

Brandy reached for a pencil. "You're saying someone killed Rossi, buried the body, then came back and ran the car into the Gulf?"

Strong nodded again. "Guess the perp thought fresh digging would show up in the graveyard, but not in a hidden spot off the park trail.

He didn't figure on your dog." He put his note pad in his pocket, stood, and swiveled the chair back in place. "But that fact's still off the record. I'm not giving out details 'til we've got a suspect."

Brandy tapped the pencil on the blank page. "Only one set of tire tracks in the cemetery? Rossi must've gone there with the killer. Rossi must've known him—or her. But why the cemetery?

A hint of a smile lifted the corners of his mouth. "A nice quiet place. Fits my drug scenario. Most likely a deal gone sour."

She paused, remembering something else. "Shell Mound dirt should be full of shell fragments. Is the spade being tested?"

He flashed one of his broad white smiles. "You don't miss much, Ma'am. But the spade's not a lot of help, either. Several folks say it belongs to the hotel, but there's no fingerprints."

"Still, it might give the crime a local connection. If the spade checks out, it means the killer knew where it was kept. Besides who besides the killer would be using a spade in the middle of the night? Handle's probably wiped clean. Otherwise you'd have the yard man's prints." She cocked her head. "Found the weapon yet?"

Strong shook his head as Brandy snapped the notebook shut and stood. She hesitated at the lounge door. "I should tell you I'm going to New York tomorrow. I want to find out what Rossi knew when he placed that classified ad."

The dark brows converged. "No law against it, I guess. I been in touch with New York P.D. They'll seal the victim's records. Come down to it, I reckon I'll go up there soon myself. Check out the drug connection."

As Brandy stepped into the deserted bar, he followed, then halted and faced her. "Ma'am, I'll tell you again. Best leave the investigation to law enforcement. You heading for a peck of trouble. Whatever Rossi knew, got him killed. The Bible say, 'The evil is sown, but the destruction thereof is not yet done.'" He winked and slid past her.

I'm never quite sure what the detective means, she thought. Was he winking to make me feel better about the scolding? Or to say he knows

I'll do whatever's necessary to get the story? Or to emphasize his warning. Detective Jeremiah Strong was a puzzle.

At the desk she stopped to offer her credit card and keys and saw a note in her box. The clerk handed Brandy the slip. "Your husband called. Says he'll be out of the office today."

Brandy glanced at the clerk's neat handwriting. "Mr. Able will be with a client on the job site most of the day. He got your message."

Brandy crumpled up the paper. "I asked you to call me. You saw where I went."

The clerk gave a righteous lift to her head. "I never interrupt anyone in Mr. MacGill's conference room, know what I mean?"

Another murder wouldn't solve the problem, Brandy thought, tempted as she was. She jotted down Thea's name and phone number. "If he calls again, be sure he knows how to reach me at my friend's apartment tomorrow."

By one o'clock Brandy had modemed more of the Rossi story to the bureau and alerted Betsy Mae Terry to expect her in about an hour. She and MacGill were discussing her historic preservation column on the lobby bulletin board when Cara's station wagon pulled up before the hotel. An almost jovial MacGill carried Brandy's suitcase through the front doors, saying, "Mind, I always treat the press with respect. Last night I felt like I'd been pulled through a ditch backwards, but no one's canceled yet and I've gotten a couple of new reservations. Maybe the poor lad's murder actually helped. Vulgar curiosity, most like." He set her bag in the back of the wagon. "Girl at the desk tells me you'll be getting back from New York around noon Wednesday. Your husband to meet you?"

The clerk has a real talent for eavesdropping, Brandy thought, laying her lap top and camera beside the bag. "Couldn't reach him. Cara can pick me up."

MacGill nodded. "You'll want to see her anyway, I shouldn't wonder. See if she got a snapshot of your man digging Rossi's grave." He slammed the hatch and leaned toward her. "Take no notice of Marcia."

The clerk again, Brandy supposed, reporting her conversation with Marcia Waters. The Cedar Key network didn't permit much privacy. "Our Cara's got no business working at what's really a skivvy's job. She deserves better." He stepped back on the curb beside a tourist couple unloading their car and waved Cara away.

Enroute to the cashier interview, they stopped in Bronson where, over a fast food pizza, Brandy explained her plan. "Our first step is to identify the woman Rossi was searching for. He said he knew her name. Once we have that information, the medical examiner can compare that woman's dental records with the basement skeleton's teeth. Even the skull size and shape tell a lot. Murder cases stay open, you know. I'm sure the police would like to close this one."

Cara wrinkled her forehead. "Then I'd still have to prove I was that woman's child."

"That would certainly be easier if we knew the woman's name."

"What Mother—Marcia—can't understand is that I need to know if my real mother abandoned me—if she walked off and left me out in a storm. That's a terrible thought to live with."

"And it would be better to know she'd been murdered?"

Cara stared at her plate, dark hair half hiding her face. "In a way, for me, yes."

Outside the town of Williston, they spotted the sign for Green Valley Haven between a gas station and a feed store. Cara threaded the station wagon through a labyrinth of narrow streets, until they found Betsy Mae Terry's trailer. She parked beside an aluminum carport and a neat square of lawn.

"You might as well come with me," Brandy said. "Listen for any fact that isn't in the old newspaper story."

The door was opened by a stout woman of about seventy with severely bobbed white hair. She wore a polyester pants suit and house slippers. In her arms squirmed a noisy Pomeranian, whose staccato yipping drowned out her first remarks. The tiny living room smelled of dog.

Once her guests were settled on the worn couch, Betsy Mae lowered herself into an over-stuffed chair opposite them and stroked her pet's silky coat until the little animal quieted.

"Cara Waters is with me today," Brandy began. "She lives in Cedar Key and has a special interest in your story. I'm writing an article about the child who was left in Cedar Key during the 1972 hurricane, alone." Cara sat forward, her eyes fixed on Betsy Mae Terry as if the elderly woman were her best chance for information. "The child's parents have never been located," Brandy went on. "Now there's another inquiry about a woman who came to town just before Hurricane Agnes. I've seen the newspaper account of your testimony in the lost child case."

Betsy Mae gave a ponderous sigh. "Lands, so long ago. About twenty years, I reckon. My husband and me had a little old café at the corner of Route 19 and Otter Creek. It's gone now and so is he. I been retired five, six years. In them days I knew most of the folks come by that corner from Cedar Key."

She set the Pomeranian on the shag carpet. With a sulky twitch of its circular tail, it crept under her chair as she reached for a filtered cigarette. "I told the police everything I could remember then."

Brandy bent toward her, her tone gentle. "Just give us a run through again, if you would. Your recollection could be important."

The older woman's eyes narrowed. She inhaled deeply and expelled the smoke toward the small kitchen, as she made an effort to drag forth the memory. "The woman was a skinny little thing. When she got off the Greyhound bus, it had already started to rain. Lots of folks were milling around in the café, or out by the gas pumps, trying to get away before the storm hit. Some going further inland, and some heading back to Cedar Key, worried about their homes."

She tapped the glowing cigarette in an ashtray and warmed to her task. "Thing I recollect about that woman the most is the way she stopped outside in the rain and looked all around her, not like she was waiting for someone exactly. More like she was scared. She looked real careful in through those big old plate glass windows before she come in."

"And the child?" Brandy asked. She heard Cara, who had been mute, draw in her breath.

"She was carrying a little girl on one hip, and she had a big old suitcase. I remember it was expensive looking leather and she was well-dressed. Looked rumpled, you know, but she wasn't wearing cheap clothes.

"I never could remember much about the kid, worse luck. I was as busy as a hunting dog with fleas. I think the little girl was tired and kind of whiny, like kids get. The woman come up to my counter and asked how she could get to Cedar Key. Well, you know, I laughed. Big headlines about the hurricane off the coast. I had the radio on, said the hurricane might turn toward Cedar Key. I told her she didn't want to go there right then."

Brandy had taken the memo pad from her purse. "How did she react to that?"

Mrs. Terry looked down and shook her head, sending a tremor through the folds of skin at her neck. "Said she had no place else to go. That when she got to Cedar Key she could get help. Of course, there wasn't no bus service to Cedar Key anymore, and not any taxis from Chiefland would take anyone there then, in case the one road in got flooded. Wasn't anything, even then, at Otter Creek except the post office and our place." Her voice subsided while she finished the cigarette.

"Did you talk to her again?"

"She come back up to pay her bill, you know. She'd gone back to set down and order something. I couldn't see her from where I was standing because we had a big old dessert case between the tables and the counter. When she come back maybe half an hour later, she told me she had a ride to Cedar Key. 'Course, I didn't think nothing about it. It was just odd trying to get there then."

"The newspaper story said you didn't see the person with the woman and child when they left the café."

The older woman mashed the cigarette end into the ashtray, reached down, pulled the Pomeranian out from under her chair, and set it again in her lap, where it settled down with a tiny snort. "I didn't, worse luck. I heard a door slam and a car pull away. The woman wasn't still carrying the big old suitcase when she come up to pay, so I reckon whoever was taking her to Cedar Key had picked up the case. I recollect she scribbled a post card, and I let her drop it in the box we kept on the counter for the mailman."

"You didn't by any chance see what was on the card?"

Betsy Mae made a shocked clicking noise with her tongue. "I don't read other folks' mail."

"Anything else you can tell us?"

"There was several folks outside, splashing around in the rain. I remember telling the cop that lots of cars was leaving. One pulled out right behind the one she was in, so I couldn't get a good look at it."

"Anything else? Especially anything that might help identify the child?"

"I told the cop that the woman had a lot of money. When she opened up her billfold, I saw a wad of bills would choke a horse. I told her to be more careful. She was wearing expensive looking jewelry. I remember a big ring, a big old diamond in the middle and a lot of little ones around the sides. I warned her about flashing that stuff around, even in little old Cedar Key.

"I didn't get much of a look at the child. Kinda dark hair, kinda skinny, too. I said at the time she wore a pinkish outfit. All I really noticed was the blue teddy bear. The little girl had her face buried in her mother's shoulder when she come up to the counter, but she was carrying a cloth bear, you know, a kind of terry cloth thing. I told the officer about it, but it didn't seem important. Wasn't anything like that found with the child that turned up in Cedar Key. I told the cop I saw a red tail light on the road to Cedar Key right after they left the parking area, but I don't know for sure it was the car she was in. Wasn't many going that way. Most folks was heading to Chiefland. I gave the police the names of everyone I could remember, the regulars, you know. I don't rightly recollect now who they were."

"The police report will list them." Brandy thought of Detective Strong. He was thorough enough to check the list, even though he didn't believe Rossi's murder was connected.

The older woman glanced at Cara, but Brandy did not explain who she was. There would be time for that if Brandy's trip to New York bore fruit. She did ask Mrs. Terry to step outside for a photograph, one with Cara beside her. If Cara proved to be the little girl at the Otter Creek café, Brandy could use the picture.

In the station wagon she noted the few new facts in her big notebook. "Didn't seem like much we didn't already know," Cara said in a low voice, plainly disappointed.

"I'm not so sure. The woman at the café had a lot of cash and expensive jewelry, and she acted frightened. No jewelry or cash was ever found. Mrs. Terry verified that the woman mailed a postcard from Otter Creek, like Rossi said. Those facts, and the blue teddy bear, weren't mentioned in the story, although people in Cedar Key probably heard about them at the time."

On the drive down country roads to Gainesville, Brandy had a warning for Cara. She turned to her. "I know how much you want to know what happened to your real mother," Brandy said, watching the scraggly pines flash by, "but don't do what the waitress suggested last night. Don't depend on regressive hypnosis." Brandy turned toward Cara, her voice firm. "I once read an article about it by a Harvard psychologist. He said we don't actually store everything that happens to us in our brains. He said if a hypnotist questions a subject about an event the subject can't remember, that person will create a memory and then believe it's true. Lots of studies have shown the process can't be relied on. The article claimed it should never be used in courts."

Brandy looked again out the window at a lonely trail that disappeared into a slash pine forest. "I'm afraid not everyone else at the table understood that fact." She thought Cara did not realize the danger. What if the killer believed hypnosis could actually make Cara remember the murder? That is, if it was Cara's mother who had been murdered.

"Maybe I can't be regressed to two years old," Cara said, "but I've got confidence in what you'll discover in New York. That's what I'm relying on, totally."

Brandy thought of Marcia's warning, and of John's. Rossi's classified ad had said "privacy assured." What if Brandy rolled over a rock and a monster crawled out. "What happens if we find your biological family? Even your father?" she asked.

Cara swallowed. For a minute she stared ahead at a field of autumn sunflowers. "I wouldn't neglect Marcia, if that's what you're worried about. I owe her more than my life." She waved one slender hand in the air. "I owe her my ambition, too. I want to be an artist with a camera." She gripped the wheel again. "But the images I see are more serene than Marcia's. I don't want to record storms and predatory birds, but I need to learn how to find and shape my own scenes."

They drove for a few minutes in companionable silence. "If we can turn up some real facts," Brandy said, "Detective Strong will listen. He's smart."

Cara's mind returned to her foster mother. "I just hope I don't learn Marcia's holding out on me. I couldn't forgive that." A cloud passed over her face. Maybe it's true I'm making things worse for her, Brandy thought. Too late now.

At a motel near the Gainesville airport where Brandy would spend the night, she handed a note to Cara with Thea's name, address, and phone number. "I won't see you until Wednesday. Call me Tuesday night and tell me what your photograph at Shell Mound shows."

"I will, I promise."

Later Brandy would remember how she waited for several minutes beside the concrete block motel, watching the shabby station wagon start back through the growing shadows toward Cedar Key.

CHAPTER 12

▼

That evening Brandy finally reached John from the motel, but she hung up dissatisfied. She'd tried to keep anxiety out of her voice, but he bridled at her questions. After dinner Saturday, he said, his feelings had been hurt. In his view she had persuaded him to come to Cedar Key and then had no time for him. Now she was off to New York. Also, he was genuinely worried about the bank restoration job.

Later she admitted to herself that she had wanted to make the New York trip, to show she could handle the job. Her father again, no doubt, telling her she was good at it. She wanted to prove him right.

Monday, as the plane lifted into the air, Brandy kicked back to think about the two murders, twenty years apart. She had to sort out the facts she knew. On the flight she had a chance to do it. From a carry-on canvas bag she took out her notebook and began to write slowly on the next blank page:

First murder: Young woman's skeleton found in hotel cistern, late 1973; only clues—shattered skull, remains of a heavy flashlight, bedspread fibers.

Fact: on the night of the 1972 hurricane, woman at Otter Creek café seemed fearful

Fact: a stranger drove woman to Cedar Key

Locals with connection to Rossi and opportunity for first murder a) MacGill: before the storm hit, said to be helping shore up houses on the gulf; owned real estate in the area; Rossi was looking for the place the woman stayed on the night she disappeared; were MacGill's Gulf cottages at that address? 1972 newspaper said some ruined by waves and flooding; could MacGill have been at the café and driven the woman to Cedar Key? he came late to the safety of the school; later he bought the Island Hotel. Could be to conceal the body.

Suspicions: Why didn't MacGill tell Rossi about the skeleton in the basement?

Motive: unknown, unless a sexual assault became fatal

Truck Thompson, then about 18, driving pick-up truck in the area, evacuating people along the Gulf; also came late to the school; could have been at the Otter Creek café and become the driver.

Motive: same as MacGill; had a reputation for wildness and violence with women; family's prominence might have protected him

Suspicions: Same as MacGill

Brandy hesitated, twirling her pencil. She could place another local name on the scene. At last she wrote reluctantly: Marcia Waters: found the lost child on road near Gulf; could have been at Otter Creek café; may have been deranged and killed the mother when she thought the child was her lost daughter, delusion heightened by similarity of storms and toddlers

Suspicions: Why is she so opposed to Cara finding out about her real mother? Is she hiding something, as Cara thinks?

Motive: fixation on recovering her dead child

Question: Rossi said someone else might be interested in the missing woman search. Who?

Brandy doodled a gravestone engraved with a question mark. She started to write Nathan Hunt's name, because he said he frequently visited in Cedar Key and was there the night Rossi made his announcement, but she crossed his name out. He couldn't have been more than nine or ten in 1972 when the woman was killed.

She began another page with <u>Rossi murder</u>—locals with opportunity: <u>MacGill</u>: at the hotel Friday night, could have lured Rossi to the cemetery, perhaps with false news of the missing woman, would have known about the spade and could have planted it by Truck's fish house; his gun is missing; was it the murder weapon?

<u>Motive</u>: to cover up the first murder; why did Rossi disappear from the hotel right after he told MacGill about his search?

<u>Truck Thompson</u>: at the hotel Friday night, later said he was out alone, guarding his oyster beds; could have panicked and discarded spade at his own fish house

<u>Motives</u>: heard Rossi's statements and knew he might uncover the first murder? also to prevent search for Cara's real parents and keep her from leaving Cedar Key

<u>Marcia Waters</u>: learned about Rossi from MacGill Friday night; both concealed classified ad from Cara; might have contacted Rossi and arranged to meet him; lives within walking distance of the cemetery; is a strong woman, could do physically what a man could; Cara said she had a gun and could use it

<u>Motive</u>: to keep Cara in Cedar Key with her, and/or conceal the earlier crime

<u>Nathan Hunt</u>: Opportunity: could have left the hotel on some pretext with Rossi; someone came and went in the hallway the night before body found; in lounge said he could uncover news of the missing woman; claimed he went fishing early, might have seen the spade in the yard and later planted it by fish house

<u>Motive</u>: unknown, unless drug connection Strong suspects

Brandy thought about the night of Rossi's murder. The killer had to shoot him in the graveyard, load the body into the rental car, drive it to Shell Mound for a hasty burial, then using the dead man's key, return to the hotel room for Rossi's clothes. Finally the killer had to set the cruise control and send the car into the Gulf.

Except for a curious golden retriever with a good nose, the scheme might've worked. At first the police believed that a drunken Rossi had careened into the water and gotten himself washed out with the tide.

She closed her notebook and shook her head. Not nearly enough data to go on, especially in the first murder. The young woman seen at Otter Creek had money to take care of herself. Why then did she seem nervous, even before she met the unknown driver? Why would she insist on going to Cedar Key in spite of the threatening hurricane? If some outside person was involved, why was Rossi killed when he came to Cedar Key to find her? One fact stood out that frightened her. Cara might've taken a photograph that would identify the murderer, and everyone at the hotel knew about it.

Between clouds she looked down at the fleeting patches of forests and towns far below. They were like the scattered elements of the murders, she thought. She just couldn't see all the pieces that made up the landscape.

* * * *

Once out of the milling crowds at JFK, Brandy hurried to curb side and joined another woman who had snagged a cab into Manhattan. In an accent Brandy couldn't identify, their unshaven driver chatted with the other passenger about the New York Yankees' current success. Brandy stared into the crisp afternoon sunlight at the Manhattan skyline as it soared into view, at empty factories, empty warehouses, and finally at a monumental traffic jam approaching the mid-town tunnel. Brandy and the other passenger supplied the toll. The cab then darted down FDR Drive, let the baseball fan out at Tudor City, and swung west. After they passed into the northeast corner of Greenwich Village, they drew up at a four story red brick building with columns beside the portico, a hood above the door, and windows bristling with bars.

Brandy mounted the stone steps and rang Thea's buzzer twice, ready to announce herself into the speaker to Thea's roommate. No response. Perhaps the woman was still asleep. A sign pointed down outside steps to the superintendent's basement apartment where a door opened below a wrought iron fence. She had turned toward this lower entrance when she heard an answering buzz.

"Brandy O'Bannon," she said, shoving open the ornamented door. Once in the hallway, she rapped at a first floor apartment door with Thea's number that fronted the street. There was another pause. Then someone rattled a lock, she heard two bolts drawn back, the door opened a crack against the chain, and a voice like sandpaper called, "Go away, bad boy!"

Startled, Brandy stepped back. Somebody giggled and the chain clattered aside. "You must be freakin' out," another voice said. The door opened into a darkened room where a young woman in a tousled dressing gown stood aside to let her in. Brandy could see an unmade bed against the nearest wall, clothing strewn across the floor, and in the corner by a window, a tall metal cage. Below it lay a scattering of bird-seed. From behind the curved bars came a murmurous, "Awk."

"Sonata," said the young woman, giggling again. Her dark hair was rolled around huge tubular curlers. Below them she batted long black lashes, eyes dancing. "Sonata and Allegro."

Brandy couldn't identify the sour smell that permeated the small apartment. Perhaps it came from the bird cage. She stood, suitcase in hand, and tried to focus on what Thea's strange but friendly roommate was saying.

"Park your stuff over there. Thea's tidier." The young woman jerked up the window shade, kicked a pair of jeans out of the walkway, plopped down on the disheveled sheets on the daybed, and motioned toward a couch at the opposite end of the long room. Brandy recognized Thea's favorite Spy prints on the wall behind a neatly spread couch cover, and an art deco chair. Beside it stood a desk, a bookcase, and a dresser that held a colorful arrangement of silk flowers. The odd couple, Brandy thought.

"Roommate Round-up," said the young woman. "Flat fee of $195. Smoke?" She pulled a cigarette and lighter out of the commodious folds of her robe. "Works fine for us. Thea slaves away all day, comes home to sleep at night." She bent plump white cheeks forward and dragged on the cigarette. An ember glowed and a tiny plume of smoke rose toward the ceiling. She jumped up, trotted over the discarded jeans, and tugged open the window above the basement entrance and the sidewalk.

"Gotta get the smoke out, like before Thea makes it home. I'm outta here about five, work my tail off in a spaghetti joint 'til ten. Most nights then we do a gig someplace near the village, 'til about three. Tonight it's an entertainment bar on East 27th. Show business, my partner and me. Allegro." She waved the cigarette toward the cage.

"I wanna be me," rasped the voice from the corner.

Brandy spotted a large parrot teetering on its perch by the window. She dragged her suitcase beside Thea's dresser. "I need to stash my things for now and get some directions. Then you can go back to bed. Sorry, but I didn't catch your name."

"Sonata. Sonata Snow." The young woman repeated the name distinctly, as if she doubted Brandy's intelligence. She was finding Thea's guest a slow study.

Brandy threaded her way across the floor to the cage. "This is your accompanist?" She had finally made a connection between Sonata and Allegro.

"Yo. Talks like an angel. Fooled you, didn't he?" Sonata tittered again. "African Gray." She moved to Brandy's side. The soft gray parrot was perhaps a foot in length, with light-colored eyes ringed by bare skin. These were now studying Brandy. Under his tail and wings ran a fringe of scarlet. He did not move as Sonata approached. "Go away, bad boy," he repeated. Sonata unlocked the steel cage and dumped seed into the feeder.

"Experts say they don't know what they're sayin'. Like, they just memorize sounds. I'm not so sure."

Brandy pulled a map of Manhattan from her tote bag, along with Rossi's address. "I haven't got much time in New York. I'm looking for an investigative agency on East Tenth Street. I need to find it this afternoon. A murder case may depend on it, and a friend's future."

Not looking impressed, Sonata stubbed a finger in the right grid on the map. "Man, you can walk from here. Go coupla blocks east until 8th Street becomes St. Marks, then two blocks north on 2nd Avenue. Watch your wallet, kid." She frowned at Allego, who was inching away on his wooden perch, a glittering eye on her cigarette. Apparently, he didn't approve of smoke.

"Awk. "Remember Who You Are," he added morosely.

"Title of a recording." Sonata tilted her head, one hand on the curve of her hip, mimicking the tilt of the parrot's head. "He cracks me up." She had wrapped her robe tighter around her waist, and below its tattered hem Brandy could see a pair of shapely ankles.

"You've heard part of his repertoire," she said. "I sing a number, he reacts. Brings down the house. Sometimes." She reached for a tape player on a shelf beside a stack of sheet music. "No back to bed for me. We both gotta practice."

$$*\qquad*\qquad*\qquad*$$

"Discreet Investigations" read the small sign in the store front window. "Anthony P. Rossi, Licensed Private Investigator." In smaller letters it announced "Financial Background Checks, Employee Reports, Skip Tracing, Missing Persons, Matrimonial Surveillance." In some ways, a rather ugly practice, Brandy thought. Not exactly the glamorous job depicted in detective novels.

Past the corner, traffic rumbled along Second Avenue. A horn blared. Brandy stepped back from the flow of pedestrians along the sidewalk and remembered a sturdy Anthony Rossi, standing bewildered in a quiet side street of Cedar Key. The memory saddened her.

She had not believed that he was a bad guy. But what did she know of New York City?

Rossi's office was in a white brick building with a green fire escape angling down the front, green trim above the hooded windows, and a matching door. Customers had to buzz for admittance. On these littered streets Brandy had passed some shabbily dressed New Yorkers and one derelict sleeping in a doorway. According to Detective Strong, she was only a few blocks from a drug infested area. Maybe a handy location for Rossi. She hated to accept that scenario. Brandy remembered Thea had warned her, the 1992 East Village was badly in need of renovation.

Through the plate glass she could see someone moving around inside. Although a New York City Police Department notice hung on the doorknob, she pushed against the door and it opened.

"Hey, you!" A head of bouffant hair jerked up behind a wooden desk near the window, and a swivel chair rounded on Brandy. "Whatcha' doing? Nobody's to come in here, know what I'm saying?"

Brandy faced an indignant woman of perhaps forty in a black sweater and red skirt. She had been collecting personal items from the lower right hand drawer of the desk and stacking them on the desk top, a mirror, a brush, three lipsticks, a comb, a box of tissues. Under the box lay a page of want ads. "Hey, I got permission from the cops to be here, pick up my things." The woman waved a dismissive hand at Rossi's sign. "Guy's dead. Beat it."

Brandy sat down in a straight chair against the wall and pulled a pen and a ragged memo pad out of her bag. "I know. I've come up from Florida. I'm a reporter and I'm looking for some information about Rossi's last case. Name's Brandy O'Bannon. Yours?"

The other woman paused and drummed red fingernails on the desk. Her eyes turned cagey. "You oughta talk to the cops, not me. I don't know squat about Rossi's business. His investigations were *private*." She came down hard on the last word.

"You were his secretary?"

"I guess you could call me that. I took messages. Typed up the notes he gave me. Only got the job two months ago. Fat chance I've got to find another, conditions like they are." She glanced down at the want ads, a few highlighted in yellow.

Inconsiderate of Rossi, Brandy thought, to get himself murdered and deprive his secretary of employment. She spoke in a voice she hoped was non-threatening "Did he give you any notes about his search for a missing woman in Cedar Key, Florida?"

"Cops here took his records, holding them for the Florida cops. But I didn't see nothing from Florida. Anyway, if you type stuff, you know you don't read what it says."

"He must've made an electronic search for the woman before he left New York."

"Yeah, sure. Used a data base. Didn't turn up nothing, know what I'm saying? That's why he hung a plane outta here."

"And you didn't talk to him again?"

Her tone became more affable. "You're freakin' nosy, lady." She considered the question, her forehead crinkling below the tall, stiff hair. "Yeah, I guess he called once from Florida. I gave him the bad news the next night. His client died the day after he left. She was an old lady, died of cancer. Her husband called, told me to tell Rossi, said he'd send the final check for Rossi's expenses and time."

Brandy's pulse quickened. "Did you get the husband's name?"

The secretary reached into her handbag, extracted a package of gum, thought about offering some to Brandy, decided not to, and popped a stick in her mouth.

"Yeah, at the time. I don't remember it now. I gave everything to the cops."

"Why do you suppose he took such a case—I mean agree to go so far away—when he knew his client was fatally ill?"

The woman snapped her gum. She still hadn't given Brandy her name, and Brandy thought she didn't plan to. "That I wouldn't know, lady. None of my business."

"I didn't catch your name?"

The secretary cocked her head and gave Brandy a shrewd look. Working for a private eye had made her suspicious. Apparently, she couldn't see the harm. "Polenski."

"He was still working on the case after his client's death, Miss Polenski. He said someone else might be interested. You have any idea who that might be?"

The gum popped again. "I told you, lady. I don't know squat about his business."

Brandy leaned forward and looked directly into her eyes. "There's talk about a drug connection between the town where Mr. Rossi was killed and New York City. You have any thoughts about that?"

The red nails tapped the desk again. Brandy waited. "Rossi had a kid brother into drugs," she said finally. "Family couldn't do a thing with the kid. Got sent to some tough school somewheres." She shrugged. "Rossi said he hated drugs."

Brandy remembered Strong had notified someone of Rossi's death. "Isn't there a wife or a family member I could talk to?"

"Poor sucker had an ex-wife in the Bronx. She'll get whatever's left." With a twisted smile, Miss Polenski nodded at the battered desk, a couple of metal files, an off-brand computer, and an electronic typewriter. "Guess she'll be sorry to see her alimony end. She knows less about his work than I do, and that's, like, zippo."

Miss Polenski stood and Brandy was surprised to see she was wearing jogging shoes. She dropped the desk items one by one into a plastic bag, picked up a sack with her dress shoes, and stuffed the want ads into her purse. "I'm done here. Gotta lock up. Gotta hit the ads." She shook the towering hair again. "Fat chance of finding something, know what I'm saying?"

Brandy felt sudden panic. She'd come all this way. Cara counted on her, not to mention her editor, but she was striking out in the first interview. As she rose she could see a postman through the plate glass at the top of the door, striding toward the letter box in the entrance foyer.

"Thanks for your help," Brandy said without a trace of irony, opened the door, and intercepted the envelopes the postman had begun shoving into the box. "I'll just hand in the mail," she added. "Might be something of interest."

"Hey!" The secretary stretched out her hand, but with rapid motions Brandy was already sorting through the letters. Bills mostly, electric, telephone, computer data base, and one legal sized envelope from an individual. The return address on a printed label read "Mr. and Mrs. Irving Grosmiller." Brandy jotted down a west side, 23rd Street address and thrust the mail at the reproachful Miss Polenski.

Maybe, Brandy thought, as the secretary threw the letters on the desk behind them and locked the door, just maybe that was the payment from Anthony Rossi's last client.

*   *   *   *

Thea Ridge arrived at the studio apartment as tall and angular and svelte as Brandy remembered. She gave Brandy a quick hug at the door and rolled her eyes at the scene. On the floor, birdseed over-sprinkled the jeans and the crumpled robe. On the foyer table the contents of a cereal bowl sat congealing beside a half glass of milk. Allegro's cage stood empty.

"God, what a mess!" Thea led her friend to her own side of the room. When Brandy gave the open cage an anxious glance, Thea added, "Sonata's got a carrying cage for the parrot."

Brandy grinned. "You've found a roommate even sloppier than I am."

Thea tucked her purse in a corner of her bookcase and sighed. "Wait 'til you see the bathroom. Ever live with anyone who jumps into the tub with her laundry? Clothes drying everywhere."

"Why put up with it then?"

With a sudden smile, her friend faced the window and flung her arms wide. "It's Manhattan! I could never afford the Village alone."

Brandy handed her the Grosmiller address. "I've got to try to phone this man. If he's not the right guy, my mission's a wash out."

Thea fluffed up her half bang, considering the street number. "Chelsea." She nodded toward the directory beside the phone on her small desk. "Give it a try." She glanced down at her plaid navy jacket and pleated skirt. "While you call, I'll change, and we'll stroll over to a Ukrainian restaurant on Second Avenue. Best cheese blintzes in New York." She paused at the bath room door. "Actually, I kind of like the parrot."

Brandy finally located an Irving at the correct address among a long list of Manhattan Grosmillers. The phone rang six times before a man who sounded tired and tremulous finally picked it up.

"Brandy O'Bannon, *Gainesville Tribune*," Brandy began. "If your wife hired Anthony Rossi to find her niece, it's important that I talk to you."

"The investigation was confidential," the weary voice said. "My wife's business. I paid for the man's time. For God's sake, my wife just died. I don't want to talk."

Brandy gripped the phone in another rising panic. Had she found the right man only to lose him? "I don't want to intrude. But I've come all the way from Florida, just to find the name of your wife's niece."

Grosmiller did not sound moved. "I'm packing up, going to my daughter's in New Jersey." Brandy could hear the irritation in his voice. "Haven't got time to see anyone. For God's sake, ask Rossi."

Of course, she thought, the story might not be in the New York papers, or he may not have seen it. Irving Grosmiller had been planning his wife's funeral. For maximum effect, she spaced her words. "Rossi is dead, murdered."

Silence. At the top of her untidy note pad, Brandy doodled a dog's head, sniffing the ground. "I'm a reporter. I think I know the niece's missing daughter. She wants to know her real name. It's a long story. I really need to see you."

Brandy listened to breathing on the phone as Mr. Grosmiller deliberated. At last he spoke. "Be at my apartment about ten."

As Thea came back into the room in slacks and a sweatshirt, Brandy faced her with relief. "I've got one small window open onto the truth. Tomorrow morning at ten."

CHAPTER 13

▼

Sunday night Cara and Marcia maintained an uneasy truce. At the dining room table Cara worked on her portfolio of photographs, devising more imaginative angles for her shots of hammocks and live oaks and snowy egrets. Did she need soft or sharp focus? More shadow? Color or black and white?

But she had difficulty concentrating. Marcia seemed upset and restless. She kept moving about the kitchen and dining room, picking up a book, setting it down, filling a glass of iced tea and leaving in on the counter, rummaging through the newspaper without reading it. No chatter about the gallery, about who bought a picture, who might commission a new watercolor. With unsteady fingers, Cara laid down her pencil. Marcia was concealing something, perhaps had concealed something for a long time. Marcia had brushed off Cara's questions ever since she was old enough to ask them.

The artist swept up her glass of tea, then stopped at the kitchen door. "Goodwill's coming tomorrow morning. I've put together a box of old clothes, mostly things of your father's." Her back was still to Cara. "I never had the heart to part with them, but the closet's overflowing. Anything you want to toss out, just put on my bed." She wandered into the hall, then turned. "I'll run home from the gallery about eleven. Are you still going to Chiefland in the morning?"

Even as Cara nodded, she had decided to act. She remembered the furtive way Marcia bent over something in the closet Saturday morning, how her face had been flushed when she swung the door closed. Tomorrow Cara would breach the privacy and trust that had always existed between them. She would search her foster mother's closet before the Goodwill truck arrived.

Cara lied. "I'll pick up my pictures at the drug store right after I serve breakfast. Might as well go straight from the hotel. I'll leave town well before eleven."

*   *   *   *

In the morning MacGill beamed through the doorway as Cara carried the last of the dirty plates into the hotel kitchen. "Mind you let us know about your Shell Mound photo."

Cara gave him a tight smile. "After I tell Detective Strong." She slipped out of her mauve apron and into a sweater. "I don't expect I'll get much. I didn't dare use a flash." She followed him into the lobby. "Going right away. Drug store usually has pictures back by ten, ten-thirty." She looked at her watch. Nine-thirty. Marcia would be at the gallery.

MacGill walked with Cara to the door and peered up at a chilly, gray sky. "For once we might luck out. Storm's moving slowly. May not get within kicking distance."

On the windy sidewalk, Cara buttoned her sweater and tied a scarf over her flying hair. But instead of starting out for Chiefland, she drove past the turn-off and set out for home. When she pulled into the driveway, Marcia's van was gone from the carport.

For the next few minutes Cara searched her own closet for cast-offs. If Marcia should come home early, a few goodwill items would give her a reason to invade her mother's room. Still, her conscience smarted as she stepped into Marcia's orderly bedroom, threw two old dresses and a torn blouse on the bed, and looked around.

The dresser held only family pictures. Wedged in the frame of a black and white photograph of her foster dad was a snapshot of him standing before the timber shack. It was taken a year before the roof careened into the wind and a flood marooned him with his men, kept him from Marcia and that first doomed little Cara. Next was her own studio portrait at about three years of age, huddled in Marcia's lap, her foster dad behind them.

No female vanity showed in Marcia's room. Her few simple pieces of jewelry were kept in a neat, partitioned drawer. Next to the bed the radio still played softly, tuned to a classical music station. Beside it lay a library book of landscape reproductions, ordered from Tallahassee. Marcia must've been looking at it last night.

Cara opened the closet door and knelt beside the tall carton marked "Goodwill." Her foster father's tarnished metal lock box had been shoved behind it. Marcia would never discard that. Cara pulled the box forward, surprised to find it unlocked. She lifted the lid and peered at his incomplete coin collection. Cara remembered him sitting for tedious hours at the table, counting, polishing, adding one now and again, an inexpensive hobby. Under them were his World War II metals, Good Conduct, Asiatic-Pacific Theater, Philippine Liberation Ribbon, Victory Metal, all earned at age seventeen and eighteen. He had said it would be ostentatious to mount them. Her eyes stung. A dear man, a thoughtful father. If she never found her real father, she could be grateful for having had this one. But the coins and metals only half filled the box. Something must be missing.

She closed the lid and peeled back the tape Marcia had wound across the Goodwill carton. On top lay her foster father's worn hunting jacket, below it his leather gloves and fishing cap. She sat back, absorbing a rush of warm memories. Then with a twinge, she pushed them aside, uncovered several folded shirts and slacks of Marcia's, some frayed curtains, beneath them a baby's stained white Christening dress, booties—these must be the first Cara's.

She could scarcely reach the bottom of the box now, and she lifted clothes out, stacked them on the floor, and tilted the box. A paper bag fell to one side. Toddler clothes—a mildewed white pullover shirt, pink coveralls. They stirred a nagging memory, something she had heard. She clawed at the last item, an old beach bag, rusted safety pins holding it together. Maybe she had a premonition.

She sat on the floor, held it for a few seconds, then began struggling with the pins. One snapped in two. Another pricked her fingers. At last they were open. She felt down into the bag. Something soft, spongy. Her fingers fastened around it, drew out a shapeless blue cloth lump. She punched it, pulled it, found two black thread eyes, a triangular mouth, straightened two tufted ears. In her head ran the interview with the cashier. She stared down at the terry-cloth bear, a sob in her throat. Mrs. Terry had seen that little girl carrying a blue teddy bear in the Otter Creek café. She had told the police. But no one ever knew Marcia had recovered it.

The next few minutes were a blur of tears and fury. Cara remembered. The cashier said the child wore something pink. What pang of conscience made Marcia keep the bear for twenty years? And the clothes? Yet hidden, probably in the bottom of the coin and metals box. Marcia had known. She had known all along that Cara belonged to the woman from the Otter Creek café. Now Marcia decided to discard the only evidence that linked them—after she sensed the reporter, and maybe Detective Strong, closing in.

Cara dropped the gaping beach bag on the floor, swept up the overalls and shirt, wrapped them around the bear, left the other clothes where they lay, and hugged the bundle in her arms. To think she had worried about invading Marcia's space! Worried about telling her she would not return to the house this morning. Marcia thought she had plenty of time to dispose of the Goodwill carton.

Now it was ten. Pulling her one large suitcase, a graduation gift from Marcia, out of her closet, Cara crammed it with pajamas, underwear, dresses, slacks and shirts, and with trembling fingers zipped it shut. She packed her few cosmetics in a plastic bag with the stuffed bear. Then she telephoned a girlfriend both MacGill and Marcia knew, and asked her to cover for her at the hotel and art gallery. Next she hesitated, phone in hand. Marcia would be home soon. She hadn't much time, but she'd better prepare Truck. She made a call to his fish house. He would be working, standing at the table beside the huge cooler, his callused hands wielding an oyster knife, the weight scales ready.

"I'm going to be out of town for a while," she said when she heard his husky voice. "Not to worry. Nothing's wrong. I'm going in to pick up the pictures this morning and then visit some friends in Chiefland." She was not good at lying, but she did not want to deal with Truck's temper this morning. "Call you later."

She hung up before he could ask what friends. No need to leave a note for Marcia. She would understand as soon as she saw the discarded beach bag and Cara's empty closet. With camera slung around her neck and purse from her shoulder, she carried her portfolio and the plastic bag to the station wagon, pulling the suitcase behind her. To the shrill ringing of the phone, Cara swung the station wagon into the street. No doubt Truck was trying to find out where she would be. She focused instead on the two Cedar Key stops she had to make, one at the bank and one at the Island Hotel. Next she would pick up the pictures, call Strong if she had a recognizable likeness, and find a place to stay. Maybe in Gainesville. Then she would phone Brandy in New York.

When Cara asked at the bank to withdraw her savings, the cashier disappeared into an inner office. In a few seconds a small man with a tweedy look and a pinched face emerged, the bank manager Cara had known ever since she could remember.

"It's not safe to carry that much cash, even in Cedar Key," he said to Cara. "If there's a problem, we're all here to help."

Cara shook her head, improvising. "I'm staying for a while in Gainesville, taking some courses at the university."

At last she agreed to take only two hundred dollars and transfer the rest to another bank after she was settled. The manager walked her to the door, eyes anxious. "But the fall term's already started."

Cara reached for possibilities. "Special arrangements. Got a job near the university." How I wish, she thought. As she crossed the street to the hotel, he still stood in the doorway.

In the lobby of the Island Hotel Cara fed a more convincing version to Mr. MacGill: she had an unexpected chance to work in a camera studio in Gainesville. She planned to enroll later for a few classes.

MacGill's square face grew pensive. "Marcia approve?"

Cara frowned. "I'm a grown woman, for pity's sake. I called Ellie Ruth Rice. She's had experience at a bed and breakfast. She'll take over for me in the dining room. Not to worry. She'll be here tonight and for as long as you need her."

"And the photographs? At the drug store?"

This small town busy-body atmosphere suffocated her. "Picking them up now. I'll call Brandy O'Bannon tonight, and I'll notify the sheriff's office if a picture shows anything interesting." She tipped her head toward the gossipy desk clerk. "Everyone in town will know where I've gone soon enough."

When Cara set out a few minutes later for Chiefland, suitcase, camera, and blue bear stowed under a tarpaulin behind her, her spirits lifted. She would contact Marcia later, after she had made firm plans. She had paid an emotional price, but she had begun to learn the truth. And she was free.

Unlike the moment before she discovered the bear, she had no warning premonition. The drug store was almost empty of customers. With growing excitement, she hurried straight to the photography section. Maybe on that moonlit night she had caught a murderer's face. As a sallow-faced young woman fumbled through a stack of yellow and black envelopes and handed her a package, someone called Cara's name. She turned to see a heavy-set man in a sports coat and tie hurrying toward the counter.

"Miss Waters?" He was close now and drew a badge from an inner pocket. "Detective Stokes. Levy County Sheriff's Office. There's an emergency." He was breathing hard now. "Just got a call from the dispatcher. It's your mother. I'm afraid she's had a heart attack."

Cara gasped. Of course. Why hadn't she thought of it? Marcia was strong, but when she came back to the house and saw that open beach bag…When she realized Cara knew, that she was gone…Cara suddenly felt faint. Memories of Marcia flooded back, walking her hand in hand to first grade, getting up early to fix Cara's favorite breakfasts, giving her a kitten for her birthday. "How is she?"

The man's speech slowed, repeating a message. "Detective Strong called in. Said we would find you at the drug store. Someone found your mother about eleven." Of course, Cara thought, the Goodwill pick up. "Medics got there right away. They've rushed her to Crystal River, Seven Rivers Hospital."

In spite of everything, Cara knew what she must do. "I have to go immediately." She fingered the fat envelope. The two shots would be near the bottom. She strode toward the door, while he lumbered along beside her.

"I'm authorized to take you to her," he said. "I've got a cell phone in the car. We'll call and get a progress report. We can use the siren if we need it."

Thoughtful of the Sheriff's Office, Cara thought. If he drove, she would save time. She could look at the photographs and call Detective Strong from the car. She paused long enough to lock her station wagon. Then he took her arm and helped her into the passenger seat of a new Ford. "Got an unmarked car, but it's equipped."

As soon as she slipped into the passenger seat, he gunned the engine, tapped two digits on the keyboard with thick fingers, and picked up the hand-held set. "Stokes here. I'm on my cell." In a few seconds he added, "Patch me in to Seven Rivers Hospital." He drove with one hand, holding the phone, waiting. "Seven Rivers? Tell Marcia Waters' doctor I found her daughter. We're on our way. Any change?" For a few more seconds he listened, then set down the phone.

Everything about the man was oversized, wide nose and mouth, massive head, coarse black hair. "Conditions the same," he said. "She's asking for you."

She'll lay a real guilt trip on me this time, Cara thought, but she was misty eyed. She loosened the glued flap of the yellow and black envelope. "I just picked up some photos Detective Strong may want to see."

Detective Stokes surprised her a little. He was well enough dressed, but sitting so close to him, she didn't find him as clean as she would expect. His hair was unruly, and his belt squeezed over an inflated stomach. The Sheriff should put him on a diet, Cara thought, and Strong could give him a few pointers on grooming. Maybe he'd been undercover.

She pulled the package open and began flipping past the first shots of a stilt house on the Gulf, aware of pines and palmettos rushing past on Route 19. Now the car suddenly slowed, spun up a dirt road on the right, and ground to a stop. With a quick motion her driver cut off the engine and lifted something out of his pocket. She continued shuffling through more pictures. Perhaps the driver had seen some illegal activity in the woods.

Then she sensed he had turned in his seat. The sour odor of sweat washed over her. She looked down. He was holding a gun level with his bulging belly, and it was aimed at her. His voice coarsened. "Outta the car. Now."

Stricken, Cara pressed her back against the car door. "I don't understand. Am I in trouble with the law? What about my mother?"

"Ain't nothing wrong with your old lady, girlie. Drop the pictures and get outta the car." The fleshy lips tilted up. "I been in the back of enough cop cars to know the lingo."

Cara stumbled out beside the road while he snatched the envelope and crammed it into his pocket, then scrambled after her, puffing, the gun still cocked at her head. When she twisted around to look for the gun, he thrust his head forward. For the first time she noticed his tobacco stained teeth. She thought of a quail, mesmerized by a snake.

"Face the other way. Hold still and you won't get hurt."

She thought of his big, blubbery body and froze to the bone. He was no Sheriff's Office detective. How could she ever have thought he was? Metal pressed against the side of her head. A car sped past, only yards away. Somewhere a mockingbird trilled. He was moving his other arm. Something metal rattled.

"One little scream and you're dead meat. Arms behind your back."

When she hesitated, he jammed the gun against her temple. She obeyed and heard the metallic click. Metal tightened around one wrist, snap, a ring gripped the other. Handcuffs, of course. Her legs went weak. She could feel her body sag. She did not control it now.

"Gonna climb into the back seat." The barrel end of the gun tapped her skull again. Somehow she crawled in. She felt a shove, and her slender shoulders fell against the other door. Then he yanked her feet up on the seat, snatched a rope from the car floor, and began knotting it around her ankles. He must've laid aside the gun, but she was helpless, drained, deafened by the pounding of her own heart.

He pulled the rope tight. "Strictly business, girlie." Wildly she thought, how methodical! A hit man, a hired thug. He reached under the front seat, pulled out a can and a rag. "You gotta keep nice and quiet."

Her eyes widened. The last thing she saw was the dirty, sodden cloth coming toward her, its sharp stench overpowering.

CHAPTER 14

▼

By the time Brandy had dressed Tuesday morning, Thea had already gone. Brandy edged past Sonata, sleeping under a pile of wrinkled clothes beside the open window. As she reached for the doorknob, Allegro swiveled his decorative head, his black eyes glinting at her. Apparently when the musical parrot act returned near dawn, Sonata didn't cover his cage.

But he only emitted a murmurous "Awk," and went back to people-watching beyond the iron grill of the front window. Stretching his dove-gray neck, he peered down into the basement entrance, where a tenant was depositing a sack in a garbage can, and called, "Go away, bad boy!"

The man, who must've been accustomed to Allegro's demands, looked up, grinned, and disappeared into his basement apartment. Brandy slipped past the cage and, taking Thea's advice, trotted down the stone steps beside the recessed basement and waited for a taxi at the curb. For the first time she noticed the coils of razor ribbon, designed to ward off burglars, between Thea's building and its neighbor.

Irving Grosmiller lived in a buff-colored brick building above a travel agency, a bagel shop, and a camera store. In the small tiled lobby Brandy stopped at a counter, where a plump young clerk interrupted his bagel and coffee to call Mr. Grosmiller on an intercom, then nodded toward the elevator.

"He's expecting you. You gotta punch the bell." The clerk smeared cream cheese on a doughy bagel half. "Number's 623." On the sixth floor Brandy was admitted to the apartment in the standard New York way. First she heard two locks turn, the slide of a chain, and finally the deadbolt release. Brandy faced a bald, elderly gentleman with thin, bent shoulders and a soup-strainer mustache.

"I'm packing," he said. From the narrow kitchen off the foyer came a shrill whistle. "Fixing some coffee. Instant." He raised bristling gray eyebrows. Irving Grosmiller suffered from one of nature's ironies, a shiny pate above and excessive hair below. "Want a cup?"

Brandy followed him while he groped in a half-empty cupboard and took down two mis-matched cups, one cracked. "Should've hired a packing crew." His faded blue eyes looked soulful. "My wife always did the packing. We hadn't moved in twenty-five years. Now on this block we suddenly got gentrification. Everything upscale." He scraped a teaspoon of dried out coffee into each cup and gave them a vicious stir. "Could've stayed, of course, because of my age. Could even buy into the co-op. It would've cost an arm and a leg."

Brandy picked up her coffee and trailed after him into what had been the living room. The sun burned through the curtainless window on several cartons and boxes and a threadbare oriental rug. "Might as well move near my daughter in Jersey. Nothing's going to be left of the old Chelsea."

With a sigh he dropped into one of two upholstered chairs beside a half-filled bookcase, set his cup on a shelf, and began stacking volumes into a narrow oblong crate. Brandy recognized a few titles, *The Ordeal of Richard Feveral, Martin Chuzzlewit, The Vicar of Wakefield.* A Victorian enthusiast, she thought. My story might appeal to his sense of drama. On the opposite wall stood a glass-paneled cabinet, crammed with sentimental ceramic figures—tiny boys and girls, puppies, and kittens, bright blue and pink birds. His wife's collection, probably. Brandy had more respect for the husband's taste.

"Mr. Grosmiller, I told you on the phone I'm a reporter from the Gainesville newspaper. Your wife commissioned a private investigator to locate her niece. I need to know the niece's identity."

"We paid the man for his time," Grosmiller said in an irritated tone. "I'm sorry he's dead, but I don't want to get involved. I'm too busy just now."

If the story of the murder even made the New York papers, it would've been a small item. He didn't understand the urgency. Brandy leaned toward him. "The investigator was murdered two days ago in Florida," she said.

His bony hand halted in mid-air, still holding a slender volume of Aubrey Beardsley. "I haven't read the newspaper in days." Finally he inserted the book into the box.

Brandy reached into her bag for a note pad, forcing her voice to sound gentle. "Tell me about your wife's niece."

He slumped back in his chair. "Her mother was my wife's sister. The family lived over on the east side, Tudor City. To start with, when the daughter was a teen-ager she give her parents problems. An only child. Sometimes ran in a crowd they didn't approve of. Then there was the tragedy."

"Tragedy?"

When he pursed his lips and glanced at her note pad, Brandy returned it to her bag. Better to trust her memory than stifle an interview. Note-taking made some people nervous.

"Both parents were killed in a car accident up in New England one summer, my wife's sister and her husband. Her niece was nineteen, at New York University." He shook his head. "Allison's her name. She dropped out of college, went through a bad time, I guess. We saw something of her for a while. My wife felt an obligation, you know." He resumed his slow packing. "The girl turned to her father's attorney for advice. Natural, I suppose. He had to close the estate, take it through probate. She got to depend on him for every decision. Turned out her father was a poor businessman, left a lot of debts and not much else. She came out with a lump sum. Not much, my wife said."

Brandy wondered where the story was leading, but at least she had a first name now, Allison.

"She didn't want to go back to school, anyway. Well, one thing led to another, and by the end of the year, she up and married the attorney. My wife was upset. He was probably twenty years older, but then he was a wealthy man. She figured that was some compensation. He was on the rebound, like they say. Divorced his first wife the year before. An ugly business. That wife told all sorts of outrageous stories about him, but he held firm. He said the woman was running around with another man. He finally got custody of their son."

Grosmiller took a long sip of coffee that dampened his drooping mustache. For a doleful moment he reflected. "So Allison and the attorney married, but I guess it didn't work out. They started having trouble early on. When she got over grieving for her parents, I guess she started thinking about having a good time again. But as you young folks say, he wasn't into her scene.

"The little girl was born about a year after the wedding. About two more years went by and we didn't hear from her. Then she called my wife a couple of times, and I think they met somewhere. Next thing I knew, Allison left her husband and took the little girl. My wife figured Allison had seen Frank Bullen as a substitute for her father, and she tired of being married to a father figure."

Allison's other name had dropped. "Why would Mr. Bullen let her leave with their child?"

"My wife said he might not want to hold Allison against her will, but Allison was afraid he'd fight for custody of the little girl. Mr. Bullen said she was running around wild. Remember, he got custody of his son after his first marriage."

Brandy reached down, opened the Beardsley volume to one of the artist's typical illustrations—a Victorian beauty with delicate features, fluid neck, up-tilted head of dark, flowing hair. "That little girl has grown up to look very much like this picture, Mr. Grosmiller. It's for her that I'm bothering you this morning."

Silently the old man stared at the page. Then he passed his hand over his eyes. "I wouldn't want to cause trouble for Mr. Bullen," he said at last. "Seems like a decent fellow. I see their pictures in the papers, at charity functions sometimes. He finally got a divorce for desertion, my wife said. A couple of years ago he married again."

"Did your wife ever hear from her niece?"

"Once, I think. A card, right after she left. My wife told Allison where to go that her husband couldn't find her, and she gave her a letter of introduction to an old friend who would help her. When she didn't hear from Allison again, she thought she'd settled in all right. I never knew where. When my wife got so ill—" he paused to get control of his voice—"she wanted to find her niece. She tried to get in touch with her old friend, but the woman had moved away. No one knew how to reach her anymore."

"Do you know what happened to the card her niece mailed?"

He thought a moment. "Might be in my wife's safety deposit box. She didn't keep much stuff. A tidy sort. I forgot about the box, and it was sealed. Now I've got to wait until later this week to get into it, look for some bonds."

Brandy steered the conversation back to Cara. "Were you aware that a woman was murdered in Cedar Key, Florida, about the time Allison disappeared? A woman who had a two-year old girl with her?"

He glanced up, startled. "My wife never knew that." He'd stopped packing now. "Name of the town rings a bell. As a kid my wife spent some time in Cedar Key. Had relatives used to live there. Talked about what a quiet, out-of-the-way place it was, miles off the main highway."

Brandy felt for her note pad again and gripped her pencil. "The murdered woman's skeleton was never identified," she said. "Do you know who Allison's dentist might be?"

"I suppose you're looking for positive identification." He rose, shuffled over to an open box, and rummaged among manila folders, albums, and small notebooks. "Methodical, bless her." He straightened up with a pocket-sized address book. "Kept important names and addresses. My wife and her sister went to the same guy for years. Allison might have, too." He carried the small book back to his chair, flipped a few pages, and peered at the neat handwriting. "It's my wife's, all right." He swallowed, fumbled in his pants pocket for a handkerchief, and wiped his eyes. "Got no idea if the guy would still be practicing. Dr. Edward Linebaugh. Had an office over on 42nd Street off Madison."

Brand jotted down the name and number. She also scrawled "Frank Bullen, attorney," and "Allison" after it. "The local sheriff's office may be interested. The murder case is still open, of course. They'll want Allison Bullen's dental records."

Grosmiller drained the remainder of his cold coffee and placed his cup on the shelf. "Sure don't want to cause problems for Mr. Bullen. He's had enough. He may not want all this business raked up again. If Allison was killed, I'm glad my wife didn't know."

Brandy doodled a tombstone and thrust her note pad back into her purse. "You'll be doing Mr. Bullen a favor. While he thought his wife was making a new life for herself, she was probably lying dead in a basement, and his child was being reared by a stranger." With a twinge of guilt she thought of Marcia Waters, but she plunged on. "The person I'm working with may be that daughter. She's grown up in Cedar Key, not knowing who she really is. She's a young woman anyone would be pleased to have as a daughter." Frank Bullen, she thought, must be the source of the money the private detective said would come to Cara. Maybe he was the other party Rossi said would be interested in the investigation.

"I don't know," the old man said, shaking his head. "There's a lot of truth in the saying, 'Let sleeping dogs lie.'"

"That would be Mr. Bullen's decision," Brandy said. "Do you know how I can reach him?"

Grosmiller pointed to a stack of phone directories on the bottom shelf of the bookcase. "Help yourself. He's a partner in a big law firm here in Manhattan. Be a shock to him, not to mention his new wife. I imagine his home phone's unlisted. Try "attorneys" in the yellow pages. He works with probate, trusts, things like that."

The bottom bookshelf was now bare. He scooted his chair to the cabinet, laid a stack of old newspapers next to it, and began wrapping the ceramic figures. After several frustrating minutes, Brandy found the trust attorneys and a firm called "Brett, Adcock, Bullen, Sturdevant, and Crye." The phone was picked up by a woman with a frosty voice. "Mr. Bullen is in conference. I can see about making an appointment some time next month."

Brandy winced. "This is a personal matter. I think Mr. Bullen will make time to see me. Will you please tell him I'm here from Florida with information about his daughter."

The superiority in her tone increased. "Mr. Bullen has a son, not a daughter."

"Mr. Bullen has a daughter he's lost touch with. She's grown now and would like to meet him."

A stunned pause followed. "Can he get back to you?"

"I'm only here through today." Brandy glanced at her preoccupied host, then at her watch. Ten-forty-five. "He'll have to call me here within the next half hour." She gave Grosmiller's phone number. "Later I can be reached at another apartment." She extracted her address book from her bag and repeated Thea's number. "I leave in the morning on an eight o'clock plane. And I won't be back."

She walked to the front window and looked down at a busy fruit vendor's cart, the crush of shoppers, the cabs and cars jockeying under the traffic light, heard the rising din of voices, horns, car engines. She remembered the razor ribbon between buildings, and felt an unexpected sadness. Cara had been raised in the still backwater of Cedar

Key. Its people weren't blood family, but they were dear and concerned friends. Marcia had been a devoted foster parent. What destiny was Brandy about to hand to Cara?

As Grosmiller continued his patient wrapping, Brandy sat down beside him, picked up a length of newsprint, and wadded it around a tiny bear. He held up a slim porcelain figure in a hoop skirt. "Almost sixty years together," he said quietly. "I won't last a year without her, you know."

Brandy raised her eyes, touched. Would John ever make such a remark about her, perhaps fifty years from now? She could not be sure. When the telephone rang, Grosmiller nodded to her and she picked it up. The same clipped female voice spoke. "The only time Mr. Bullen can see you today is during his lunch hour. What did you say your name was?"

"Brandy. Brandy O'Bannon, *Gainesville Tribune.*"

"He says it would be best to meet him at his apartment, Miss O'Bannon. His housekeeper will be there to let you in. His wife's out for the morning. He'll meet you there about twelve-thirty." Brandy wrote down an address on Sutton Place.

At the apartment door she shook Mr. Grosmiller's frail hand. "I'd as soon you didn't mention me when you meet Mr. Bullen," he said. "I'd like to stay out of this whole wretched business."

In the elevator Brandy had a sudden feeling of insecurity. She was out of her depth. What was she doing in Manhattan, preparing to talk to a powerful New York attorney, to tell him his daughter might lay claim to him after twenty years?

She comforted herself with the thought of Cara, safe in the cocoon of Cedar Key.

CHAPTER 15

▼

Cara was conscious of a vise-like headache, of being prone and joggled in the back seat of a car. She longed to cry out for help. When she was twelve, she had broken an ankle playing soccer. It was Marcia who comforted her in the jolting ambulance. But Marcia was not here now. Cara had shut her out of her life.

She tried to lift her hand to her head, and remembered that her wrists were bound behind her. Rigid with fear, she waited several minutes while her memory flooded back, afraid to speak, afraid the thug who drove would bind her mouth as well. She'd read that a captive had once suffocated because of a clumsy effort to stifle her voice. Cara couldn't sit up; she couldn't move her ankles or legs. By twisting her neck, she could see the tops of trees flashing past in growing darkness. The bumpiness of the road must mean the driver had veered off the highway, away from any town, and onto a dirt road.

At last the car ground to a halt. The brute who drove snapped open his door, stepped out, and slogged around to the passenger side. Cara stiffened.

Her door swung wide. "Okay, girlie. Time to get out. We gonna switch cars. Move!"

"I can't move," Cara said, her voice soft, non-threatening.

"Damn. I ain't gonna carry you. I'll loosen the ankle rope some. One false move, you know what'll happen."

Cara rolled out of the seat and wobbled to her feet. She stood in a sandy road, tall trees rising around them, no lights, no sounds except the sighing of the wind. She could see before them the square bulk of an open vehicle. Rough hands shoved her the few feet to a swamp buggy, and half lifted her onto the passenger seat.

Cara whispered, "Someone will find my car."

He looked at her, his grin wolfish. "Don't count on it, sister. No one will find your car for a long, long time. And nobody knows where you've gone." She had seen to that herself, she thought bitterly, her heart sinking.

The car keys were in her purse and it was gone. Anyway, thugs like these would not be stopped by a locked car. Surely she was dealing with more than one person. Maybe, she thought, the homicide detective was right. Maybe Rossi had crossed a gang of drug dealers, and she had taken the leader's picture. If true, she and Brandy were wrong about a connection with her. Brandy's trip to New York would be useless. Cara slumped down in the seat, her chest knotted in a tight fist.

After the swamp buggy swerved around a curve in the two track road, its dim headlights shone on the broad, black waters of a river. The Suwannee, she thought. No other nearby body of water stretched so far across. She could see the distant shore, thick with bald cypress, slash pine, and red cedar. When her driver jammed on the brake, the tires slid a few feet in the wet soil.

"Out!" He grunted, lifting his bulk out of his seat.

The passenger seat was too high for Cara to jump down. When his fingers tightened around her arms, she almost fainted with fear before he half dropped her to the ground. A small skiff had been tied to a tree by the shore, and beyond it, anchored off a small island, a houseboat rose and fell with waves kicked up by the wind. She could not look at him. It was bad enough to be next to his sour smell. "What are you going to do with me?" she asked.

He did not answer, and instead half pushed and half carried her across the damp river's edge and over the side of the little boat. He yanked the rope on a small kicker, waited for the engine to catch, then steered across to the houseboat. In the failing light, Cara stumbled up the short ladder though a gate onto the deck and was hustled past the wheel house. She glimpsed a whiskey bottle and a wall phone. Then he pushed her though a pocket door, and into a cramped bedroom with bunk beds, one dresser, and a tiny bathroom off the short hall.

"My hands," she said, trying to steady her voice. She nodded toward the head. "I've got to use my hands."

"Shit." He grabbed a small key from a jacket pocket and unsnapped the handcuffs that had rubbed her wrists raw, in a hurry to waddle out of the room, slam the door shut, and lock it. Probably eager to get to the whiskey and the phone. She didn't know whether to hope he'd get so drunk he'd pass out, or to fear the liquor would inflame him. By pressing against the door, she could hear his gruff voice rise and fall on the cellular phone, but she could not make out any words except "bitch." He was reporting to a superior, she thought. He had told her no one knew where she would be. Only a few people in Cedar Key would have known that fact.

Through two high, narrow windows, locked tight, she could see a thin strip of sky, heavy with moving clouds. The hurricane was beginning its rush up the coast. The bushy-haired brute in the next room was not the only horror she had to confront. There would be wild winds and lashing rain. Too petrified even to cry, Cara fell on the lower bunk and curled into a fetal position.

*   *   *   *

After Brandy emerged from the subway at 59th Street on her way to Mr. Bullen's address, she turned east. The streets grew wider, cleaner, the shops more elegant. Canopies blossomed above sidewalks patroled by uniformed doormen. Beside a small park, floored with brick overlooking the East River, Brandy found Frank Bullen's townhouse, walled off by a wrought iron fence and a grassy terrace.

When she gave her name to the doorman and explained that she was expected, he ushered her into a lobby of black and white marble, made a call, and then showed her to a bank of elevators. The aura of wealth intimidated Brandy. She had given little thought about dressing to meet Mr. Grosmiller, but now she brushed off her pleated navy skirt and straightened her white collar and the narrow sleeves of the matching jacket.

After she exited the elevator, she stopped to gaze critically into a full length mirror beside the doors, ran a comb through her coppery hair, and dabbed on a touch of lipstick. Maybe, she told herself, this visit means financial aid for Cara. She also reminded herself that people with large amounts of money were usually expert at keeping it.

The door was opened by a woman in her sixties with a blue uniform, a white, lacy apron, and a permanent wave like steel wool. "I'm the housekeeper, Louise Gruber," she said. "Mr. Bullen's secretary called. He'll be here soon." Brandy stepped into a foyer with a black marble floor. Under a row of tall windows, a vista of ivory greeted her—ivory Berber carpets, ivory brocade on the couches and chairs, ivory satin paint on the walls, and ivory embossed fleur-de-lis on the drapes. After the housekeeper showed her into the living area, Brandy perched on a Hepplewhite chair beside a glass coffee table and a grand piano, clutched her shabby cloth bag, and tried to look at ease.

Her glance strayed to the polished bar set against one wall, decanters of amber-colored wine reflected in its soaring mirror. Maybe the faithful Louise would offer her a sherry, bolster her nerve. Maybe Brandy was going to miss lunch altogether.

After fifteen minutes, when her anxiety had peaked, Louise re-appeared, not with the hoped for sherry, but with a message. "Mr. Bullen's here. He'll see you in his study." More opulence, Brandy feared, and followed her down the hall into another room, smaller and oak-paneled.

The attorney rose from behind a desk and motioned Brandy to a leather couch. "Miss O'Bannon, I believe."

Frank Bullen was a man of medium height, and judging by his neat, well-trimmed white hair and the slight sag beneath his chin, Brandy estimated him to be in his sixties. But in his smartly tailored suit he looked solid, even athletic for his age. As she sank into the soft cushion, she was aware that he had seated himself several inches higher. He confronted her, arms crossed. From a high window behind the desk, sunlight fell on an angular face with sharp planes and watchful blue eyes.

"Now then. I'm interested in the story you have to tell me." His gaze gave nothing away.

Brandy set her bag down beside her and folded her hands together. "I'm a newspaper reporter, Mr. Bullen. I explained that. I'm also the friend of a young woman who's trying to identify her missing mother and find her father." He nodded without speaking.

"I discovered that a woman came to Cedar Key, Florida, with her two-year old daughter at the same time your wife and daughter left New York." She waited and he remained silent. "The dates in 1972 seem more than a coincidence. The day the woman was seen near Cedar Key, she mailed a post card from that location to her aunt, her mother's sister. We have the date. It was right before Hurricane Agnes." For a moment Bullen closed his eyes and sighed. "I know this must bring back painful memories," she added.

When Brandy did not go on, he spoke, his voice quiet. "My wife never contacted me. Not once. It's sad to think she might've written her aunt instead. That fact was never communicated to me. At least I would have known she and little Belinda were all right." His fingers closed around the only object on his desk, a brass paperweight, the muscles in his jaw tight. Clearly the subject was still emotional.

Brandy spread her hands in her lap. "That's the tragic part. She wasn't all right." She lowered her voice. "I'm sorry to be the one to tell you. Your wife may have been murdered shortly afterward."

He paused, released the paperweight, and sat up straighter, his lips drawn in. "That's a terrible thing to suggest." He turned away. "Is there proof?"

Brandy reminded herself she was talking to a lawyer. "Someone, we don't yet know who, drove her from the bus stop to Cedar Key, right before the hurricane struck. The next thing we know, the child was found wandering in the storm, alone. No one ever claimed her. Months later a young woman's skeleton turned up in Cedar Key. It had been cleverly concealed. We should be able to establish the dead woman's identity, now that we know who she probably was."

Bullen stood and looked out the window at the East River, where a tugboat pulling a garbage barge was crawling under the Queensboro Bridge. For a few seconds he remained silent, stroking the back of his neck, perhaps calming himself. At last he said, "I certainly hope it wasn't Allison. And what happened to Belinda, *if* the child was Belinda?"

"If I'm right, your daughter's been reared by a local artist, a woman who's devoted to her. The girl was placed as a foster child. She could not be adopted because no one knew who her parents were. Her name's now Cara. She calls herself Cara Waters." Brandy felt in her bag. "Would you like to see a snapshot?"

He looked up again, as if studying something on the ceiling. Then facing her, he held up his palm, a stop signal. "It's all of great interest to me, if it's true. If this young woman is really Belinda, I want to see her, of course. I'll be very sorry about Allison...if the story checks out." He sat down again and crossed his knees. "Do you have the card that Allison is supposed to have sent?"

Brandy shook her head. "We haven't found it yet. We have testimony verifying it." She did not take out the photograph. Perhaps he did not want to get his hopes up and then find Cara was not his daughter. Attorneys were schooled in skepticism. "Allison's dental records would be helpful."

"I discarded such information years ago. You can understand that." He met her eyes. "You have local authorities working on your theory, then?"

"Not yet. I only discovered your connection today. The Sheriff's Office has other concerns right now." Exasperated, she thought of Detective Strong and his search for a drug ring. "Mr. Bullen, you probably don't know that an investigator was recently hired to find your wife. Three days ago he was shot near Cedar Key. I hoped he had called you. Allison's aunt was his client. He said someone else was interested in finding Allison."

The attorney shook his head again. "Cedar Key? An old town on the Gulf, isn't it? A sad business about the aunt. I believe I saw her obituary in the paper. I was sorry to see it. I didn't know them well, but they were nice people." Then, perhaps because of past hurt, his tone hardened. "Allison had lots of friends, some very close." He looked away and passed his hand across his lips. "One of them may want to find her. But you realize, this unidentified woman may not be Allison at all, and your young friend may not be her daughter."

His blue eyes clouded, the bitterness in his voice eased. "Miss O'Bannon, I once married a very lovely girl who seemed to need me, but it turned out, she didn't. Not really, not for long. I wouldn't hold her against her will and I wouldn't take her daughter from her. She had already suffered too many losses. End of story, except that now I am finally married to the right woman." That sentiment seemed to end the conversation.

"Does your son still live with you?" Brandy asked, standing.

"No." Bullen spoke in a decided voice. "He doesn't."

Voices sounded from the foyer. Brandy recognized the soothing tone of the housekeeper and heard another, more melodious. Then spike heels clicked down the hall. A slim beauty, perhaps a carefully tended forty, appeared in the doorway, carrying a large, elegant shopping bag.

"Just checking in," she trilled. Her gaze lit on Brandy and the shapely eyebrows arched. She wore her chestnut hair shoulder length, a black sheath over a long, supple body, and three exquisite ropes of pearls. Bullen rose. Even erect, he was not quite her height.

"A visitor from Florida, my dear. Family business. Miss O'Bannon, my wife." He bore down on the last word. "Miss O'Bannon tells a tragic story. It may involve me."

The woman stepped forward, smiling. "Welcome to New York," she said to Brandy, then turned to her husband. "What's this about, Frank? Tell me about it."

"Not now." His curt reply resounded in the marble hall. "Later tonight." It's still too hurtful a memory, Brandy thought.

His wife accepted the rebuke. Instead of asking any more questions, she held up, quite tenderly, the large sack with an Oriental logo. Lifting out a cloisonné vase, she slowly rotated it to reveal the green enamel base, emblazoned with a fire-breathing dragon. She turned to Bullen. "Quite a find at the Japanese antique gallery. For the side table in the foyer."

Bullen gave the vase a bored glance. On her slender left hand she wore a diamond and platinum wedding band, above it an unusually large, square cut diamond with a distinctive ladder of smaller diamonds on each side, and on one wrist a bracelet that matched her pearls. Brandy thought he might have tired of his wife's expensive tastes.

"We'll talk about the vase another time," Bullen said. When he continued standing, Brandy rose, too.

"Had lunch?" he wife asked.

"I'm late now. I'll have fruit and yogurt at the office. You'll be home this afternoon by five?"

"I'm playing tennis at the club." Mrs. Bullen led the way back down the hall toward the front door.

He paused, his hand on the knob. "No later than five-thirty, then. Don't disappoint me." He turned again to Brandy. "I'm afraid with such short notice, we both have lunch plans."

The expression in his eyes was still unreadable. "We must stay in touch. You understand, a man in my position can be subjected to false appeals. It wouldn't be the first time someone has claimed to be Belinda. But if you've truly located her, well…I'll have a lot of plans to make. It would be a pleasant shock after all these years, having a daughter again. Do let me know how your investigation turns out."

Brandy looked into the impenetrable blue eyes. He doesn't believe Cara is his daughter, she thought, but she is. Maybe he'll believe the sheriff.

"You'd better tell me how to reach you," he said.

Brandy delved into her bag for her card with the *Tribune* bureau address. "I leave New York early tomorrow, but if you think of anything that might help, you can always reach me at this Florida number."

As the door closed, Mrs. Bullen gave Brandy a look that mingled curiosity with concern. "You must be starved. It's almost two. I'm meeting a friend for lunch, but I'll ring for Louise." She pushed a buzzer. "Our housekeeper will be glad to give you some lunch. There's no decent restaurant nearby."

Brandy blessed her for thinking of food. "That's very kind," she said. "I'd like that." Frank Bullen had been polite but, lawyer-like, he had learned far more from her than she had from him. Her only hope now was Louise. A servant, left alone all day without much to do, might prove talkative, and Louise Gruber acted as if she had worked for Frank Bullen a very long time.

A door opened down a carpeted stair off the hallway. As Mrs. Bullen excused herself and disappeared into the bedroom wing, Louise's frizzled permanent came into view up the steps. In a few minutes Louise had seated Brandy at a breakfast table on street level, facing a kitchen that was a decorator's triumph—soft, peach-colored tile on floors and walls, an island of hardwood with a marble top and wine racks on the side, hardwood cabinets and table.

But something had been missing from Frank Bullen's costly living room and study, something she'd expected to see. She couldn't think what it was.

As Louise placed a plate of fresh fruit and finger sandwiches before her, Brandy looked up. "Come join me, Mrs. Gruber. It's lonely eating by myself. Tell me about life in New York City."

The housekeeper rinsed her hands at the sink and faced Brandy with a look of surprise. "Always heard you Southerners were friendly folks." She slumped into a straight chair on the other side of the table. "I had my bite already, but I could set a minute before I start things for dinner. Main thing you need to know about the city, is be careful. Don't trust nobody. Don't carry a bag like that one. First thing a mugger will snatch." She sat back and nodded with vigor.

"Do you live with the Bullens?"

"Oh, no. I have digs in Queens. Nice little apartment. My old man and me been there fifteen years. I serve an early dinner here, then zip across the Queensboro Bridge."

"You've worked for Mr. Bullen a long time?"

Mrs. Gruber smiled. "Twenty-five years this summer." She fumbled in her apron pocket. "Cigarette?" Brandy shook her head. "I have one now and again. Truth to tell, so does Mrs. Bullen. Hides it from him, of course." She trotted to the nearest cabinet and lifted down a cheap glass ashtray.

"You must've known the last Mrs. Bullen. She's the one I came to see him about. The one that just up and left town."

Louise pursed her lips with disapproval. "Flighty little thing. Not real stable, truth to tell. We all thought so." She dragged on the cigarette. "Only Mr. Bullen didn't see it at first."

"She'd suffered an awful tragedy, I hear."

"Lost both parents. A car smash. Well, we all felt sorry for the poor thing. But after a while, a person has to grow up." She wagged her head sagely and tapped her cigarette on the ashtray.

"What sort of things did she do? I mean, what made her seem immature?"

"Well, now. She wasn't used to running a home like Mr. Bullen's, of course. Didn't know the first thing about it. Wasn't this place then, but plenty nice. Truth to tell, I had to take over and I was pretty green still myself, but then I'd already learned a lot. Mr. Bullen's first wife wasn't no better. I started working for him then, and that woman, she wasn't never at home. I did it all." She puffed on the cigarette again, her eyes turned upward. "I got no complaints. I'll retire this summer. I'll get my social security and a nice retirement from Mr. Bullen, too."

Brandy tugged her back to the topic. "And the second wife, Allison?"

"Well, at first he was just crazy about her. Because of her tragedy and all, he tried to make a kinda shelter around her, protect her from the world, you know. But after a while even Mr. Bullen noticed she was strange. She either stayed in her room all day, or she'd sneak out and be gone 'til all hours. I remember once he went to someone's house where they were having a noisy party and brought her home. Drunk, he said. Finally, he said, 'Louise, you got to help me with Allison. I can't be watching her all the time. I've got to be at the office.' So I kept an eye on her, you know.

"She had some awful people over in them days. Men with long hair and earrings, that sort." Louise took a last drag and snuffed out the cigarette. "Well, Mr. Bullen and me, we cleared them out. I got an idea of who she was phoning and where she planned to go. It worked. After a while she kinda quit seeing them."

"What about their little daughter?"

Louise carried the ashtray to the sink and dumped the butt down the disposal. "That baby was cute. I had to take care of her some of the time, though, to tell the truth, Allison was pretty good with the baby.

She'd take her when she went out, but she didn't go out much that last year. She didn't pay much attention to her step-son, but then he was usually away in boarding school."

"Were you here when she ran away?"

Louise washed the ashtray and returned it to its hiding place. "Well, I wouldn't exactly call it running away. She left, but it wasn't no surprise, not really. I heard her talking to someone, a relative I think. Sounded like they was making trip plans. She called the bus station and the bank. She had a little money of her own."

"Then Mr. Bullen knew she was planning to leave?"

"'Course he knew. He'd asked me to keep him posted. You don't put nothing over on Mr. Bullen. He's too sharp. But he just decided not to interfere. 'Louise,' he said, 'let her go. I can't take the child from her mother after she's lost so much already. I won't keep Allison here if she's unhappy."

"Why didn't he give her a divorce and ask for visitation rights?"

"He thought she'd listen to reason after a while, for the child's sake. I don't think she even asked for a divorce. Just lit out one day. Allison never gave him a chance to get close to the little girl. Kept the child with her all the time. There was no reasoning with Allison when she got a notion in her head, so he just let her go. Made some business trips about that time to take his mind off her, but she broke his heart, poor man."

"And he finally divorced her?"

"Never heard a word from her. I said, 'Ask the police to look for her,' but he said, 'Louise, a grown woman leaving home is not a crime. Not the police department's business. They don't bring foolish wives back to their husbands.' So that was that." She turned a shrewd gaze at Brandy. "You know something about Allison and the little girl? That why you're here?"

"Maybe. She may have come to a town I know in Florida. Looks like he would've tried to find his daughter."

Louise drew herself up, looked over her shoulder, and leaned toward Brandy. "Truth to tell, I don't think he was sure she was his daughter. Not with all the funny business the year before. There was one young fella, someone she used to disappear with a lot…" She let her voice trail off suggestively. "Legally, of course, Belinda was his daughter."

Bad news, maybe, for Cara, Brandy thought. Louise had explained why Bullen seemed restrained about Cara. "At least Mr. Bullen had one child to raise," Brandy said. Then she realized what was missing from the town house. Where were the portraits of his son by the first wife, the boy who had stayed with his father? "What happened to the son?"

Louise drew her mouth down and frowned. "A big zero. Could've had any career he wanted. Mr. Bullen could've got him in law school. But the boy was like his mother. Running around, flunking out of schools. Went to a coupla prep schools in New England. Then started in at a partying kinda college, but he finally just quit. Dabbles now in this and that. Importing business, last I heard. Mr. Bullen settled an allowance on him several years ago, and we don't hear nothing much from him anymore. Lived in Las Vegas for a while, then down around Miami. Likes boating. Oh, he tries to butter Mr. Bullen up now and then. He'd be over thirty now."

"I wondered why there weren't any photographs."

"Mr. Bullen had as soon forget about Blade, I think. Nice looking boy, though."

Brandy recalled a monogram B.B. on a pair of socks worn by a Miami fisherman. "I used to know a Blade Bullen in Miami. Got a picture handy?"

Louise scuttled upstairs and returned with a dusty album. She wiped it with a cloth, then flipped to a page in the middle of the book. Brandy noticed several blank pages. "Allison," Louise said. "Mr. Bullen took her pictures out. Said he couldn't bear to look at them." She settled on a page and held it open for Brandy. "There's the little blister's prep school picture, before he was kicked out. Drunk as a skunk."

Brandy drew in her breath. The boy's eyes were unfocused, the lips sagged in a silly grin, the blond hair was disheveled. But she was looking into the adolescent face of the man she knew in Cedar Key as Nathan Hunt.

CHAPTER 16

▼

When Brandy opened the door to Thea's apartment that afternoon, Sonata was emerging from the bathroom, her arms laden with lingerie and hose, her smile sunny. "A Libra," she announced, "like sensitive, artistic, entertaining. Tonight will be a sensation." Brandy set Thea's key on the foyer table, beside a newspaper open to the astrology section, and scrambled to make a connection. With Sonata, Brandy always felt as if she'd stumbled into a conversation already in progress. Probably Sonata was referring to her daily horoscope. Brandy wondered if Allegro's mattered, but she didn't ask.

The parrot was whacking away at his cuttlebone and barely cocked his head at her. Sonata began poking her slips and underpants and stockings into any drawer that would hold them. "What's your sign?"

Brandy crunched over the scattered birdseed and picked up the telephone book. "Scorpio, I think." Sonata peered at the newspaper page and knitted her pencil-thin eyebrows. "Big thing for you is unexpected danger. Like, Look out!"

Brandy stacked her notebook and note pad on the table. "Everybody in New York wants to warn me." She thought of Cedar Key's three man police force. Despite what Cara believed, small towns had advantages. Still, even in tiny Cedar Key there had been a drug bust at the dock. She picked up one of the telephone books on the shelf in

Thea's area, studied the yellow pages under Manhattan dentists, and found a Dr. Edward Linebaugh. A call netted some concrete information. This Linebaugh was the son of the original dentist, now retired. After a wait of several minutes, the appointment secretary came back on the line and reported that records were kept for at least twenty-five years. If proper authorities contacted the office, she would fax the charts.

Next Brandy placed a call to Detective Strong at his Bronson office. She was not so fortunate this time. The detective was in Cedar Key. She left a message that she had exciting news and asked that he call her in New York about nine that night. She wondered what he would make of Nathan Hunt's real identity. At least it might raise questions. Why was Frank Bullen's son sniffing around Rossi's missing person's investigation? Maybe he was the other interested party, trying to keep the relationship hidden. Whatever his father's suspicions, legally little Belinda Bullen would be his half-sister.

The Sheriff's Office could request an exhumation order. A comparison of dental charts and teeth would show if the Cedar Key skeleton with the cracked skull was Allison Bullen.

Brandy had scrawled a record of her interviews across several notebook pages and decorated the margins with a square cistern and an oval tombstone when a familiar voice startled her. "I wanna be me," Allegro rasped, one shiny eye following someone up the stone steps.

"And so does Cara," Brandy murmured.

Sonata giggled. "A freaking feathered watch dog." She reached for the locks to admit Thea.

That night, after Tandoori Chicken at an Indian restaurant on East Sixth Street, Brandy returned to find no message from Cara on Thea's answering machine. Disappointed, Brandy decided that Cara didn't snap a recognizable picture at Shell Mound. But the agreement had been that she would call either way. Brandy dialed Marcia's number and let the phone ring ten times. No answer. Both out. She would ask about the photograph tomorrow.

Next Brandy phoned the car service Thea recommended, making certain she had a ride to the airport early in the morning.

Then she called home again. John answered, still disgruntled. "Busy as hell. Are you ever coming home?" A waltz played in the background. It didn't reflect John's taste, and she could hear a woman's voice. Maybe the radio was on. Brandy vowed to stay cheerful. "I'll be home tomorrow. I didn't know I'd have to come to New York. We'll take a weekend soon, go to that place on the Suwannee you liked. Promise." In the end she couldn't help asking, "Do you have company?"

John paused a beat. "Tiff and I had to re-do some computer drawings. She's just leaving. We had problems to solve before the contractors start work tomorrow."

So it was "Tiff" now. Brandy's grip on the receiver tightened, but she knew better than to start a quarrel a thousand miles from home. "Cara's to pick me up about noon. She'll drop me off." Brandy drew the mouthpiece close to her lips and tried a more sultry tone. "Try to be home early. Love you."

"I hope you do," he said, stressing the second word; then the other receiver clicked down. If this investigation doesn't end soon, she thought grimly, my marriage might.

It was nine-thirty before Detective Strong returned Brandy's call. He listened without comment to her report, but she thought his breathing quickened. "I'll have me a good talk with Mr. Blade Bullen, AKA Nathan Hunt. I'll also contact the medical examiner. That New York dentist—give me his name and number."

Brandy called out the information. "Maybe you can close two cases for the price of one."

Strong's grunt sounded skeptical. "In the Rossi case, we think we found the murder weapon. But I'll follow up on the dental exam. A judge has to order an exhumation." He paused while she imagined him slowly shaking his head. "Jesus do say, 'Thou shalt do no murder.'"

No argument there. "I hope the judge grants it. Mainly I want to help Cara Waters. I'll be back in Gainesville tomorrow."

"Your friend Cara's mama, she's a basket case. You know anything about her daughter leaving town?"

Brandy steadied her elbow on the desk, and her voice raised an octave. "Left town? When? She's supposed to meet me at the airport."

"Likely will. The mama don't tell us much. She called, all tore up. Said her daughter got mad, pulled a couple of hundred dollars out of her savings and cleared out. Wouldn't tell me why the girl was mad. Wanted us to drop everything and look for her. She'd already called all the girl's friends. 'Now, M'am,' I told her, 'the law can't go after every grown woman reckons she'll leave town.'"

Brandy began jotting down a quick list of Things to Do Tomorrow. Item one was "Ask Cara about argument with Marcia."

"I'm sure Cara will meet me. She'll want to know what I learned in New York. I'll call you and Mrs. Waters when I see her."

Brandy hung up, disturbed. Like mother, like daughter, I hope not, she said to herself. There was an eerie similarity in Cara and Allison's running away. She could understand that Marcia's possessiveness might finally drive Cara out of town. But why hadn't she called Brandy afterward?

In the morning Brandy was up by five-thirty, almost two hours after the parrot act returned, and dressed in the bathroom, breathing in the warm, soapy smell, and ducking Sonata's drip dry costumes. She'd asked that the car pick her up in front of the building at six. She left a thank-you note for Thea on the table, slipped into her jacket, and quietly opened the door. Allegro turned his dove-gray head, then without comment, resumed sentinel duty by the window.

Outside a cold, misty darkness still hung over the deserted streets, and a dim pocket of light glowed behind clouds to the east. On the lookout for the hired car, Brandy trotted down the long flight of stone steps, vaguely conscious of a movement below the wrought iron gate and railing of the basement well. Early for the tenant to be there, she thought, remembering the man with the garbage.

She had started across the narrow sidewalk toward a street lamp when she heard the scuffle of footsteps behind her. She whirled. A thick figure was rising from the basement entry, its face grotesque, a blur of mashed lips and flattened nose. Brandy dropped her suitcase. Her heart thudded and her fingers tightened around the straps of her bag. A stocking mask, of course. Gasping, she stumbled backward, even as the figure covered the pavement between them in a few clumsy strides, one gloved hand outstretched, in the other a short, ugly cosh like a club. Her brain flashed all the warnings. A mugging. Give up the handbag. But she thought of her airline tickets, her credit cards, her driver's license, and she clutched it, too stunned to cry out. From somewhere behind her, she could hear a car engine.

In the split second that the weapon whipped higher, a command rasped from the first floor window, "Go away, bad boy! Go away, bad boy!"

The mugger paused, twisted around, stared upward, and in that instant the hired car swept up to the curb and the driver leaped out. For a second the mask hesitated, glanced at the razor ribbon between the buildings, and then sprinted down the sidewalk, tugging off the stocking as he ran.

Brandy tottered back toward the building and sagged against the railing. "You okay, lady?" The driver took her arm.

She nodded, swallowing hard, suddenly sick. A window opened in the basement apartment and a man in his undershirt looked out. "Dammit," he said crossly. "Got to remember to lock the gate."

"Go away, bad boy," said Allegro.

Brandy smiled at the driver's puzzled expression. "Don't ask." She stood for a second, trembling. "I'm all right now."

On the sidewalk he recovered her fallen suitcase and the tote bag with her notebook. "You wanna call the cops? I seen the guy, but I don't think I could I.D. him."

Brandy shook her head. "I've got a plane to catch. I'm not hurt."

The driver stooped and retrieved a piece of paper blown against the metal posts of the basement entry. "The guy was in one big fat hurry. Dropped something."

He settled Brandy in his car and laid the paper beside her on the back seat. As he stowed her suitcase in the trunk and climbed behind the wheel, Brandy closed her eyes and leaned back, still shaken. In her mind she saw her father again, rumpled and grinning, among his students' papers and his books. "You'll be a first rate journalist, Bran," he was saying. "First rate. You care about people." But researching Cara Waters' story had become too strenuous.

She opened her eyes and with an unsteady hand picked up the strip of newsprint. It took her a minute to recognize the historic restoration column with her photograph. She'd given it to Angus MacGill when she arrived at the hotel and he'd tacked it on the bulletin board. They'd talked about it Sunday. How did it come to New York? Oh, Daddy, she thought, what have we gotten me into?

*   *   *   *

At the Gainesville airport Brandy stepped into warmer, damper weather. Heavy clouds were gathering to the west. At the gate and the luggage carousel she scanned the line of cars for the old station wagon. No Cara. Uneasy now, she located a phone booth in the terminal, reported in to her bureau, and asked for her messages. They did not include one from Cara. Immediately, she placed another call to Strong and reached him at the Sheriff's office.

"Cara didn't show," she said. "I'm concerned."

"She'll turn up. Just been gone overnight. She knows your office number." Brandy did not feel comforted. The detective probably wouldn't tell her, even if he were worried. "I also want you to know," she added," that I was attacked this morning, right outside my friend's apartment building. Man with some kind of a blunt instrument. He was scared off. There's got to be a connection with this case."

"Lots of folks get mugged in New York."

"But most muggers don't drop their victim's photograph. The clipping came from Cedar Key, from the hotel.

The detective paused, then he said quietly, "Fed Ex or a fax, I reckon. You gotta be more careful, young lady. Someone's mighty anxious to shut you up."

"They might have reason to shut Cara up, too."

"Looks like she cut out her own self. But I ought to admit, we got evidence that connects Rossi and the old hotel murder. Before the autopsy on Rossi, we found a list stuffed in his wallet. Got overlooked in the first body search. Handwriting checks out. It's headed 'Search for Missing Woman,' then lists the things he did, like check the drivers' license records, the local school, the library, the police department. Last thing he wrote was 'Hunt missing woman at cemetery.' Sounds like somebody tipped him off, told him she'd been murdered."

Brandy felt a rush of sympathy for Rossi, a fellow list-maker. That's why Strong was willing to talk yesterday about a quick exhumation order. "So now you don't think Rossi was a drug dealer who crossed someone?"

"We're still looking at that, but the case got lots of angles. I pulled the skeleton case folder outta the cold case file, and got the old HRS records on the kid that turned up in Cedar Key during the hurricane. Cops tried to find out if the kid was the same one left the café with her mother. Cashier's statement's interesting. She could recollect most of the folks she saw in the café. Couple of your buddies turned up on her list. MacGill stopped on his way home from Chiefland. And she says Truck Thompson came tearing up for gas in his daddy's pick-up. A wild young punk then, still in high school."

Brandy's mind raced to the Rossi killing. "I've always thought the private eye was shot because he was about to uncover the earlier murder. Last night you said you had the gun might've shot Rossi."

"Ballistics is running tests. The weapon was buried in the hotel basement. Belongs to MacGill." He paused. "'Course this is all off the record. I oughtn't to be talking so free to a reporter, young lady."

"Trust me. I promised none of this goes in print until you've given your okay. Have you talked to the sport with the alias, Blade Bullen?"

"Says he's having woman trouble. Using the phony name to give some gal the slip. Says he comes to Cedar Key a lot to fish, and it's just coincidence he ran into Rossi. Says he got interested in Rossi's story and hung around because his step-mother disappeared with his half-sister about the same time. Allows as how he was curious."

"Do you believe in coincidences?"

"They do happen. But I told him to stick around. Ran a rap sheet. He's been in a few scrapes. DWI, first time marijuana possession, little stuff."

When the detective hung up, Brandy felt cheated. No Bible quotation. Maybe the Good Book didn't have much to say about coincidences. She retrieved her laptop from a storage locker and had dragged her suitcase to the curb, when she spotted a trim, familiar figure hurrying toward her—Angus MacGill, harried and apologetic.

"Sorry, lass. I'm a wee bit late. Clerk reminded me your flight was due about noon today. We don't know where Cara went. I was afraid she mightn't get here." Breathless, he stooped to help with her suitcase. "Nice trip? Any trouble on the way?"

A harmless pleasantry? She wondered if he expected her still to be in New York, nursing a split head. The clipping had been on display in his hotel, and his gun was being tested for Rossi's murder. She reverted to her chief worry. "I'm awfully puzzled about Cara. When was she last seen?"

He pointed with his free hand toward his Ford and they started toward it. "She picked up her pictures at the store in Chiefland. Marcia established that. Seems strange she'd leave before you got back, though. Cara was dead keen on your going to New York. Expected some kind of miracle. You find out much?"

Brandy decided to take a leaf from Frank Bullen's book. "Nothing definite."

He opened the passenger door for her. "Where to?"

Brandy frowned. She couldn't go back to her bureau office, not without knowing about Cara. Even if Cara had unaccountably lost interest, where was Brandy's story without her? There was John to think of, but he couldn't possibly come home until well after five. "I'd like to see what I can turn up myself. The Sheriff's Office doesn't have a reason to look for her. Not yet, anyway." Quickly she calculated her time. "Mr. MacGill, I truly appreciate your coming to meet me. But I'm going to take a detour. I'm going to rent a car here at the airport and snoop around a bit before I drive home."

From the driver's seat, his blue eyes studied her. To Brandy he looked older than he had last Friday, the square face more drawn, the bright gaze more anxious. "Suit yourself, lass. I've got to get back to the hotel. The storm's been upgraded. It's moving north again in the Gulf. Need to batten down the hatches." He shook his head. "Marcia's already checked with all Cara's friends. No one's seen her or the station wagon since yesterday morning. Seems like she just got fed up and chucked it all. Told me she had a job near the university, was going to take some classes, but Marcia's called every photo studio in Gainesville. Fine Arts Department at the university never heard of her. Doggett's even made some unofficial inquiries around town. Cara's by no means in Cedar Key."

He scowled up at the sky. "Mind, I do feel sorry for Marcia. She's that upset. She'd bring tears to a glass eye." He parked beside a car rental counter and helped Brandy unload her suitcase and lap top. "Marcia's a fine woman, even if she keeps too tight a grip on Cara."

"You two have a lot in common, I'd think."

His nod was a trifle wistful. "Been a lonely life since the wife's gone."

Brandy grasped the lap top and the bag with her notebook. She didn't want to feel too much empathy for MacGill or Marcia Waters.

Everyone was a suspect. "Where's the drug store?" she asked. "That's a good place for me to start my search."

"Biggest strip center in Chiefland, north of the center of town on 19."

She thought of the long drive MacGill had made from Cedar Key and smiled at him. "I really appreciate this." Then she thought again of the clipping. "One other thing. Whatever happened to that column I gave you, the one about historic preservation in Lake County?"

He thrust out his lower lip, concentrating. "Can't say. Thought it was still on the bulletin board."

Brandy's smile died. "It's not," she said.

✳   ✳   ✳   ✳

The jaundiced looking young woman at the camera counter suffered from a cold, and she was not eager to talk. She glanced up with suspicion when Brandy identified herself as a reporter. "Miss Waters' mother was in here this morning. I told her all I know." Sniffling, she held a tissue to her reddened nose. "I wasn't paying no special attention. Miss Waters comes in here a lot. How I know where she is?"

Brandy's voice was calm. She did not want to raise the clerk's anxiety level. "I'm looking for Cara Waters because we're working together on a story. I don't plan to use your name. Anyway, I'm with the Gainesville paper."

Relaxing a bit, the girl stuffed the tissue back into her pocket and looked down. "She wasn't here but a minute."

"Before people pay for their pictures, sometimes they check to see if a roll came out. Do you remember if Miss Waters looked at the photographs you gave her?"

The clerk rolled her eyes up to the left and compressed her lips, trying to recall. "I can see her standing there...No, she didn't. She just paid and walked out."

"Anything special you can remember about her leaving?"

Again the eyes went up. "There was a man came in. He spoke to her. I remember that. They left about the same time."

Brandy held her breath. "This could be important. Do you remember anything at all about that man?"

At first the girl shook her head. "Ordinary looking guy. Well," she amended after a second, "kinda fattish, tall."

"Can you remember how he was dressed?"

"Nothing special. Didn't have on work clothes." She squinted, concentrating. "Had a kinda ugly face, really, a lotta dark hair, pretty long."

Brandy handed the girl one of her cards. "You've been a big help. If you think of anything else, call me." She leaned closer. "Don't tell anyone but a law enforcement officer about the man you saw speak to Miss Waters, all right?"

The girl nodded, sniffled, and re-applied her tissue.

From a newspaper dispenser on the sidewalk, Brandy bought the Gainesville paper and scanned the weather news. A small hurricane now, winds eighty miles an hour, moving slowly. At the present rate, if it didn't stall again or take an unexpected turn, it could pass on up the Gulf tonight, most likely make landfall near Apalachicola. Brandy sat in the car for several minutes, her notebook in her lap, recording the details Strong had given her on the phone, and the few from the drug store interview.

Then she looked at her most recent To Do list: Ask Cara about argument. Call Strong. Call Marcia. She crossed out two and three, waited with pencil poised, then started a new list: 1. Unknown man may be with Cara. (Clerk would recognize most locals.) 2. Cara may have picture of someone digging grave. 3. May be in danger from that man 4. Connected to attack on me?

She added a fourth item on the To Do list: search for station wagon. No point in looking in Cedar Key. That area had been thoroughly covered. She would need to question people near Chiefland, perhaps people in isolated areas. She thought of the caretaker at the Shell Mound campground, of the bleak farm house where she'd telephoned the Sheriff's Office, of the woman who ran the shabby little store on the Suwannee at Fowler's Bluff, all only a few miles away. Other such places existed along the lonely roads of Levy County.

She glanced again at the thickening sky and remembered Cara's phobia. How would she react if she were helpless again in the path of the hurricane?

CHAPTER 17

▼

Brandy slipped a Florida map out of the pocket flap of her notebook and figured time and distances. Now it was two. In an hour and a half, even allowing for brief interviews, she could make a sweep of the Shell Mound campground, the road past Fowler's Bluff, duck down a few dirt roads, and still be home to greet John.

She drove away with hopes high. No one had really searched yet. Marcia had accepted the notion, like the police, that Cara had simply moved away. But soon Brandy's optimism faded. The roads around Otter Creek yielded no clues and Brandy's first stop was a disappointment. The caretaker near Shell Mound had no information. He had not heard from Cara since she asked to leave her car in the campground Friday night, had seen no sign of the station wagon among the few campers and fishermen. Brandy's excursions among the scattered houses on nearby side roads were equally unproductive. By the time she reached Fowler's Bluff the clouds were piling higher in the west and a whiff of rain hung in the air.

She pulled the rental car under the long limbs of a live oak and trotted up the steps of the clapboard store. Behind a counter stacked with hunting and fishing guides, tide tables, and a rack of chips and nuts, the manager was listening to a radio and stuffing a flashlight and some soft drink cans into a tote bag. She didn't pause when Brandy asked about Cara's 1980 station wagon.

"Just a few fishermen at the cabins over the weekend. Last of them cleared out this morning." A friendly, wide-lipped face looked up. "No station wagons." She was a tall, skinny woman in a shapeless cotton dress, hair stringing down over one eye, tone apologetic. "Most generally, I'd be proud to pass the time of day, but I'm fixing to leave myself. Radio says they's hurricane winds out in the Gulf, and they turned this-a-way a coupla hours ago. Locking up soon and going to my sister's in Chiefland."

Brandy glanced out the dirty window at the choppy waters of the Suwannee. Tied to the pier, a skiff with an outboard kicker rose and fell with the waves. Perhaps three hundred yards across the river a thick, unbroken band of trees lined the shore. The county map showed mile upon mile of the Lower Suwannee National Wildlife Refuge along both riverbanks.

Her memory reverted to Saturday morning—a houseboat chugging down the channel, a fat man on deck. A tall man. A man with dark, bushy hair. "A houseboat went by here last Saturday. Seen anything more of it?"

The woman rubbed her chin, frowning. "I recollect it ain't come back. Most generally, the fella ties up at a little bitty island about a mile down river. On the north side, before you get to Little Turkey Island. Probably better shelter there than near the Gulf. We're twelve miles up river, but we'll still get some flooding."

Brandy opened her purse. "My friend may have gone for a ride with him. Could I rent your boat for about an hour, run down there and pick her up?"

The frown deepened. "Pretty rough out there already. Be getting rougher."

Brandy slid a twenty dollar bill onto the counter. "It'd just take me about an hour." She looked down at the slack suit she'd worn on the plane. "I'd like to use your rest room and change first."

The woman's plain face still looked doubtful, but she picked up the bill. "Better hurry, then. I aim to be gone in an hour."

Once in her jeans and jacket, Brandy settled herself on the skiff's rear seat, zipped her camera into the roomy plastic bag, stowed it in the stern along with the boat's line, and pushed away from the pier. When she yanked the starter rope, the kicker coughed a few times, then sputtered into life. Gripping the tiller, she guided the skiff away from the dock and jolted across the waves down river.

Her plan was simple. Find and observe the houseboat. Obviously, more than one big stranger with bushy black hair could be in the Chiefland area, but if she saw any sign of Cara, she would get a picture. Her cover story was simple. She was a reporter winding up a feature article about life on the Suwannee.

Her real task was to reconnoiter and return before the gusts of wind began carrying rain. On the return trip the waves, if not the current, would be running toward Fowler's Bluff. Her hair whipped around her face, the little boat slapped up and down, bucking the waves, and she often needed both hands to keep it on course.

She had almost decided to start back, that the sky was too dark, the island too far, when she rounded a sweeping curve and saw the houseboat to her right. The stern rocked near the western end, about a hundred yards from the north shore, a mass of pond cypress, river birch, and water oak, thick with undergrowth. Brandy eased back on the throttle, maneuvered closer, and peered upward. No one was on deck. Not surprising, given the weather. She steered closer. A small jalousie window near the stern would mark the bathroom, or head. Next to it should be a bedroom. A moment later she caught her breath.

Outlined against the closed side window was a woman's slim form. Backing around, Brandy cut into the protected strait between the opposite end of the island and the mainland, pointed the skiff's bow toward a barren spit, throttled back again, and as the boat nosed up onto the tiny beach, killed the engine and leapt out with the bow line.

In a few minutes she had fastened a clove hitch around the slender trunk of a young cypress.

A splash startled her, and she whirled to see the ridged back of a large alligator slither into the water behind her. She shuddered. Mid-October, she thought, most 'gators are already dormant. She drew a long breath and paused, remembering other warnings she knew: Keep an eye out for rattlers and water moccasins, too. They get nervous before an approaching storm. She tucked the cuffs of her jeans into her socks. Then slinging the tote bag with her camera and the extra line over her arm, she edged past a wax myrtle shrub and a spiky tangle of saw palmettos, until she could see the hull of the houseboat, tapered like a fishing vessel. At its bow stood a wheel house with tall, three-sided windows. A sturdy metal rail encircled the boat, beginning at a wide forward deck, running beside a narrow walkway on each side, and ending on the stern, where a dinghy lay bottom up. A thinner rail looped around the cramped top deck.

Someone had once spruced up the hull with a decorative blue band, but now the entire rig looked unkempt and in need of painting. The place where Brandy had seen the figure was in the lower section. She crouched among waxy white myrtle berries as a massive man in a tee shirt emerged from the wheel house and stumbled out on deck. His stomach bulged over his belt. Heavy black hair blew around his low forehead and across his wide nose and mouth. In one ham-fist he carried a roll of duct tape. He looked toward the clouds, shook his head, and zigzagged to the front window. The boat wasn't yet rolling enough, Brandy decided, to account for his gait. Maybe he was drinking. Up went a length of gray tape. Of course, she thought, he's getting ready for the storm. He had two anchors overboard already, fore and aft, and a thick rope sagged from the trunk of a pond cypress.

Brandy watched him tape the three windows on the outside, then lurch back through the door. Before it closed, he took something out of his pocket, held it against the front window glass beneath the outside tape, and plastered tape over it on the inside. She waited while he slouched down behind the helm and lifted a bottle to his mouth. He did not strike her as the sort who would welcome a reporter.

Being careful not to step on any twigs, she worked her way through the underbrush to the boat's stern, waded out, tossed the line over the metal railing, and secured it with a bowline. Then holding fast, she pulled herself up onto the deck. There she dropped the line, lifted the Nikon out of the bag, hung the strap around her neck, and switched it on.

Now for the hard part. The woman might not be Cara, but surely taking a picture of the oaf's girlfriend wouldn't be a crime. She stepped around the dinghy and inched down the catwalk toward the window. Even before she reached it, she heard a sound like sobbing. Finally, by putting her nose against the pane, she could see into the room. Below the window stood a cheap looking cabinet and across from it, bunk beds. On the lower one lay a slim form. As Brandy watched, the woman stirred, raised one arm, then sat up, shivering, her head bent forward. Brandy recognized the cascade of long, dark hair. She raised the camera. Best to get proof, signal to Cara, and come back for help.

She had clicked the camera and was tapping gently on the glass, when to her right, she heard labored breathing. In nightmarish slow motion she turned. The bulky figure was lumbering down the walkway toward her from the bow. To run or to brazen it out? For a nano-second she hesitated, and while she was deciding to make a break for the line, the man lunged forward, one huge hand grabbed her, an arm closed around her neck. She could not make a sound, could only smell the liquor and the sweat.

"What the hell you think you doing?"

He dragged her, struggling, backward to the front deck and into the wheel house, where he relaxed the arm choking her so that she could breathe, could squeak out her pitiful explanation. "A reporter. Writing a story about life on the river. Looking for people to photograph and interview." She glanced wildly around, saw the wheel and console, a table with a bottle of tequila and another of vodka, a shabby couch, a galley with a butane stove, a small refrigerator, dish cabinets, a fire extinguisher bracketed to the wall.

"How stupid you think I am, sister?" Twisting her head against his shoulder and the ropy muscles of his neck, he yanked the bag from her arm. She heard the Nikon hit the floor. "Shit, a reporter wouldn't be sneaking up on a boat, wouldn't be out when a freakin' hurricane's coming in!"

He jerked her by the arm into the tiny galley, and with his free hand pulled back a panel above a counter, picked up a hand held transmitter, and pushed a few buttons. "Moose. Yeah. Guess what I got? Some bitch, nosing around the boat. Says she's a reporter."

After a minute, he grinned. "Reckon she's the same one. Yeah, I can. Gonna be rough tonight. Coming in around nine o'clock. Yeah, yeah. Taped the windows. Gonna move the boat out a little, gotta be able to swing away from the island. Don't wanna get beached." A moody silence followed while his arm tightened again around her neck. "Yeah," he said at last. "When the freakin' storm's over. We'll do it then."

His voice fell, took on a wheedling tone. "I told you I got it. Reckon it's worth a lot, ole' buddy. I just need my fair share. Yeah, yeah, we'll talk tomorrow." Her fingers stretched, touched the red cylinder.

"Hey!" He dropped the transmitter, grabbed both her arms, and whipped them behind her. His voice took on its familiar rasp. "No funny business, sister. And can the bullshit. We know who you are. Looks like ole' Moose got two guests tonight." He dragged her beyond the galley toward a wooden door with one small glass panel. "You go in here with your buddy."

Holding her arms immobile with one hand, he retrieved a key from a peg on the wall and unlocked the pocket door. Then he shoved her into a darkened passageway, tossed the unzipped plastic bag after her, and slammed the door. The key turned in the lock.

When Brandy was next fully aware, she had sprawled at the foot of two steps, her face pressed against a damp carpet rank with mildew, with Cara kneeling beside her. "Oh, God, Brandy. What have I gotten you into?"

Brandy raised herself on her elbows, her head splitting. "We're in this together." Her voice shook and she paused a second. "First, tell me how *you* got here."

Cara helped her up and they sat side by side on the bunk. Wiping her eyes with her skirt, Cara blurted the story of the blue teddy bear, the shock of finding it in Marcia's closet. She had meant to leave for good, to find a place in Gainesville. She knew that's what everyone would think she'd done. She knew now that she was wrong, that she never meant, deep down, to hurt Marcia.

After the drug store, she remembered the chloroform, and coming to, sick. Then she was hoisted into the swamp buggy, still with the man called Moose. They jostled along a two-track road that ended at the river. He had hauled her aboard yesterday afternoon, and later he'd brought her canned soup. So far he'd stayed on the other side of the door. "But he's drinking, Brandy, saying nasty things. I'm scared to death of him!" Cara's voice sank to a whisper. Her dark eyes widened. "And there's going to be a hurricane. I don't think I can stand it."

Brandy put her arm around Cara's thin shoulders. During the storm, she had to force herself to be the strong one. "Let's take inventory," she said, her voice calm. "At least we know more than we did. We know you belonged to the woman at the Otter Creek café." She stood, her hand pressed against her bruised forehead, and looked at the tightly closed panes. "But knowing that won't help us much unless we can get out of here."

"There's no window latch on the inside."

Brandy took a few steps around the small room, checked the solid back door—locked—the tiny bathroom and its toilet, shower, and sink, above the toilet its high, narrow jalousie window.

She looked back at Cara. "Did you get the picture at Shell Mound?"

Cara gave a sad shake of her head. "I don't know. He took my purse and my pictures. Never saw them."

"I think he did, from what he said just now on the phone." Brandy sat down again, her gaze fixed on the window, and patted Cara's slender hand. It was trembling. Rain pattered now against the pane, and they could hear the wind rising in the cypress trees. She took Cara's chin in her hands and turned her away from the window. Here was a young woman who could hike alone into the woods at night, but could not stand the sound of heavy rain and wind. "I found some useful information in New York. I'm pretty sure I know who your father is. A wealthy attorney." No need to tell her about Frank Bullen's paternal doubts. Legally she was his daughter. "The oddest thing I learned is about Nathan Hunt. You remember the good-looking guy at the hotel with the ducktail haircut?"

Cara swallowed and nodded.

"Nathan Hunt is not really Nathan Hunt. His name is Blade Bullen, and I think he's your half-brother. Probably he was shadowing Rossi. Your father re-married a few years ago. His name is Frank and yours was Belinda, Belinda Bullen. He wants to know about you."

Cara raised her head, for the moment distracted from the whine of the wind. "I knew you'd find out. My mother?"

"Allison Bullen. Dental tests should confirm that." Restless, Brandy rose again. "We're probably here because of the photograph. Somebody thinks you got a picture of them burying Rossi. It's possible Rossi's murder doesn't have anything to do with your mother's, although now Strong thinks it might." She opened a folding door into a narrow closet. Rain slickers, a torn life cushion, a can of tobacco, three pairs of dirt-encrusted fishing boots, and the lingering, sweetish smell of marijuana.

"Looks like Strong was right about the drug connection. Our brutish friend is into running pot." She looked at her watch. Five-thirty. They had to act before the hurricane hit, or it would be too late. "When do they feed the animals here?"

"Oh, God, how can you think of food?"

"I'm not thinking of food. I'm thinking of escape."

"We couldn't overpower that gorilla, drunk or sober."

Brandy slouched again on the bunk. "We got one thing he doesn't. Brains. That ploy at the drug store—somebody programmed him. He's working for someone. Could be anybody. Except the person had to know when you were going to the drug store. That narrows it a bit—John and me, MacGill, Truck, Blade Bullen, and, of course, Marcia. We know the hotel clerk has a big mouth."

Tears trembled again in Cara's voice. "I wonder why he didn't just shoot me? Why are they holding us?"

"Could be lots of reasons. Some of those people care about you." Brandy didn't add aloud another reason. Maybe someone doesn't want to dispose of more bodies right now. She rummaged in her large tote bag. Camera gone, of course, but she still had her plastic film pouch. Both could hold useful things. Outside the line was still tied to the rail. "We've got to think of a plan."

But she thought first of John. Right now he should be walking through the door of their cluttered apartment, or listening for his key in the lock. She hadn't seen him since Saturday night. This was Wednesday. Almost a week since she had lain in his arms, since she had last felt loved and secure. He would pour himself a beer and begin waiting. Would he worry that something had happened to her and call the police? Or would he be angry, think once more she had abandoned him for her job?

Cara clasped her hands to keep them from shaking. "If we tried to break a window, that devil would be on us like a flash. He might tie us up. He did that to me. I can't stand that again."

A blast of wind and rain rattled the panes. The boat began to rock. "We ought to make our break before it's completely dark. Before the hurricane makes landfall."

Cara's gaze was again drawn to the window. "If he's not too drunk, he'll probably bring our food by six. He did yesterday. After that, he'll be busy with the storm."

"I wouldn't count on his seamanship." Brandy's eyes brightened. "There's one real hope. The woman at Fowler's Bluff. She'll report that I didn't come back with her boat, and the rental car's still there. She knows where I was going. Someone will contact the Sheriff's Office, and Strong will call my husband. He'll find us, at least after the storm passes."

She felt a rush of warmth for John. He might be annoyed with her, might be fascinated by Tiffany Moore, but if he knew Brandy was in trouble, he would be an absolute bloodhound.

Cara pointed toward the window. "Brandy, look."

Moose had clamored down from the houseboat. They watched him crash through the wet underbrush toward the end of the island. They waited, pulses racing. Maybe he had deserted his post for safer shelter. But in a few minutes they saw him tug Brandy's skiff along the island shore, saw him throw its oar far out into the roiling water, turn the boat upside down, and with a mighty heave, send it sliding into the river. They watched it twist and turn until it bobbed around the bend out of sight.

Cara's hand flew to her mouth. "They'll find your empty boat. My God, your husband will think you drowned in the storm."

CHAPTER 18

▼

At 5:45 Brandy heard the lock turn again. The pocket door slid a foot to one side and Moose thrust his perspiring face against the opening. He had grown a bristly stubble, and for the first time Brandy noticed a missing tooth.

"Chow time." He stooped and with thick fingers set a pan of tomato soup, two slices of stale bread, and two tablespoons on the top step. Unsteadily he straightened up and hoisted a vodka bottle before the opening. "Have us a little party. Soon's I move the damned boat out a-ways. Gonna be a helluva blow tonight. Hurricane party." He peered again at Brandy and Cara, huddled together on the side of the lower bunk. "Two of you be fun." He dangled a rope from one big hand, his heavy brows contracting. "I'll make sure you gonna cooperate." They looked back with faces of stone. Nausea rose in Brandy's throat. A demon from hell, Brandy thought, remembering Dante's *Inferno*, the classic she'd packed to re-read over the weekend—a weekend that seemed eons ago.

After Moose slammed the door, Brandy stepped forward and peeped through the square glass panel.

Pale, Cara whispered, "Remember, he's got a gun." Brandy could see him sitting at the wheel, fingers drumming on the console. Then he stood, yanked a yellow rain slicker from a rack in the galley, pulled it on, and opened the wheel house door. The wind was rising, and she could make out his yellow bulk bent against it in the rain.

Brandy carried the pan across the swaying floor to the bunk, handed a spoon to Cara, and took a sip of the tepid soup. "Got to keep up our strength." Suddenly she gazed at the heavy handle, then into the open bathroom, up at the narrow window, and felt a surge of excitement. "Keep a watch on Moose."

Dropping the toilet lid, she climbed onto it, holding the spoon. She estimated each jalousie pane's width at about five inches. Removing at least three might give them an escape route. On tiptoe, she pried with the handle at the metal flange that held the bottom glass in place. "Maybe we have a chance. This is one way burglars get into a lot of Florida houses." She had worked one side of the pane loose when the handle snapped. "What's he doing?"

"Re-tying the line, giving it more slack."

"Come, take this." Brandy handed down the narrow glass. Water spattered her face. Forcing herself to be more careful, she loosened another strip with the other handle. She was getting the knack. "We have to move fast. He'll be taking the houseboat farther out. Make it a lot harder for us." She lifted the second pane down and started feverishly on the third. "Cara…" Brandy looked down at the slim face staring up at her, at the slight body. "You know what you've got to do. I could never get through this opening. I think maybe you could."

Cara shrank back against the sink. "Go out in the storm? I couldn't!"

Brandy climbed down and took her by the shoulders, wanting to shout at her, to shake her, to ask how else they could possibly get away. Her own heart was pounding, but she tried to think rationally. Their only hope was Cara. In a psych class Brandy once heard about overcoming phobias. The feared thing should be associated with someone or some object the person liked.

"Look, as a little girl you were horrified by a storm because you were deserted, alone, helpless. Now you've got me. I won't leave you. Would you rather hang around for Moose's party?"

Tears of horror filled Cara's brown eyes. Time was passing. Where was Moose? Brandy slipped over to the glass panel in the pocket door, Cara behind her. The wheel house door swung open. Moose shambled back in and peered between strips of duct tape toward the shore. They could see his big lips move. Probably swearing. Then he pulled out a small drawer, picked up a handgun, stuck it in his belt, and lumbered outside again.

Cara's fingers fastened around Brandy's arm. "He's carrying a gun!"

Brandy shook loose, rushed back into the bathroom, climbed up, and peered into the blowing rain. Moose had plodded below the empty window, head down, to the rear deck. Here with a wrench of his arm, he righted the dingy, carried it to the side, threw it over, and begun climbing down. "He's going over the side," Brandy reported.

Cara's face glowed with relief. "My God, he's leaving."

"Probably won't be gone long. He must've seen something. He's rowing around the island to the right, toward shore. Come on! It gives us a little time." Jumping down, Brandy turned to Cara. "It won't be easy. I'll boost you through the opening. A jail deputy once told me if your head fits, the rest of you will. You've got a hole, maybe fifteen inches wide."

Cara pulled herself up on the lid and then began to cry. Brandy fought her frustration. "You're brave. You went out into the forest alone at night. But I know this is hell for you." When she thought of the ghoulish Moose, the connection clicked again, the story of a journey through hell.

"Ever hear of the *Divine Comedy*?" Cara looked down, puzzled. "In the *Inferno* Dante was afraid of hell, but he had a guide. That guide took him through all the circles of hell and never left him, no matter how awful things were. They saved themselves. Cara, we can be like that. I'm your guide."

Cara nodded, turned back to the wall, and with an effort raised her arms, and with trembling fingers gripped the sill.

"Now listen carefully. The key is on a peg above the door. Get any keys you see. Maybe the swamp buggy's still around. I'll be getting ready. Let me out and we'll make a break for the shore."

When Cara had pulled herself part way up the wall, Brandy leaped up on the toilet lid and pushed her farther. "Does your head fit?" She could see the dark hair flying. "Twist your shoulders through the opening and sit on the sill."

At last Cara inched her lean body through the slot and rested for a second on the window ledge. Through the opening her voice came back muffled. "Some kind of deck above me. Maybe I can grab the lowest rail." She stretched above her head with one arm. "Got it!" Drawing her legs after her, she hung suspended for a second from the outside rail, then dropped to the lower deck.

Brandy's heart hammered against her chest. Where was Moose? From the closet she snatched up the plastic slickers, rolled them tightly, stuffed them into two pairs of fishermen's boots, crammed the boots into the big plastic bag, and zipped it. How to carry it? Quickly, she removed her belt, ran it through the handles of the bag, threaded it again through the belt loops, and buckled it. She would have to try to swim with the extra weight. They would need the boots to hike through the swamp along the river, and hurricane winds would hit in three hours. By then they wouldn't be able to drive or walk.

Through the door panel she saw Cara sidle into the wheel house, saw her shaking fingers pull the keys out of the boat's ignition, then dash to the door to lift down its key. When the pocket door slid back, Brandy slipped through and closed and locked it behind her. "When Moose gets back, maybe he'll think we're still here."

On the galley counter she swept up some packages of cheese and crackers, dumped the extra roll of film out of the plastic pouch in her bag, replaced it with the crackers and her watch, and re-locked the pouch. Cara's face was ashen. Her teeth chattered. God, Brandy thought, don't go into shock. The worst hasn't even begun. "We've got to let ourselves down with my line, get across the island, and swim to shore." She took Cara's cold hand. "The channel isn't wide. Maybe twenty yards. It's protected."

They crept down the narrow walkway facing the river to the stern. Still no dinghy in sight. The only sound was the pounding of the waves against the hull, the whistling of the wind. In the fading light, Brandy looked toward the knotted wall of trees beyond the island, Wildlife Refuge for bobcats, alligators, snakes. Maybe they could find refuge, too.

She led Cara to the line slung from the railing, and obediently Cara slipped over the side, held on, and dropped into the coffee-colored water, Brandy close behind. Working her fingers furiously, she untied the wet line, and thrust it into a pocket. They might need it. Then she led the way to the left, around the edge of the island, past dripping spines of saw palmettos, through clumps of wax myrtle, her bag catching on low branches of pond cypress and river birch, until they halted before the strait that separated them from the mainland. And then, near the houseboat, they heard a loud crackling. As one, they turned. A giant yellow shape came blundering after them. Cara gave a little shriek.

Moose had beached his dinghy near the houseboat, had heard them or seen their tracks. Brandy was moving again, even as she called to Cara, "Into the water—fast! If you don't see me on shore, run!"

When she hit the water, she gasped with the sudden cold, with the strength of the current. She struck out in a modified crawl, trying to glance behind her on every third breath. Soon all she could do was struggle forward, dragged down by the plastic bag and her own tennis shoes. Even in this sheltered backwater, waves dashed against her face, filled her mouth, blurred her eyes. If she could stay afloat, the current should wash her ashore, maybe several yards upriver.

She hoped the splashing near her was Cara. Her friend would reach land more quickly, and by now the afternoon's large alligator should have found its hole. Even the thought of the ridged back she had seen earlier made her feel faint. She forced herself to think of Moose instead. Would he swim after them? Surely not. He'd go for the dinghy. Above her head she heard a zinging noise and something hard hit the water to her left. A bullet? He did have the gun. But she didn't dare duck under water. She might not be able to surface again. She'd decided to jettison the bag, when, through the filter of rain, she saw trunks looming ahead, gnarled roots.

She stepped down and her foot plunged into the pulpy river bottom. She breathed in the acrid smell of riverbank mud. Before her, Cara was crawling forward among a nest of blunt cypress knees. Brandy staggered up beside her, looked back, saw Moose crouched like a demon monster in the dinghy, yelling, his words lost in the wind. Once again Brandy grabbed Cara by the hand, found an overgrown trail, maybe an animal's, ducked and scrambled up the marshy riverbank. She looked back from the partial shelter of a bald cypress trunk. Moose was ashore now, his gun drawn. Again they hurled themselves down the dim track.

The keys from the boat ignition—she had fingered three keys on the ring. Maybe one went to the swamp buggy. Another shot. Wide. It slammed high into a tree behind them. Moose had not yet floundered up to level ground. Through the rain Brandy could see a square bulky shape like a Jeep in a clearing ahead.

At that moment her wet fingers slipped from Cara's hand, she heard a loud crunch, and Cara screamed. Brandy's first thought was, Cara's been shot! But as she whipped around, she saw Cara's arms flailing, her mouth stretched in terror, one leg plunged to the knee in a pile of sticks and branches. She managed to cry out, "Oh, God, Brandy! A 'gator hole!"

In an instant Brandy recognized the tell-tale depression, the tangle of leaves and stems. Time shifted to slow motion. She reached out as Cara's leg sank lower. Eyes wild, Cara babbled, "Something moved!" Even as Brandy grasped both Cara's hands and tugged, she remembered the full brute length of the afternoon's alligator. Cara, white face frozen, slid upward. A split second passed like a hour. Then she scrambled to her feet, and they bolted toward the Jeep.

Over her shoulder Brandy heard a thrashing noise, turned and saw the huge snout protrude, the rutted moss green back heave upward, tail lashing, jaws open, saw the long shining teeth. She had read that for short distances a person couldn't outrun an alligator—certainly not as burdened as she was. Even as the beast lunged forward, hissing, on powerful legs, the yellow rain slicker surged up from the river bank. A bullet hit a cypress trunk behind them.

Ahead Brandy could make out the mammoth wheels, the open metal body of the swamp buggy. Again she glanced back. Another shot. The beast careened around in the path, its tail sweeping a giant arc, and raised its massive head to the new menace. Brandy vaulted onto the running board and into the driver's seat. Behind her Cara clamored into the back seat, then tumbled over into the front. Brandy's hand shook so hard she was afraid she could not switch on the ignition. Even if Moose didn't hit them, he could puncture the stubby engine or the monster tires.

Willing her fingers to work, she tried one key. Wouldn't fit. Maybe it was the one to the houseboat. The next slid into the slot, turned. The engine barked to life. Behind them down the trail, Moose had halted, retreated a few paces, and fired again at the alligator. Brandy jammed down the clutch and the gas, shifted, and whirled the wheel. The buggy jerked backward, then leapt down a slick, two track road. Rain pounded the steel chassis; limbs swung overhead.

"A timber road. It must go to the pavement," Brandy called. The buggy twisted around hammocks, under live oak branches, the heavy wheels grinding deep into sandy ruts. A clump of Spanish moss blew across the windshield. Brandy slowed, and Cara climbed over the gear shift, swept the hood clear.

"My money's on Moose, not the 'gator," Brandy said above the roar of engine, wind, and rain. "He has the gun. He'll go back to his boat, call his friend. They'll cut us off."

She rounded another hairpin curve, through the gathering dark saw a trough in the road, tried to swerve around it, and mired the front wheels. She gunned the buggy backward and tried to rock out. Sand and debris flew up, but the wheels spun deeper.

"Just as well," Brandy said. "We can't stay on the road. They'd find us in a minute. Buggy probably doesn't go more than thirty miles an hour." She opened the soaked bag and drew out the boots. "Put on the rain gear—it'll be some protection—and the boots. We'll hike north, toward the road that connects the main highway to the town of Suwannee. Before it's completely dark, maybe we can turn toward town. It's our best chance for help." With our luck, she thought, we'll probably stumble on the Shell Mount ghost instead.

The sky was a seething, charcoal mass, lit by a sulfurous yellow. Here the flat-topped cypress had thinned and they tramped, heads lowered, through stands of slash pine, cabbage palms, and red maples. Rain stung their faces, leaves and twigs fell in showers around them. Wind pushed against them from the west. Their boots squished, left huge sandy tracks that Brandy hoped the rain would wash away. When she stepped on a small pine limb, she picked it up.

"This'll do to poke under shrubbery when we stop." Cara's eyes widened. She knew why. To scare away rattlesnakes. Ahead to the left through the growing darkness and rain, Brandy saw two lights moving steadily closer, away from the Gulf. Soon she heard the drone of a car engine. They must be near the paved road to the town of Suwannee. Quickly she pulled Cara beside her, thrust the stick into a thicket of palmettos, then drew Cara closer. Water spattered up from the asphalt as the car neared.

"We can't take a chance. Might be Moose's friend." They squatted and watched the car vanish through the rain. At least they knew roughly where they were. "We'll push a little farther, parallel to the road. On the map it's straight. But we've got to find a safe place to stop, get ready for the big blow." Brandy had lost all track of time, but there was no way to look at her watch, even if it had survived in the plastic pouch.

"I'm thinking of rattlers," Cara said through her teeth. "How about climbing up in a live oak?"

"Can't risk it." Brandy raised her voice above the wail of the wind. "First things to go down in a hurricane. We need a low spot, someplace to flatten out." She'd never heard of lightning during a hurricane, but she didn't want to be near tall trees. They came upon an open field, then one reforested with slash pines, and finally reached a slight rise where a clump of young cabbage palms bent forward in the gale.

"Here," Brandy called. "Behind this little hill." She couldn't walk any farther. Shuddering, she prodded the grasses and tall weeds around the palms with her stick. Then they dropped, gasping, onto the sodden grass. As blackness descended, they huddled together in the pocket of earth, engulfed in the sharp smell of wet soil. Brandy could scarcely make out the swaying white trunks above them. Somewhere near, a pine snapped in two, its top crashing to the ground. Brandy opened the dripping bag and rooted in the bottom for the plastic pouch. So far Cara had borne up well, driven by terrors even greater than her fear of the storm. But until it passed, she had to take care of them both. One step at a time.

Fumbling with the opening strip of a cracker pack, she handed Cara a handful of crumbs, a distraction from the descending blackness. "Where's the Shell Mound ghost's light when we need it?" Brandy asked, trying to raise a smile from Cara.

From the west swelled a gigantic roar. Brandy pulled the line out of the bag, circled it around Cara's waist and her own, and lashed them to the trunk of a short cabbage palm.

Now the real test would come. She put her lips against Cara's wet ear and shouted, "Dante passed through all the circles of hell safely. We will, too." Water streamed by, puddled at their feet. They flung their arms around each other, closed their eyes, felt the ground shake. The shrieking wind tried to tear them apart or knock them against the palm trunk. They heard the wood creak and bend. The howling and gnawing lasted until Brandy thought they could not endure more, would surely break like the long limbs of the live oak.

And then, suddenly, the wind stopped, the drenching rain became a patter. Ceased. Brandy looked up and saw a patch of clear sky, the glow of the rain-washed moon.

"It's over!" Cara sat up, struggling against the cord. With wonder, Brandy saw a dark quick shape spring from a nearby thicket, eyes like coils of fire, a tawny flash of bobcat, too busy to worry about humans. Brandy laid a restraining hand on Cara's arm. "Wait. Could be the eye is passing over." She had heard of the calm in the center of a hurricane's deadly rotating winds. By the faint light, she shook her watch out of the pouch and peered at it. Eleven o'clock. In the eerie stillness the cabbage palms righted themselves, the pine branches fell silent.

But Brandy could sense the coming change. A movement in the air, a quivering among the palm fronds and palmettos, a rolling cloud. She unsnapped her slicker, slipped her right arm out, and threw the plastic around Cara's shivering body. And then the hurricane struck again— total blackness, raging wind, the drumbeat of torrential rain. She tucked in all the ends of the rain slickers as best she could, wrapped her arm around Cara's rigid shoulders, and gripped the line. The plastic lifted, fought to break free, but the line held. Brandy rested her head against the rocking trunk and prayed.

Sometime during the long night, she dozed. First she was in the vestibule of hell, being blown along with sinners who would not commit to moral rightness. Then her dream changed. She was covered with water, two year old Cara in her arms, sandbags falling around them down cistern walls.

Once she thought she heard John call her name, and a thrill ran through her. He would come out of the darkness and find her. But when she tried to go to him, she woke to the roar of wind and water.

CHAPTER 19

▼

Dawn came with the dying wind, a smoky glow under thick clouds in the east. Gusts still shook the palm fronds and ruffled the tall grass. Beside the road lay a huge oak, its roots a knotted tangle in the air. Brandy untied the line and shook Cara gently by the shoulder. "We'd better hit the road, the sooner the quicker."

Cara raised her head, wonder in her eyes. "We survived." She held up the plastic tote bag. "I saved this." Faint color now tinged her cheeks. The stiffness had gone from her mouth.

Brandy smiled for the first time and slipped on her watch. Six o'clock. Separated from the road by marsh grasses and a wide ditch, they passed under a line of pines, scrub oaks, and an occasional soggy maple. Gradually the sun rose at their backs, screened by clouds. One car flashed by, going toward Suwannee, but they hid, afraid to hail it. Any car might carry Moose's partner.

In two hours they skirted a fallen restaurant billboard, slogged through a heavily forested area, then a burned field. At intervals dirt roads branched off toward the river. Next came hardware store and fish camp signs, a few manufactured homes, a trailer without a roof. But no cars or people. No signs of life. Brandy took an irrational comfort from the slender white steeple of a tiny church.

Ahead rose a water tower, then cabbage palms and a few cottages on a network of brimming canals that forked toward the river. To the north lay a marsh of saw grass and needlerush and a distant stilt house, to the left a road that crossed a small concrete bridge. A hand-lettered board with an arrow read "Lazy River Marina. Dawn to Dusk. Open now."

Cara halted. "Let's see if the sign's really true. I've got to sit down." Brandy looked again at her watch. Ten o'clock. Beyond the bridge she could see the high metal roof of a boat hangar, shut off by a locked gate. They shuffled to the bridge and collapsed on its low concrete side. Brandy pulled off the boots she had taken from Moose's boat and set them at the edge of the bridge.

"We shouldn't need boots now."

With a sigh, Cara removed hers while Brandy turned to examine a structure at the river's edge beside the metal boat hangar, a smaller frame building with open shelves for dry storage, a few boats in the slots. In front stood a seedy looking store on concrete blocks. Water ran level with the back steps and flooded the area around a lone pick-up truck. In the weeds inside a chain link fence lay the broken hull of an old fishing boat. The gate to the store was open, and when Brandy stood and peered more closely, she saw that a door beside a boarded window was open, too. Above it a second sign announced the Lazy River Marina. Brandy read aloud, "Storage and Service Seven Days a Week."

Her whole being trembled with joy. "We've found another human being. There'll be a phone and a safe place to wait."

Cara raked her fingers through her stringy hair and glanced down at her muddy jeans. "Think what we must look like."

"The least of our worries."

As they skirted the smaller hangar, Brandy glanced up and recognized a familiar boat, a walk-around with a console amidships and the name "Fisherman's Fling" on the prow. She remembered that Blade Bullen, AKA Nathan Hunt, fished this area, that he'd been coming to

Suwannee to store his boat before the storm. Her heart lifted. Maybe they would find a familiar face.

They trudged up wooden steps between corner pilings and into a wide entrance area, its walls posted with marine charts. Before them stretched a long, dank room crammed with displays of fishing lures and rods, cans of oil, sweatshirts, bathing suits, shorts, and tee shirts. Everything reeked of mildew. Beside a cluttered counter near the front, a black Labrador retriever sprang to his feet and barked. But the man pulling duct tape from a plate glass window turned and gave them a huge smile.

"L-land, l-look what the cat dragged in! My God, w-where you girls been?" He dropped the tape and came forward, a stocky, middle-aged man with a gap between his front teeth and a slight stutter.

Cara saw a straight chair beside a stack of plastic foam minnow buckets and sank into it. Brandy clutched the counter. "We were caught in the hurricane. We need to use your phone to call the Levy County Sheriff's Office."

"L-lands, girl. Of course. L-lucky the phone's back on. I'll make the call for you. You look hungry. Let me get you something to eat. You still wet?"

While the lab, calm now, sniffed her leg, Brandy glanced down at her damp and wrinkled shirt and jeans.

"I'm the owner here. Got a little office in the b-back of the store. It's got a couch and some hot coffee. You g-girls go right in there. Clean up and take a load off your feet. You l-look bushed. I'll call now. T-tell them to come get you."

Scuttling toward the rear door, he showed them a small room with a desk, a battered leather couch and chair, a window covered with plywood, and wonder of wonders, an adjoining bathroom. "Just give me your n-names."

Giddy with gratitude, Brandy paused in the office doorway. "Cara Waters and Brandy O'Bannon. They're probably out looking for us now."

"Sure thing. L-lands, glad I stayed last night. Worried about my c-customers' boats, you know. It was bad, but I reckon they mostly c-came through all right. C-customers will be along any minute to check. Be right back. Soon's I make the call, I'll rustle up some sandwiches been in the cooler."

He retreated to a corner of the counter and picked up the phone. "S-sheriff's Office? Lazy River Marina in Suwannee. Yeah, okay. Say, I g-got two drowned looking gals here, but they's all right. O'Bannon and Waters, I believe they said they names was. Yeah, you can c-come get them. I'm gonna give them some grub and let them clean up a bit here. Yeah. S-soon's you can make it."

Brandy was sprawled on the couch with a hot cup of foul-tasting coffee when he came back with the sandwiches. "You wouldn't have a comb, would you?" She had taken a fleeting and horrified look in the cracked mirror above the sink.

"Well, now, I'll look. K-keep a few supplies for c-customers. I found these." He handed her two tee-shirts that said "Shark Mania" and two women's cotton shorts of uncertain size. "Y'all can pay me back l-later. At least them's dry. I got a c-customer coming in now. Picky about his boat."

Brandy accepted the clothes with thanks and heard the door click shut behind him. While Cara changed in the rest room, Brandy pulled off her sticky jeans and shirt and struggled into the fresh outfit. Both top and shorts sagged. After Cara emerged, trying to straighten her wild, dark hair with her fingers, they hunched together on the couch, bone-weary, devouring the stale bread and baloney.

"I've got to call John," Brandy said. She wondered if he had learned about the overturned skiff. Maybe divers were already searching the river. She was overwhelmed by the need to hear his voice, even that bland tone on the answering machine.

Cara looked down, sheepish. "I ought to try to reach Marcia."

"MacGill said she was frantic with worry." Brandy turned the knob, but the door did not open. Maybe it was stuck. No, through the crack she could see the bolt. She felt a stirring of anxiety. "Why would the guy lock the door from the outside? We'd do the locking." It was an old door with a sizable key hole. "Must be a dead bolt on the other side." Lowering her hands, Cara stopped eating and stared at the door. With growing panic, Brandy rattled the knob. "Hey, let us out!" She realized they did not even known the proprietor's name.

Silence. She pounded on the door with her fist. At last they heard footsteps growing louder, then halt before the door. Their host bent down with a self-satisfied chuckle and put his lips close to the key hole. "Soon's the storm passed, I had a c-call from a buddy. Wasn't hard to figure out where you g-gal's would head. Now t-take a close l-look." There was a pause. He was backing up. "Got me a right handy little piece here." Brandy could see the black nozzle of a revolver. "J-just as soon use it on y'all, if I hear another peep. Stay quiet, you won't get hurt. G-got one customer out front. If he hears a thing, y'all are dead meat."

Brandy slumped down on the couch. "Oh, God, we walked right into a trap. Twinkle-tongue suckered us in here with those damn handwritten signs. He didn't call the Sheriff's Office. He called Moose. He's part of the drug ring. I've known some wonderful people who stutter, but he sure isn't one of them."

Cara stifled a sob. "Maybe his customer heard us."

"Not likely. He's been out by the dock."

Brandy shuffled to the door and squinted again through the key hole. At the front of the room she could see a plate glass door open. The marina owner came in and turned to talk to someone else. Behind the squat shape of the proprietor loomed a tall, slim figure. She held her breath.

"If the river calms down enough, I'm taking the boat out this afternoon," the man said. "I told the Sheriff's Office my father and I would join the search." The voice sounded familiar. When the stout owner disappeared to the right of the doorway, Brandy clearly saw Blade Bullen standing in profile before the counter.

Frantic, she turned to Cara. "A note! Find a piece of paper. Look on the desk!"

Cara rummaged through the top drawer and pulled out a legal-sized envelope. Fingers shaking, she scrawled a line in pencil and handed it to Brandy. It read "Help! Look in the marina office. Kidnapped!" She signed it "Cara."

The younger Bullen still lingered at the counter, his wallet in his hand. Brandy slipped the envelope under the door, gave it a mighty push. Through the key hole she could see it slide across the floor. The wind from the open back door caught it, sent it skittering farther. Cara knelt beside her.

"He's the guy who's probably your half-brother," Brandy whispered. Bullen turned, took a step toward a display of lures, and stepped on the envelope. When he moved, another gust blew it against the chair. The black lab raised his head and watched it flip over, face down.

A heavy weight settled in Brandy's stomach. Cara crawled up on the couch and covered her face with her hands. They heard the front door bang shut. "Blade Bullen's planning to look for us—you, mainly," Brandy said. "That's ironic." She stood and dusted off the baggy new shorts. "Frank Bullen—I think he's your father—must be coming to Cedar Key."

She sat next to Cara, her mind washed clean of ideas, too tired to think anymore. "You know what the last circle of Dante's hell is?" she asked at last.

Numbly, Cara shook her head.

"The circle of deceit. The one sin that only man commits. Fitting, isn't it?"

Cara's brown eyes looked up, wet. "And how did Dante and his guide get away?"

Brandy thought for a minute. "They climbed down," she said. "They climbed down Satan's flank."

Cara stared at the plywood nailed across the window frame on the outside. "We can't wait here like fish in a barrel for Moose." Brandy looked at her drawn, purposeful face and remembered the young woman who had gone alone into the night time forest to photograph a ghost. The hurricane had passed. She was strong again. Maybe from now on. "Help me move the couch over by the window," Cara said.

That done, Brandy could see the seat was about level with the sill. She managed to open the latch of the double hung sash and force up the lower pane.

Cara gritted her teeth. "We're going to sit here with our backs braced and kick as hard as we can."

Brandy's spirits rose. "True, these guys we're dealing with aren't mental giants. Plywood's not all that strong."

Brandy gave the lowest slat a vicious kick. "If we're lucky, Twinkle-tongue will be gassing an engine or moving a boat with the fork lift."

Cara joined her and the bottom plank splintered, tore loose from the nails, dropped into the water below, then the next. "One more," Brandy said. "Then it's over with the line again."

When the third plywood board splashed down, Brandy pulled the nylon rope out of her bag, tied it to the leg of the couch, and threw it over the sill.

"Okay, you first. The water can't be deep and the store's on pilings. See if you can get up under the floor out of sight. We'll try to make it to the back steps."

Cara ducked her head and straddled the sill, gripped the line, and let herself down. Brandy heard her slosh into the standing water, then followed her out the window. Once more she was hit by the acrid smell of damp, polluted mud. When her shoes sank into the muck, she looked up and shook her head. No way to pull down the window or retrieve the line.

They huddled for a minute, up to their knees in the cold flood, then struggled between concrete supports under the building, dragging their feet across a bottom of weeds, mud, and sand.

Cara shuddered. "Wish we still had our boots."

"They wouldn't have stayed on." At last, half squatting, they worked their way through the shallow water to the concrete blocks at the back door. They could see the broken hull, and beyond it, the fatal bridge. Their boots still lay beside the road, the gate still hung open. Moose would be expected. No other customers or cars were on the street.

"Got to try to get away from the store," Brandy whispered. "We can hunch down and make a run for the old boat. Keep it between us and the store. Then dash through the gate and make for the canal, duck down under the bridge again."

Cara nodded, her face rigid. Brandy willed her legs to keep moving. She ran first, along behind the derelict boat, and crouched at the corner of the gate until Cara charged up behind her.

"Now!" Brandy spurted through the gate, hit the bank of the canal beside Cara, and stooped into the shadows under the concrete arch. Once more they huddled together.

"Thing is," Brandy said, "people ought to start coming back soon." She scanned the few boarded up cottages along the canal. "Watch for a car with kids in it, a family."

They sat for several minutes in shivering silence. "It'll be strange to meet a man who might be my father," Cara said at last. "How can I prove he is?"

"Tests. First, the dental records will verify the skeleton is Allison Bullen's. Then we have to show she's your mother. DNA testing can do that, prove he's your father, too. Tests shouldn't be a problem. Frank Bullen's a wealthy man."

A few more minutes passed. "I don't need tests. I've got the blue bear. Or I did."

"I don't know if that would be legal evidence."

The strain of the last two days showed in Cara's eyes. Her voice broke. "Where in the world is everyone?" Brandy patted her hand, trying to think what to do next. As a guide she had not been a rattling success. "I think you said Dante finally got out of hell."

"He did." Brandy looked at Cara thoughtfully. Finding her biological father would force hard decisions on Cara—about Marcia, her career, her whole future. "But Dante had to reach his final goal by himself."

On the road several yards away a car stopped, but no one appeared at the few houses they could see. What kind of vehicle would Moose come in? Surely not the swamp buggy. A pick-up, probably. When Brandy crawled to the edge of the arch and peered back toward the store, her legs almost gave way. The owner now stood in the doorway, glaring out at the parking lot. Then he trotted down the steps, knelt, and looked under the building.

Shaken, Brandy scooted back to Cara. "The guy knows we're gone." If they ran, he would spot them. If they waited, maybe he wouldn't think of the bridge."

And then Brandy heard barking, throaty, excited. She remembered the black lab. The proprietor might not be smart, but he had an assistant, a skilled searcher.

"The owner's dog," she breathed. They sat paralyzed, hearing the rapid patter of paws, the nails scratching on the road bed, the little yelps of discovery. Tightly they held each other and listened to the dog come clawing down the embankment, its cry exultant.

CHAPTER 20

▼

Brandy spun around, grasping for a stick, a rock, any weapon. But retreating water had swept the concrete slab clean. In her panic she thought of the car that had stopped on the street. If it was Moose, if they faced Moose and the marina owner, they were done for. Someone was scrambling down the bank behind the dog. She heard loud panting. As the animal bounded into their dim sanctuary, she ducked and threw one arm around Cara's shoulder, the other up before her face. Her mind raced with images of salivating Dobermans and pit bulls and her body tensed for the attack. She braced herself and shut her eyes.

Then something moist touched her cheek. Her heart gave a sudden leap. A dog's wet tongue? She opened her eyes and looked into a soft, cream-colored mask, saw a flash of feathery tail. Burying her face in Meg's red-gold coat, she wept.

When Brandy raised her head, a tall, familiar figure was half sliding down the last few feet into the culvert, arms lifted to keep his balance, dark hair tumbled over his forehead. A wave of emotion surged in her chest. She saw John's eyes widen with relief, heard him calling her, as he had the last night in her dream. Dripping and muddy and wordless, legs weak, she rose and ran to him, laid her head against his tan jacket, clung to him. For the first time in two days she felt safe.

His arms closed around her. "My God, I've been frantic."

She tried to speak and found to her surprise that she was crying. Turning, she took Cara's cold hand and choked out the words. "We were kidnapped. The guy in the Lazy River Marina. He has a gun."

John's lips tightened. "We'll take care of him."

Thank God, Brandy thought, he's not alone. With John's arm steadying her, she held Cara's hand and stumbled up toward the bridge, while Meg bounced ahead, her tail like a banner. When they reached the road, she could see Detective Jeremiah Strong standing beside his Ford Taurus, hands on his hips, watching with an enormous grin.

"Guy in the marina," John called. "He was holding them both."

While Strong put in a call on his radio, John waited, one arm still around Brandy's waist, and rubbed his forehead. "How in the world..."

Brandy nodded at Cara. "We escaped out a window. Twice. Couldn't have done it without Cara."

Her friend leaned her slim body against the Ford, holding high her head with its tangled mop of hair. Gone was the shaken figure who had cringed before the wind and rain. Even in the soiled shirt and shorts, she had dignity. She knows, Brandy thought, that she conquered a storm and two kidnappers. Now perhaps she's ready to face Marcia and Truck.

As the detective closed the car door, John lifted Meg's leash from the Ford's hood and snapped it onto her collar.

"Dixie County deputies been searching this whole area," Strong said. "Ever since we got the report this morning you was missing. They'll be here directly."

Brandy caught a flicker of motion in the marina doorway. Cara whirled and pointed toward the parking lot. "He'll get away!" A squat man had bolted down the steps and was trotting across the pavement toward the pick-up. The proprietor had seen the detective's car.

"Remember the gun," Brandy said.

Strong's hand moved under his jacket toward a slight bulge at the small of his back. "Only way to get out is past me."

Strong crouched and took a few steps forward before Brandy heard the squeal of brakes, and three Dixie County cruisers pulled across the road behind them, armed officers spilling out of each. While the black lab barked through the screen door, they converged on the parking lot. Several hands yanked the marina owner from the pick-up cab, threw him against the door, removed his revolver from an ankle holster, and half dragged and half walked him toward the bridge.

"This the guy, M'am?"

The chubby proprietor sagged between two deputies, wild-eyed, gap-toothed, the corners of his mouth dribbling. "D-didn't do nothing! Just t-tried to h-help them two ladies!"

Brandy nodded to the deputy. "He's the one. Helped us by locking us up and threatening us with the gun. There's another one, even more dangerous, on a houseboat across from Little Turkey Island. Moored on this side of the river—if he's still there."

The tension in Cara's face relaxed as the marina owner was hustled past.

"Marine Patrol can pick up the second guy," Strong said. "The dispatcher will be glad to call off the divers. They was fixing to look for you." He moved again toward his radio, then motioned to the corporal in charge. "Meantime, you might cover those logging roads this side of the river. In case the guy takes off."

Cara giggled. "His swamp buggy's bogged down on one of those roads. We got away in it."

For the first time John flashed his lop-sided grin.

While two deputies secured the marina site and waited for a search warrant, another pair tucked the marina owner into the cage in the rear of a cruiser. Strong opened the passenger door of his own car for Cara, while John ushered Meg, then Brandy into the back seat and climbed in last.

"This area's under Dixie County jurisdiction," the detective said, sliding under the wheel. "I told the corporal how to reach you both. You'll have to come back and make full statements."

One deputy started his engine, then leaned out the car window and called to Strong, "Got a message here for Mr. Able. Dispatcher says there's a contractor in Gainesville trying to reach him. Called our operations center in Cross City."

John was reaching for the door handle when Strong spoke. "You can't call from the marina. No one can go in until it's searched. You can use the phone at the store in Fowler's Bluff. We got to take you there, anyway, for your car."

While Strong drove back down the narrow highway, John moved in close to Brandy. "Damn it," he said, frowning. "The call's got to mean a problem on the bank restoration job. I had to leave in a hurry, and I left things to Tiffany. The first crews started today." He lifted a strand of water weed from the back of her neck, looked around, and finally deposited it on the floor mat. "Left my car next to your rental at the store." He pulled her head onto his shoulder. "When the woman at the fish camp got back this morning, she called the Levy County Sheriff's Office. Her boat hadn't been returned, and your car was still there."

"Bless that woman," Brandy murmured.

John's lips brushed her dirt-streaked cheek. Then he drew back and scowled. "Any idea how crazy that news made me? The woman said a young lady had rented a boat to look for a houseboat near Little Turkey Island. Said the water was already rough. After her call, her empty skiff washed ashore." He rubbed his forehead again and sighed. "I never doubted the missing woman was you. Who else would go out in that weather? Detective Strong confirmed your name at the rental agency. He let me come with him."

Brandy felt like a child who'd been rescued from danger by her parents, but still faced their wrath. John looked down at the retriever cuddled up beside Brandy. "We were hoping somehow you'd made it to

Suwannee. I knew Meg's nose might come in handy. She went wild over those boots on the bridge."

Strong glanced in the rear view mirror. "I reckon the kidnapping hooks in with the Rossi murder." Brandy lifted her head and noticed the white steeple floating past, then the roofless trailer. Strong grinned. "Reckon it turned out to be drugs, after all, right?"

Brandy rested her head again on John's shoulder. She felt bone tired, her arms and legs limp. "Marijuana had been stored on the houseboat, yes."

She wondered if she would recognize the clump of cabbage palms where she and Cara had found shelter, where the bob cat had sprung forth. A weak sun glowed through a thin cover of clouds. It all seemed unreal now.

"But I gotta hand it to you, O'Bannon," Strong added. "You was right about Miss Waters here being snatched."

Cara had slumped against the passenger door. Now she nodded. "I never got to see the photograph. Maybe it did show the murderer."

"The Dixie County guys will be looking for it, for sure." He turned right at U.S. 19, drove through the tiny community of Old Town, and crossed the brimming Suwannee at Fanning Springs. "Got to thank Mrs. Able for another tip," he said in a few minutes. "Before the storm we took up the woman's skeleton. Carried it to Gainesville and faxed the dental records. Preliminary report came in early today. It's Allison Bullen, all right. I called the man used to be her husband in New York. Wasn't any other family."

Cara faced him, her voice clear. "Except me. Allison Bullen disappeared during Hurricane Agnes." She frowned. "I found the blue teddy bear her little girl was carrying. My foster mother had it hidden. She knew I was that woman's child all along. That's why I left. Brandy says my name's really Belinda Bullen."

After a pause, Strong spoke more quietly. "If that's the case, I reckon you'll see your daddy and his new wife later this afternoon. Flying into Cedar Key in some kinda private jet. I told him he could claim the remains in a few days. He wants to talk to you and that son of his. Says Rossi called him about the search, and he sent his son to check it out. Didn't want anyone to know who they were, not 'til he was sure Rossi was on the right track."

"Mr. Bullen was afraid of a false claim," Brandy said.

"He's a wealthy man." She could see Cara's narrow shoulders go tense. In the pale light her eyes looked enormous. How would it feel to meet a father you'd never known, a man who might not acknowledge you? "He plays his cards close to his vest," Brandy added, "like a lawyer would." She glanced at the detective. "What did you tell Mr. Bullen?"

"Nothing," Strong said, "except that we identified the skeleton."

Brandy remembered her own halting interview in Bullen's well-appointed study. "I told him the medical examiner thought his wife had been murdered."

"Come down to it, I'll likely see the man today myself. I aim to go back to Cedar Key this afternoon. Got to question a certain someone." Brandy remembered MacGill's gun was being tested for Rossi's murder. Angus was probably in for a grilling.

Strong swung off Route 19 and made the final turn toward Fowler's Bluff. In the fish camp parking area he pulled around a fallen oak limb beside John's car, switched off the engine, and heaved his long legs out from under the wheel.

"Wait while I run in and call Gainesville," John said. He opened his door and looked down at Brandy, nestled beside him, at her ragged shirt and damp shorts, at her wan eyes. He shook his head. "You're in no condition to drive the rental car back to Gainesville."

Strong leaned against the Ford while John sprinted across a yard littered with twigs and Spanish moss, up the worn steps, and into the store. "Be patient and long suffering," the detective said, mostly to himself. "So shall thou have dominion over all wicked works."

Brandy nodded with satisfaction at his words. She had closed her eyes when John came back, the muscles in his forehead taut, anger plain in the tilt of his chin. "All work at the construction site's stopped.

Contractor's mad as hell," he growled. "We had to redesign a steel support system to preserve the old structure. Something about it's not right. I never should've left an intern in charge." There'd been a problem with Tiffany Moore's renderings, Brandy knew. That was why she'd called John Saturday at the hotel.

Even though Brandy did not want John blamed, she felt a twinge of vindication. The architectural profession was replete with excellent women, but she had never thought one of them was Tiffany Moore.

With gentle pressure John took Brandy's hands in his and helped her from the car. "I've got to get to the bank building as soon as I can. I can straighten out the problem. The contractor can't go on without me. It could mean my job with the firm."

Cara leaned over the back seat, appealing with her eyes to Brandy. "Brandy, come home with me this afternoon. Clean up and get a good rest. You could make a fresh start tomorrow." Her voice became more urgent. "You could meet my father with me. You talked to him in New York. I wouldn't know him if I saw him."

Without looking at Cara, Brandy took John's hand. "Do what you have to. Go on to Gainesville. Your work's more important right now. I'm safe. Anyway, I don't want to wait at the job site while you solve the problem. And I need to return the car."

John drew her to him and kissed the top of her head. "I don't want you driving back alone, not until I'm sure you're okay. Take a room at the hotel and rest." He pulled back and looked into her eyes. "In the meantime, I'm asking Detective Strong to follow your car to Cedar Key, in case you get any other looney ideas."

For a second longer he held her. "Call me tomorrow morning when you leave. I'll pick you up at the airport car rental." His tone softened, and turning away from the others, he murmured, "Then we'll have a real celebration." She gave him a final hug.

It was not until Brandy had settled behind the wheel, Cara beside her, that she realized he would spend another evening working with

Tiffany Moore. She wondered if the intern would be part of their celebration.

As John pulled out of the parking lot, Strong strode over and shook
a finger in Brandy's window. "Go straight to Miss Waters' house first.
Her Mama's wore out with worry. She's waiting there now." He
straightened up, hands again on his hips. "You got nothing else to concern your head about. This Rossi case will go down soon. And maybe
the murder of Allison Bullen, too. No more messing, M'am, in police
business." He flashed a quick smile and winked. "Unless I ask you."

Strong, master of the mysterious comment, she thought.

*   *   *   *

Marcia Waters came to the door of the frame cottage with haunted
eyes. As she held it open, her gaze never left Cara's face. With shock
Brandy realized how the artist had aged. Her confident stance was
gone. She was more stooped, every gesture more tentative. Between
foster mother and daughter now lay the tattered teddy bear, a barrier as
clear as a physical barricade in the room. Cara gave her an awkward
peck on the cheek and strolled into the living room. What Marcia had
lost in self assurance, Brandy thought, Cara had gained.

Cara's eyes fastened on her foster mother. "I got through the hurricane okay. We have a deeper problem. You know you kept me from
finding out who I am."

Marcia's long fingers spread helplessly toward Cara. "I can try to
make you understand."

Brandy stopped in the doorway. "Look, you two have a lot to talk
about. I'll go on to the hotel."

Marcia turned toward Brandy as if aware of her for the first time.
"Detective Strong was good enough to call me. I've been briefed about
the kidnapping. I'm just so grateful to you..." Her voice twisted into
silence. When she clasped her hands before her, Brandy realized it was
to prevent their shaking. She looked from Brandy to Cara. "Cara and I

have to talk, yes. I have to try to explain. But there's something else. Officer Doggett called. Mr. Bullen—Mr. Bullen and his wife are due at the airport at four-thirty." She can't say "Cara's father," Brandy thought.

Cara glanced at Brandy, an anxious pitch to her voice. "Don't go. I need you at the airport. You can have a good soak in the tub here, and you've got fresh clothes in your suitcase. You can take a nap in my bedroom while I clean up. I'll rest in Mother's room. Then we'll go together to meet the plane."

Brandy checked her watch. Already two-thirty. It would be quicker to stay until the Bullens arrived. She'd call the hotel now, then check in later. Marcia laid a timid hand on Cara's arm. "I'll fix some sandwiches. You both must be starved." Brandy had started back to the car for her suitcase and notebook when she overheard Marcia's soft request. "Fact is, I'd like to go to the airport, too."

✳   ✳   ✳   ✳

After Brandy surrendered the bathtub to Cara, she lay down in her young friend's room, closed her eyes, and thought about Rossi's murder. If Cara was kidnapped because of the damning photograph, what had happened to it? Moose had said on the phone that he "had it," that "it" was valuable, that he wanted his "fair share." Would he have destroyed the picture, or had it instead given him sudden power? Not for a minute did she think Moose or the stuttering marina owner had dug Rossi's grave that night. And not for a minute did she think the picture explained the attack on her in New York.

She sat up, drowsy now, and leafed through her bulging notebook, then scribbled what she could remember of the houseboat. Somewhere in her notes must be a lead. When she had jettisoned the marina shorts and shirt in the bathroom, she found she still had Moose's key ring and its set of three keys. She held them up now and studied them, trying to remember. She had seen something on the houseboat that might be important. Now what was it?

CHAPTER 21

▼

The airport lay on a spit of land between a marsh and a patch of weeds and wild flowers, a 2,400 foot strip two miles from town with no directional lights, no fuel, and no personnel. At four-thirty Brandy, Cara, and Marcia waited beside the field in the rental car, Cara's new-found confidence waning by the minute. The strain of Marcia's break with Cara was clear in her foster mother's hollow eyes.

Above the orange wind sock they heard the plane's engines, saw the sleek little jet slow, bank, settle into a long glide, and strike the ground with a light bounce. In a few minutes Frank Bullen in a gray business suit emerged from the plane's doorway and came down the metal steps. His wife's tall figure sidled along behind him in a beige silk pants suit with wide, billowing legs. Bullen's features were as bland as Brandy remembered, perhaps a trifle plump, his mouth small, his manner deliberate. He glanced at the first familiar face, Brandy's, and raised a gray eyebrow.

"The newspaper woman?" He emphasized each word. "I hadn't expected you here. This is a private matter. We don't want publicity."

Cara's fingers shook as she took Brandy's arm and extended the other hand, brown eyes shining. "I'm Cara. Brandy's been helping me find you. She's kind of been my guide."

Bullen's voice dropped. "Well, then." He paused, his eyes appraising Brandy. "We all have a lot of catching up to do." He took Cara's hand, studied her with a subdued smile, then moved in beside her, deftly replacing Brandy. Mrs. Bullen halted at the bottom of the steps, her chestnut page boy lifting in the slight wind. As she began ankling in high-heeled pumps across the uneven asphalt, Bullen stepped forward, held out his arm, and turned again to Cara. "My wife, the current Mrs. Bullen." He gave Cara a tight smile.

The last Mrs. Bullen, Brandy thought, was presumably Cara's mother, and her mind turned to "My Last Duchess" in Browning's famous sonnet. She wondered if this next wife had a first name. She'd never heard him use it. The current Mrs. Bullen offered Cara her hand. "Such a charming young lady," she murmured, bending her elegant head to Cara's level. Then standing tall again, she stared at the bleak airfield around her, breathing in the fresh smell of green plants and salt water, a startled expression in her eyes.

Marcia stood humbly to one side in her plain white blouse and long skirt, her strong artist's hands folded before her, her cheeks drawn, her lips pressed together.

"This is my foster mother, Marcia Waters," Cara explained, touching Marcia's arm. "She's been very good to me."

Bullen inclined his head toward her. "Someone from the Sheriff's Office told me you've reared Belinda. Of course, under the circumstances, that was a generous thing to do." Again the careful smile. "I'll certainly see you are appropriately compensated."

Marcia opened her mouth, then without making a sound, closed it. In her anguished silence, Brandy heard the cry of a frightened toddler alone in a storm, the voices of the school girl and her devoted foster parents, the pleas of a mother now for her grown daughter's love.

But Bullen's attention was no longer on Marcia Waters. His glance swept the desolate airstrip and its fringe of scrub oaks. An osprey swept through the faded sunlight to its nest in a longleaf pine. Someone will need to pick up the pilot and our bags later," he said. "Don't see any taxis or much of anything else."

The trio followed Brandy to her car, where the Bullens climbed into the rear with Cara, and Marcia slid into the passenger seat. "I can come back," the artist said. "I have a panel truck." In the rear view mirror Brandy saw Mrs. Bullen's eyebrows lift.

Marcia appeared not to notice. "Would you care to stop at our house? You could visit with Cara there."

Bullen wiped his forehead with a monogrammed handkerchief, leaned back, and sighed. "That's very kind—Mrs. Waters is it? But I think we need to go to the hotel. It's been a tiring day."

Brandy thought of Cara's last two harrowing days and bit her lip.

"Drop Marcia off, then," Cara said, "and we'll take them to the Island Hotel. I used to work there. It's quite historic, and it has a gourmet restaurant."

Mrs. Bullen turned her stately profile and gazed out the car window at the cedars and live oaks, at the Victorian homes and the Gulf, at the dark outline of Atsena Otie Key. "Quaint." She looked at Cara beside her. "Our Manhattan townhouse will be quite a change, of course."

Cara gave her a look of faint surprise. "I'd look forward to a visit," she said.

In the hotel, while Cara stopped at the counter, Mr. Bullen looked around the lobby, then turned to Current Wife. "Go to the desk and explain the accommodations I need. Perhaps the clerk can recommend something modern."

Brandy went in search of MacGill. She wanted to give the pair and Cara some space, and to find some time alone to update her notes. Something she'd already jotted down kept trying to surface, and she still couldn't remember the elusive detail about Moose's houseboat.

Without locating the proprietor, Brandy returned to the sound of Mrs. Bullen's distinctive trill. While Bullen himself waited just inside the double doors, his wife was poised at the counter, speaking to the awed clerk. "The hotel's charming, but of course, Mr. Bullen needs a phone in his room. Clients may need to reach him." Her gaze swept over the plain wooden chairs, the iron stove, the time-worn staircase rising in shadows at the end of the room. She shrugged the shoulders of her silk tunic. "We really prefer something a bit more contemporary."

It would not matter to the Bullens, Brandy thought, that Civil War soldiers on both sides had trod those steps, and wealthy long-ago merchants, and a railroad magnate of the early 1860's who expected Cedar Key to be the prime port on the West Coast.

As Current Wife rested her hand with its expertly manicured nails on the counter, Brandy noticed she was wearing, in addition to the exquisite diamond she'd had on her left hand in New York, a gold and pearl pendant with matching earrings. Probably needs a safe, she thought. Not likely in Cedar Key, not since the 1860's.

The young desk clerk, much impressed, peered over her glasses and then telephoned a new motel at the end of the street. To Brandy she announced that Mr. MacGill was not feeling well and couldn't see her, but that her room was ready. The clerk also had messages: Blade would meet his father for dinner at the hotel, and Doggett had called to report that a deputy was bringing Cara's station wagon home. It had been found, Doggett said, at an abandoned hunting camp. Because of the hurricane, the owner had gone to check on his property. Otherwise the camp would've been deserted for months.

Bullen turned to Cara. "Splendid. You'll have your car tomorrow. I've asked your stepmother to take you shopping in the nearest good-sized town. She'll pick out the smart clothes I want you to wear in New York."

Cara had no chance to react. As Bullen was speaking, Brandy could see Truck Thompson's fish house van careen up to the curb. The hotel doors burst open, and the oyster man's solid body hurtled into the lobby. "You lied to me!" he shouted at Cara. "You didn't go to no friend's house! I been crazy with worry." Brandy wondered what Frank Bullen and his wife would make of the soiled black jacket and fisherman's boots.

Cara put one slender hand on the oyster man's arm. "Someone should've told you. I was kidnapped. The Sheriff's Office found Brandy and me today." She looked up at Truck's scowl. "This is my father, Frank Bullen from New York."

Truck swung around to face the older man, close-set eyes ablaze. "Don't figure on taking her off somewheres, like New York. Cara belongs in Cedar Key. We took her in. I been watching out for her ever since she was a shirt-tail young'un. Cara and me got an understanding. I got a fine business. She can have whatever she wants right here."

Bullen shook his head, unperturbed, like a person watching an exotic species. "I'm afraid we've made our plans, but since you're a friend of hers, you must join us for dinner. My daughter will bring Mrs. Waters, and my son will be here, too. About seven at the hotel, shall we say?" Bullen ignored Truck's reddened face and looked at Brandy. "Will you be able to drive us over to the motel? Perhaps Belinda—Cara..." again the bleak smile—"will be kind enough to bring us our suitcases." He looked again at Cara. "It's been an extraordinary day. We'll have a real talk in private tomorrow."

As the Bullens settled into her car's rear seat, Brandy wondered if this man had any real emotions at all. Perhaps a lifetime of steely control had merely blunted their expression. But when he took out the monogrammed handkerchief again to wipe his forehead, his hand shook.

Brandy watched in the rear view mirror as he stared out at the deserted gazebo in City Park. "Belinda's mother could've had any luxuries she wanted." His voice softened. "The best of everything, the both of them. At home I protected her. She turned her back on it all. Chose to run off to the other end of nowhere, get picked up and bludgeoned to death in some cheap tourist cabin. I imagine she was meeting some man." Then the bitterness seemed to drain from his voice. "Her daughter seems more reasonable."

*   *   *   *

When Brandy returned to the hotel, she met Detective Strong coming out of the sitting room between MacGill's apartment and the lounge. He towered above her, a half-smile on his lips. "You're a first class note taker. I expect you're a good observer, too. Got a favor to ask."

Brandy halted, surprised. But he had hinted he might need her.

"What I want you to do is this. I gotta question MacGill, and I don't wanna take notes right in his face. A tape recorder makes a guy clam up." He dropped his voice. "I got no deputy with me. I want you to sit quiet-like in a corner and write down what the guy says, how he acts. You know MacGill, and I don't. You're more likely to know if he's telling the truth. Anyway, I need a witness."

Brandy nodded, feeling bad for the Scotsman but good for the feature story she would eventually write.

"Likely I'll carry him into Bronson for more questioning tomorrow, but he'll talk better now, here in his own place."

When Brandy returned with her notebook, Strong led her into the darkened sitting room and placed her in the shadow of a tall Japanese screen. "We won't try to fool the guy. He'll know you're here, but I hope he'll forget about you." He hesitated. "Guess I could tell you the latest development. I had a call from Dixie County. They've finished going over the houseboat. Moved it to a pier near Old Town. Bad thing is, the guy called Moose is dead. They found him in the river, shot. Best guess is late morning or early afternoon."

"No big surprise there," Brandy said. "He's got another partner, I figure, more dangerous than the marina owner. And the Shell Mound photograph?"

"Couldn't find it. But they don't think the killer did, either. Everything in the boat was a mess, like there'd been a right smart search."

Brandy looked thoughtful. "Sounds like Moose got greedy. I heard him try to make his partner pay for the picture. He forgot he knew too much. Not too bright of him, but that was typical Moose behavior. He went ashore and left us alone on the boat. That's how we got away." Her mind raced back to the interior of the houseboat's cabin. She would have to think of a place the deputies didn't.

When MacGill appeared in his doorway, Strong explained that, for MacGill's own protection, Brandy would make a record of the interview. Thrusting out his lower lip, MacGill gave Brandy a long look, then seemed to accept her role. He sat down, rigid, crossed his legs, and folded his arms across his chest. "You're a canny lad, Detective Strong. Shouldn't I have a lawyer?"

Strong leaned forward, his big hands relaxed between his knees. "Well, technically you could, but I don't suppose there's anyone handy now in Cedar Key. You've got nothing to hide, and this is just a preliminary talk, sir, very informal."

MacGill kept his arms folded, but after a few seconds, he nodded.

The detective began by complimenting the proprietor on his civic pride, the work he'd done on the hotel, his reputation for helping people. Gradually the Scotsman's arms dropped to his lap, his tension faded.

Strong went on in a calm voice. MacGill's testimony was valuable, he'd be better off telling everything he knew about the Bullen case. MacGill tilted his head, wary.

"We think you can help us with Allison Bullen's disappearance," Strong said, his voice earnest. "I looked at the report the officers made at the time. That cashier gave them the names of everyone she saw in the restaurant that night. It's a pretty long list, but your name's on it."

MacGill started. "That proves nothing. Before the storm, mind, lots of people were there. Truck Thompson, for one."

Strong smiled agreeably. "A wild kid then. The cashier said he got gas that night. But you're more the kind wants to help someone. A woman with a little child, frightened and caught in a storm."

When MacGill looked down, Strong pursued. "And you with some empty beach cottages. Everyone gone because of the hurricane warning. Most natural thing in the world. You gave her a lift, put her up for the night free." Strong shook his head in admiration. "The good Samaritan."

MacGill stared at the floor.

"'Course, something unexpected coulda happened. We found the fabric from the cottages with the woman's bones. We got folks say it's the kinda bedspread the housekeeper used on the couches. Got the remains of a big old flashlight like the ones in each cottage." He sighed. "I been in touch with Allison Bullen's uncle. The bank just opened his wife's safety deposit box. She died a few days ago. Can you think of any reason Allison Bullen would've sent a post card that said she was staying at your place?"

He paused and MacGill sat silent, head again tilted forward. At last he looked away; his shoulders slumped. Then he shifted his body and slapped one thigh. "She was helpless, scared to death. I should've told someone. I meant to help her and the wee bairn."

Strong nodded sympathetically. "'Course you did. You probably never even knew her name." His voice grew more intense. "But the medical examiner thought that big flashlight was the murder weapon. A misunderstanding between you, maybe? You never meant to hurt her."

MacGill's head shot up and he drew in his breath.

"You panicked. You thought no one would understand. You put her body in the cistern. Bought the hotel a few months later. No one the wiser. No need to explain. Even when the skeleton was found, no one knew who she was, and the kid had a good home."

Strong raised his brows and shook his head. "Then after all these years. Rossi comes snooping around. He's about to find out. Your reputation's at stake."

MacGill's gray eyes widened and locked with Stong's. "No! Not a bit of it!"

Strong held up his hand. "We got your gun, we got your spade. They were wiped, but the fingerprint guys think the new laser process will bring out latent prints."

Again MacGill sagged in his chair. "I had a reason, mind."

"Sure you did," said the detective, his jaw firm.

MacGill looked up. "You don't understand. I didn't use any gun or do any digging." He brought his hand down hard on his knee for emphasis. "Years ago, when I left that woman at the cottage, she was fit as a flea. When the storm got worse, I came back to take her to the school house. She was gone. So was the bairn. Blood all over the floor. Bedding gone. I ran to the school for help, and there's my friend Marcia, full of herself, hugging that same little girl. Looked just like her own, everyone said, lost those twenty years. Marcia talked like the child was hers, brought back by the storm."

His eyes misted. "What was a body to think? She drove past us when I took the woman and child to the cottage. Maybe when Marcia got caught in the hurricane, her memories flooded back. She might've lost it. Saw the woman with a bairn she thought was hers." He pulled a handkerchief from his pocket and wiped his eyes. "Mind, I don't know that she did it. I thought she might've. What good to tell someone? The bairn's mother was surely dead."

"So you dropped the body in the cistern?"

The Scotsman sat up straight. "I never saw a body, as God's my witness."

When Strong finally let a shaken MacGill go, and the hotel owner had dragged himself through the door into the lounge, Marcia was waiting for him. When she took his arm and led him to a table, Brandy heard her say, "You look like you could use a drink, a strong one."

Brandy thought of the postcard Allison Bullen had mailed from Otter Creek, the one her uncle said his wife received in New York. "Lucky Mr. Grosmiller sent you that card," she murmured to Strong from her chair beside the screen.

He flashed a wicked grin. "Look at the record. I never said what she wrote in the postcard. I asked if there was any reason the dead woman would say she stayed at his cottage. Come down to it, M'am, the man couldn't find it."

Brandy glanced down at her notebook. "Clever little trick. Anyway, you've established a possible scenario, but I'm not convinced you've proved it yet. Never mind MacGill's gun. Remember, as yet no fingerprints. Almost anyone could've stolen it and hidden it in the basement."

She ticked off the other candidates. "You've got a jealous boyfriend who didn't want Cara identified. If she found her lost family, she would surely leave Cedar Key. Truck Thompson wasn't too young to be involved in Allison Bullen's death. We know as a younger man Thompson was rough on women. Maybe gave a pretty little woman a lift in the storm, and then thought she ought to return the favor. Maybe he got enraged when she wouldn't. He wouldn't be the first teenager to turn violent.

"You've also got a half-brother who has every reason not to want his half-sister and fellow heir discovered; and then there's the devoted foster mother who treated the baby like her own lost child. MacGill suggested her motive. Maybe she killed the mother in a psychotic state, and now she's trying to keep the grown child."

Strong stood and stretched his long arms. "Don't forget something, young lady—the perp's got to be connected to a drug ring." Frowning, he looked down at her. "Speculation's fun, right enough, but the captain wants evidence."

Brandy flipped back a few pages in her notebook and studied her scrawl. In a few minutes she brightened and looked up. "Something I'd written bothered me. I couldn't put my finger on it. I know what it is now." She snapped the covers shut. "I think I know who killed Rossi, but I can't prove it unless you help me."

Hands on his hips, the detective thrust his head forward. "And how do you know?"

"Rossi told us," she said.

CHAPTER 22

▼

Brandy's conference with the detective in the hotel sitting room took only a few minutes. Strong's first reaction to her plan was scathing. "What you mean, girl, Rossi told us who killed him? Rossi didn't tell us squat."

Undeterred, she picked up her notebook and spoke with deliberation. "I'm almost sure he did. I can prove it. If you cooperate, we can nail Rossi's killer tonight."

Strong hesitated, doubtful, and scratched the back of his head. He's trying to think of a way to let me down easy, Brandy thought. He knows I'm not worried enough about proper police procedure. She hurried on. "Say yes, and this evening will be the last time I meddle in either murder case. I promise." That statement garnered his attention. He dropped his hand and straightened up, watching her like a skeptic watches a magician and his hat.

"I swear," she said, "after tonight I'll disappear until your captain calls a press briefing. That's the next time you'll see me." When his eyes brightened at the prospect, she seized her advantage. "If my plan works, even if I'm wrong about Rossi's killer, you'll still bag the one who's guilty."

The detective visibly weakened. Brandy pressed on. "It can't do any harm to try. You didn't mind fooling MacGill. This won't be that dif-

ferent. Look, tonight you've got the perfect opportunity. All the suspects will be at the same table. Just listen. You're the main participant
in the scheme. It'll be a law enforcement operation."

Her promise to stay out of the Sheriff's Office business, she thought
afterward, and not her logic finally convinced him. For several minutes
Strong listened to the plan, raised a few half-hearted objections, and
then capitulated.

"I've got to make a call to Dixie County, you understand," he said at
last. "Got to have their cooperation, and at the last minute. Give me
two hours to get my ducks in a row."

She shook her head. "An hour and a half max. The Bullen dinner
won't last long. MacGill was whacked out after the grilling, but he'll
recover fast if he needs to. And remember, everyone's got to believe
you're going back to Bronson tonight."

The detective heaved a sigh and turned toward the door of the
lounge. "Better hustle, then. I missed my kid's Little League game last
Saturday, thanks to this case. I can say I'm not going to miss another
tonight." He gave her a rueful glance. "Even though I will."

Brandy remembered something Marcia had told her about her expe-
ditions in nature photography, something that would help Brandy's
scheme. "Before you leave town, I need to give you something you can
signal me with. I can get it from Cara."

While Strong left to find a secure phone, she rushed to call Cara
before she and Marcia left their house. "Cara, I haven't time to explain,
but I need the audio tape you and Marcia made of the Great Horned
Owl. Can you slip it to me before dinner?" Cara's puzzled tone implied
Brandy had finally gone around the bend, but she could deny Brandy
nothing. "I'll bring it," she said.

"Don't tell Marcia."

Brandy had still not seen MacGill. She would catch him or leave a
message. A half an hour later, Strong and Brandy watched the Bullen
party pull into the parking lot and enter the dining room to join Cara,
Marcia, and Truck. Two small tables had been pushed together for the

six members of the group. Mrs. Bullen had changed into a sleek, glittering bodice with an ankle length skirt. As Bullen pulled her chair out for her, Brandy heard him hiss, "You're overdressed. If we weren't staying at another hotel, I'd have you change. For God's sake, this isn't the Rainbow Room in New York." His wife glanced down, for the moment embarrassed.

He's stressed-out and neither is in their element, Brandy thought. Cara sat next to Blade and across from Marcia, Truck between Marcia and Mrs. Bullen, who was poised at one end of the table, opposite Mr. Bullen at the other. Soothing, bread baking smells wafted in from the kitchen and overlaid the tension in the air.

Current Wife had moved her chair as far as possible from the neighboring oyster man, whose idea of dinner clothes was a Windbreaker and a tee shirt. She stared with a puzzled expression at the life-sized, soft sculpture of a manatee and diver suspended in one corner of the room. Marcia sat with bowed head, folding and re-folding her napkin in her lap. Blade had turned up in a natty blue and ivory check sport coat with a red tie. When he arched his eyebrows and smiled down at his new-found half-sister, Truck's wide face settled into a look of sullen hostility. In the dusk beyond the closed-in verandah, the dry seed pods of the mimosa tree rattled against the screen.

After they were all settled, Brandy waited near the door while Strong strode into the dining room. When he approached the table, Cara introduced him to her father as the homicide detective on the Rossi case. Frank Bullen stood and shook hands.

"I'll brief you tomorrow, sir," Strong said. "I missed my son's last two little league games, and I don't aim to miss tonight's. Be back in the morning. The Rossi case is about to go down, and we may know something more on your..." His gaze traveled across to Current Wife. "On Allison Bullen's case in a few days. Waiting for tests. I'll keep you posted."

Nodding, Bullen seated himself again. He pursed his small mouth and picked up a menu. "We can't stay in Florida more than a day." He glanced out the window at the broken sidewalk and the old homes across the street. "This is hardly the place I would've chosen to rear a daughter. I want to make arrangements for a cremation and take my daughter back to New York."

Cara set a glass down and looked up quickly. "Nothing's quite settled yet," she said and then noticed Brandy.

Brandy slipped across the room and hovered beside Cara's chair. The young woman turned, reached into her pocketbook, and murmured, "I want to return this," and passed Brandy a padded envelope.

Bullen was sweeping on. "The Sheriff can reach me at my Manhattan office," he said to Strong. "I'll leave my card. After so many years, I don't expect a full resolution."

Strong cocked his head to one side and gave him a sorrowful glance. "Could be you're right. The Bible say 'That which is far off, and exceedingly deep, who can find it out?'"

But as he turned away from the mystified host, he winked at Brandy, and added in a low tone, "I've still got to find a secure phone, call the Dixie County guys."

"Don't leave town yet," Brandy whispered back. "I've got something to give you. I'll meet you outside." Strong gave her a decisive nod and disappeared through the lobby and into the gathering darkness of Second Street.

Cara waved to Brandy. "Please join us. None of this would be happening if you hadn't investigated." Her invitation had the sound of a plea. Cara looked again at her father and added, "We're talking about our plans."

Brandy didn't need to see Marcia's bleak expression or Truck's scowl to know how welcome she would be, and she already knew Frank Bullen's disdain for reporters. It was Cara who surprised her. Cara's somber eyes had lost the glow they had after their rescue in Suwannee. Perhaps the discoveries had all come about too rapidly, or perhaps John had been right, after all, and she had not helped, but had hurt Cara.

"I was just about to explain my career plans," Cara said, leaning toward Mr. Bullen. "I'm going to take some courses in photography at the University of Florida. Work toward a degree in Fine Arts. The University has a great program…"

Bullen gave her a slight, sad smile. "I'm afraid that's just a state school. You'll want a private arts college. Best in the world, right in New York." He bent toward Cara. "I hear you've had to work waiting tables and even cleaning hotel rooms." He shook his head. "I won't have any more of that." While he turned to consult Current Wife about the wine and the soft-shelled blue crab, Cara's cheeks flushed and she sat back, dark eyes troubled.

Next to her Blade lifted a highball and shot Brandy one of his appraising looks, lips tilted in a smile but the expression in his gray eyes flat. "Dad and I just missed sharing in the glory today," he said. "We would've found you two. My God, I was at that very marina this morning, getting my boat out."

"Would've been the first time you put that expensive rig to good use," his father muttered.

But Cara turned to Blade, eager. "You'll never know how hard Brandy and I tried to get your attention."

"Well, it turned out okay," Brandy said. "The Sheriff's people got the bad guys." She knelt beside Cara. "I won't join you, but I want to share some news." The strained table talk ceased. She felt sure everyone was listening. "Sergeant Strong just told me the marine patrol moved the houseboat to a pier near Old Town. Moose is dead. Shot. I guess someone higher up was afraid he'd talk. Or maybe he was trying his hand at blackmail."

Cara's lips tightened. "I won't pretend I'm sorry."

"The deputies didn't find the photograph you took at Shell Mound, though," Brandy added. "But someone else had been searching for it." Except for her voice and the rustle of the mimosa tree, the room was silent. She glanced around. "I know where that photograph is. I saw Moose hide it."

Cara drew back, frowning. "You don't mean to go there yourself!"

"For heaven's sake, Cara, child's play after what we've been through. Twinkle-tongue's arrested. Moose is dead. The pier's right off U.S. 19. There's always a lot of traffic. Anyway, I want to get my camera back."

"Are the deputies still there?"

"No, but look…" she held up Moose's key ring. "I've got a key. You're busy. I'll give you a call when I bring it back for the Sheriff's Office." She dropped the key in the pocket of her slacks.

When she rose, she was reasonably certain the rest of the table had overheard, but she had one more base to touch. All the suspects needed the same information. At the counter she leaned on her elbows and spoke to the hotel clerk. The woman's curiosity about Brandy and the Bullens should have reached fever pitch. She could be relied on to spread the news.

"I'll be gone for a couple of hours," Brandy said. "If my husband calls, say I've already gone to bed. I don't want to worry him. I haven't gone to my room yet, but tell Mr. MacGill I'll be late. I'm going back to the houseboat to get my camera and an important photograph Cara took. I don't want to be locked out of the hotel." She gave the clerk a Mona Lisa smile, tucked her notebook under her arm, and strolled to the door where Strong stood beside his car.

The air barely stirred. After the violent wind of the previous night, it now hung moist and heavy over the quiet street.

"You'll need a small tape recorder and this audio tape," she said to Strong. "Play it near the houseboat, so I'll know you and your guys are covering me. It'll sound natural. Probably at least one owl nests along the river there. I'll start on board when I hear it."

Strong stepped into his Ford Taurus. "I got a tape player in my kit. Use it sometimes for interviews. We'll nab the perp when he shows up. He'd be trespassing, for starters. You shouldn't need to get on the boat at all." He sat for a moment, shaking his head. "I must be out of mind, letting you try this."

"Not to worry. It'll be easy, but the suspect's got to believe I'm going to get the photograph."

After he drove down the street, Brandy started the rental car. Strong would need time to stake out the houseboat and her suspect time to exit the hotel, she pulled into the café across the street.

At a booth she re-read her notes, wolfed down a hamburger and a cup of coffee, and stalled for an hour. Before she left the table, she lifted her pencil flashlight out of her purse and thrust it into her pocket.

On the road again, Brandy drove down Second Street, rolled across the three bridges out of Cedar Key, and swung northeast. Between thin clouds a ghostly moon appeared and disappeared like a pale Cheshire cat. She took the shortest of three routes to Chiefland. Old Town on the north side of the Suwannee River was only a few miles farther. The whole trip should be about forty miles, even on back roads, less than an hour. She slowed, remembering again she must give Strong a chance to prepare.

CHAPTER 23

▼

Brandy and Cara had survived on pure adrenaline for two days. Brandy still felt energized. One last surge was all she needed, and she was confident. They had already outwitted two clods in two days. By comparison this scenario was easy. All she had to do was present herself on the houseboat, after she knew Strong and his men were ready, pretend to go for the picture, and leave the rest—as Jeremiah Strong would say—to the professionals. John wouldn't approve, of course, but this would be her last act in the case.

She picked up more traffic when she hit U.S. 19. After the lights of Fanning Spring vanished from her rear view mirror, she crossed the river, passed through tiny Old Town and curved west, then south on a sandy road that wound down to a deserted pier. Next to the wooden dock lay the shadowy bulk of the houseboat. A restaurant that once served riverside meals was shuttered, and no light shone from a trailer that sat under a canopy of trees by the shore. One dim bulb burned at the end of the pier. Across the water, the bank lay in utter darkness, and above her the wind sighed through cypress leaves.

Brandy waited for half an hour, her bravado leaching away with each minute. Where was Strong? She didn't see his sedan, but she knew how skillful these law enforcement officers were. They were all probably concealed in the trailer or vacant buildings, Strong's car hidden behind the scraggly row of scrub oaks. He might even be in the houseboat itself, where he would be closest if Brandy needed him.

For a few minutes longer she listened to a deep throated chorus of frogs. The hull's rubber fenders crunched against a piling, and from the bank came the rank odor of rotting water weeds. At last, when she had almost decided something had gone wrong, she heard the resonant five hoots of the great horned owl—hoo-hoo-oo, hoo, hoo-oo—fainter than she had expected, but distinct. She couldn't tell if the mournful sounds came from the houseboat or the riverbank, but they were the signal. Obviously their suspect had not yet arrived. With a deep breath, she slipped the key ring from her pocket. She recognized the swamp buggy key and the one to the boat's ignition. That left the key to the houseboat door. She padded down the dock to the houseboat's metal gate. Under her tennis shoes an aged board groaned. Slipping up the latch, she stepped aboard.

Again she waited. No sound now but the croaking of the frogs. She tried the key in the cabin door. At first it balked, then the lock clicked. Probably nothing will happen, she thought. Her suspect might not have swallowed the bait. Too smart. Either way, she won. If she found the murderer's picture, it wouldn't matter whether she lured her suspect aboard or not.

She sidled into the wheel house and into almost pitch blackness. Pulling her small flashlight from her pocket, she swung it around the room. The deputies had not straightened up the cabin since they last searched, or someone had come after them. Debris had been tossed everywhere—pots and pans on the galley floor, the compass wrenched loose from its housing, the sofa bed pulled out, cushions strewn across the floor. She hoped the wide strips of duct tape still covering part of the windows would blot out the glow from her flashlight. In a corner lay her Nikon, proof the ransacker wasn't hunting for valuables. Better not touch anything yet, she thought. The hard part will be waiting to spring the trap.

It was then that she heard a soft movement behind the closed pocket door. Someone breathing? A foot shuffled on the step. Her heart gave a giant leap. But it must be Detective Strong or a deputy, signaling again from the bedroom. Still, she held her breath. Don't look for the picture, she thought. Give the suspect plenty of time to come aboard. She crept to the window, peered out at the darkened pier. Silence. And then she heard the noise again behind her, a scratching. The door shifted and slowly rolled back. Instinctively, she backed into the hard, cold surface behind her, pressing her spine against the bow window. Surely Strong would identify himself now. Instead, a low, muffled voice came from the doorway, the words clear. "Get the picture. Now."

With trembling fingers Brandy flicked off the flashlight. From the pocket doorway another thin shaft of light probed the wheel house, inched toward her. Behind it a head emerged, encased in black knit. Nauseated with fear, knees weak, she clutched the back of a chair. A ski mask, of course. The figure's whole lithe body was sheathed in black, commando fashion. Now she saw the gun. The tone was sharp, urgent, as she had expected, but she'd thought the detective would hear it.

"You've got one minute to get the picture or you're wasted." She strained to hear Strong or the deputies and heard a shuffling noise on the pier.

"Strong!" she yelled. "Now!"

A squirrel leapt from the dock onto the boat railing, then bounded away. Silence again. A short ugly laugh from the doorway. The figure stooped, glided closer, leveling the gun, its barrel like a cannon. "Get the picture!"

If she found and gave over the picture, she would surely die. She could identify a murderer, one who had already killed at least twice. Her frantic gaze flitted from item to item, sorting, rejecting, at last seizing the one chance. She forced herself to speak. "I was mistaken." Her voice quivered. She tried to control it. "I looked when I got here. The picture isn't here."

The gun moved closer. "Maybe I won't shoot you." Again the hard laugh, razor-like. "Some deaths are worse than shooting. Old Moose kept lots of knives in the galley."

She could see the row of knives in a wall mount. The blades glinted in the narrow beam. "You win," she quavered. "You searched every place but the right one." She edged toward the galley. Her fingers touched the fire extinguisher. "Look at the brackets." Was that low, shaking voice hers? She wanted to dash for the deck, dive into the black water. But the tall figure blocked the only exit, still pinned her with its flashlight and its gun.

Her voice steadied. "I watched Moose through the door panel. Look carefully. He was clever. Right behind here, taped to the bracket. It's hard to see, but it's here." The ski mask head tilted. Eyes gleamed through the slits, following her fingers. "I've got to move the unit to the side." Her voice dropped to a whine. "Then you'll let me go?"

Another snort of laughter. "Sure." The gun didn't waver.

With a silent prayer, Brandy grasped the bottom of the red metal cylinder in one hand, lifted it up, grabbed the pin out with the other, and in one quick motion, aimed and mashed the lever. Liquid foam spurted in an arc. She heard a startled cry, heard the gun fall. "Shit!" a black gloved hand shot up to the eye holes.

But as Brandy spun to sprint across the room, the other gloved hand jerked the fire extinguisher from her fingers. She felt a crashing blow to the side of her head, felt herself crumple, then slam down on the hard floor. As the lights in her head went out, she was conscious, nearby, of an owl's plaintive call.

*   *   *   *

Brandy's eyes opened to a blinding glare. She had felt darkness and pain. Now she heard too much noise. For several seconds she could not think what had happened. If she had climbed down Satan's flank out of hell into the light, there shouldn't be so much noise. She was confused. Finding salvation from Dante's *Inferno* was Cara's task. As she closed her eyes again, she remembered someone had struck her. No one was hitting her now. Perhaps this was paradise, and the figure bending over her, an angel.

"Holy Jesus! What's her old man gonna say?"

Another voice, light years away. "You oughta called sooner, detective. Hell, we ain't got that many guys for back up."

Brandy opened her eyes again and looked into the dark, anguished face of Jeremiah Strong. "Your timing was off, M'am. You didn't give me time to round up the Dixie County deputies. You were supposed to wait for the owl tape."

"I guess the owl around here," she whispered," didn't know the plan."

While Strong was speaking, he peeled off his sport coat and tucked it under her head. "You okay? Stay flat and turn your head to one side. You got some blood up side your head, but we bandaged the cut, and your mouth is clear."

"The best laid plans o'mice and men," Brandy murmured. Another voice called out from the open door. "An ambulance's on the way, detective."

Brandy's head felt like it was pressed between steel plates, but she managed a faint cry, "Did the guy get away?"

The outside deputy again, "We're holding some dude in black. Caught him hiding under the pier." Angels, all right, Brandy thought, in uniform. All she could see were black shoes and olive green cuffs. She tried to focus. What was it she must remember? Something terribly important had brought her here.

"Duct tape," she said suddenly and tried to sit up. Her head exploded.

Strong spoke softly. "Just lay quiet, M'am. I figure you got a concussion. You're not making a heap of sense."

Brandy eased her head back onto his coat, but her mind had cleared. "Listen, Strong. It's important. The window is taped in strips on both sides. Pull the duct tape off on the inside." With exaggerated patience she formed the words. "The photograph, remember?"

Strong rose and spoke to someone near the front window. "Do like the lady says. She's got a good track record."

A sticky sound ripped across the glass. A more distant voice said, "Gal's right. An envelope's stuck under the tape."

All she could see was the bottom on the wheel console and a barometer that had fallen beside it. "Moose put something there before the hurricane. I saw him do it before I climbed aboard." She remembering kneeling among the wax myrtle while he plastered strips on an outside window before the storm, then lumbered into the wheel house, laid something against the glass inside, and covered it with more tape. She'd thought it odd at the time.

Everything was coming back to her now, except the last few minutes before she banged down on the floor. "The tape will be stuck to the envelope, but you can slit it open. The outside strips concealed it. Very bright for a guy with the brains of a bagel." She waited while Strong produced a pocket knife. There was a momentary silence. The deputies must know the importance of the photograph.

"Be damned," said the other voice.

Strong knelt again and put the slit envelope in Brandy's right hand. "You said you knew who shot Rossi and buried him. Now tell me, who's gonna be in this picture? I don't even know yet who the deputies got in the cruiser."

A challenge. In spite of her position on the cabin floor, Brandy prepared to enjoy herself. "Remember Rossi's list? The one you found in his pocket? Rossi wrote *'Hunt missing woman in cemetery.'* We didn't get the real meaning. An English teacher could explain."

In her mind's eye she could see her mother at the dining room table, correcting a stack of student themes. "We've been confusing a proper noun with a verb. *Hunt* is used here as a proper noun, a name."

She paused for breath. Strong frowned. Grammar had probably never been his forte. "*Hunt's* the name Rossi knew Blade Bullen by, we all did. The notation meant Rossi was going with Nathan Hunt to meet the missing woman in the cemetery, not to search for her body there.

"He left out punctuation and little words, like you do when you take notes. On the original there's likely a space or comma or dash between the words *Hunt* and *missing woman.* The item is the last one on his list. The last thing the poor guy did was go to the cemetery with the man he knew as *Hunt.*

Brandy tried to raise her head again and quickly decided against it. "I figure Blade persuaded Rossi he could produce the woman Rossi was looking for. He said as much to us all in the lounge that night. Probably told Rossi the woman wanted to meet in a quiet, deserted place, that she suggested the cemetery. It wouldn't surprise Rossi. He knew she might have a new identity, might not want anyone in Cedar Key to know her past. That's why he wanted as little publicity as possible."

Strong lowered himself into the captain's chair and shook a finger at her. "Take it easy, M'am. You're talking too much."

Brandy took a deep breath again. Her head throbbed, but she was far too excited to be quiet. "I'm sure Blade said he'd go with Rossi and take a gun for Rossi's own protection. The investigator didn't carry a weapon. Blade could've picked MacGill's gun up from the hotel desk. He was often behind the counter with the desk clerk. Remember, you found Rossi's broken glasses in the cemetery. Later he would've had no problem burying the gun in the basement, where it would surely be found, and planting the hotel spade at Truck's fish house. Both seemed to implicate MacGill."

Brandy pulled out the photograph and held it up for the detective. In the glow of a hurricane lamp they both recognized the pale, startled face of Blade Bullen, the spade handle in his hand. "Blade Bullen," she said, "sole heir to the Bullen fortune—unless Rossi produced a long-forgotten sister."

Strong stood and placed his big hands on his hips. "Blade Bullen, also drug runner and marijuana broker. The guy tried hard to stop you. Left a fake message at the hotel, telling you to come back to Gainesville. Later faxed your picture to his thugs in New York. Probably said you were a reporter or an under cover cop, fixing to expose their whole operation. Then he planned to zap you and Cara both this morning. Instead he got the blackmailer you call Moose. Moose and the guy at the marina were cogs in his marijuana wheel." He shook his head. "Tonight he must've left the dinner early and drove like thunder to get here first. Thought he'd finally get rid of you and the photograph."

Brandy tried to nod and immediately stopped. "Yeah, three routes to the main highway and he took the one that beat me."

Footsteps pounded up the pier. Someone entered the cabin and called out, "Medics are here with the stretcher."

Strong stood and held open the door. "Carry her to the emergency room in Gainesville."

Her blue eyes clouded. "You've cinched the case against Blade. But you still have to unravel the first murder." The detective rolled his eyes toward heaven.

Before the medics could reach her, Brandy grasped the leg of a chair and wobbled to her feet. "Don't need help," she said, and sank in a heap on the floor.

CHAPTER 24

▼

When Brandy awoke at last in broad daylight, she first saw a curtain on rings, hanging from a rolling metal stand. Still groggy, she realized she must be in the emergency room. Where was Strong? Never around when she needed him. She glanced about for her clothes, and then heard a heavy tread and a low voice speaking to a nurse. The woman pulled back the curtain. "Visitor."

Brandy looked up. "Have you called John?"

"Look, M'am," Strong said, formal again. "Lady here says you been held for observation, but you seem okay. They'll turn you loose on the world this morning."

Brandy grinned. "I see. No need for John to know the whole scenario, right? You'd rather I met him at the airport late this morning, just like we planned yesterday." She put a tentative hand on her bandaged head. "Could've had a nasty fall on the hotel stairs, being tired and all. My own fault, of course."

He shifted from one foot to the other. "Something like that."

She eased herself up on her pillow. "It could work. All anyone has to know is that you guys caught Rossi's killer at the houseboat. All my things are still in the car." She glanced up in appeal. "I'll make you a trade. I won't explain how all this happened if you do two more things for me. The first is easy. Have the rental car driven back to the airport. But there's another."

When Strong's eyes widened in alarm, she smiled.

"Like MacGill would say, don't get your knickers in a twist. I need to see some pictures, that's all. I've been lying here going over everything that happened. Blade was only about eleven and in New York when his stepmother was killed. That means he didn't kill Allison Bullen."

She chose her words with care. "I don't have my notebook, so I've been remembering things I heard yesterday and haven't had a chance to write down. Do you realize this whole case turns on images? The artist in Marcia and Cara would be pleased."

She ticked off the list on her fingers. "First I saw Allison Bullen's wedding portrait at the police station, and then Marcia's powerful hurricane scenes. They showed her both losing and finding a child. There were also her portraits of the little girls. I saw the photographs of the Island Hotel refugees after Hurricane Agnes. My photograph in the newspaper column turned up in New York. Last, Cara's picture of the murderer at Shell Mound was worth killing for."

She sat up straighter and tapped the sheet for emphasis. "Can the Sheriff's Office make enlargements?"

He nodded, his eyebrows up.

"Where's my purse?"

In silence he handed it to her from the drawer of a bedside stand. She pulled out her small notepad and pencil, scrawled a few lines, ripped out the page, and handed it to him. "I need to see these photos enlarged. There are only two. And I'd like to have my notebook. It's in the rental car. I want to look at the notes I took when I interviewed the Otter Creek cashier." She leaned forward, coppery hair falling in tangles over the top of the bandage. "If the pictures show what I think they will, and my notes say what I think they do, we'll also know who murdered Allison Bullen."

*   *   *   *

For Brandy the following weeks passed in slow motion. In the bureau news room she worked with one ear cocked for Strong's occasional call. She hadn't forgotten her ambition to be transferred downtown, but she had flubbed the Shell Mound ghost story, and now the Cedar Key crime features didn't seem as important as Cara's well-being. The detective did keep her posted. A few days after Blade's attack on Brandy, she was able to report his indictment for the murders of Moose and Anthony Rossi.

In the meantime, the two photographs Brandy had requested were enlarged, enhanced, and studied. Jeremiah Strong saw what Brandy predicted he would. Then a battered flashlight, preserved by the Sheriff's Office for nineteen years—ever since it was found in the hotel cistern—was dispatched to the FBI's fingerprint lab in Gainesville. Finally, when Brandy thought she could not endure another minute's wait, the results came back. A latent partial print on the metal handle had yielded to the laser.

Detective Jeremiah Strong made another arrest, his captain held a press briefing, and at last Brandy wrote the story of Allison Bullen's murder. She had kept her word to Strong.

On the mild January day that her feature blazed across every edition of the *Gainesville Tribune,* she folded the newspaper, shoved aside a stack of envelopes, catalogs, and books that were about to topple across the breakfast room table, and smiled at John over their grapefruit and English muffins.

"It's time to keep another promise." She stretched out her arm and patted his hand. "One I made in October, before I ever heard of Anthony Rossi and a missing woman. It's also time I gave an explanation to some friends in Cedar Key."

Later that morning Brandy's benefactor at Fowler's Bluff was surprised by her call. Brandy could picture the woman in her shapeless print dress, bending over the rotary phone, could remember her wide, pleasant mouth. "Yes," she told Brandy, she had a vacant cabin at the fish camp, yes, for the next weekend. Clearly she was relieved that Brandy and John would bring their own boat. She would probably not be eager to rent Brandy her skiff again.

*   *   *   *

When at last Brandy lounged beside John on the rear seat of their pontoon boat, Meg at her feet, she wondered why she had ever found the broad, sepia-colored Suwannee menacing. Tied to a post at the pier, their eighteen foot aluminum boat rose and fell with the current like a floating patio. On the opposite shore the bare limbs of tupelo and sweetgum spread under an umbrella of cypress.

John exuded contentment. On the grill at the bow lay the remains of a speckled trout picnic, and in the live well swam two Suwannee bass. Brandy opened her notebook and leaned across the small table, where Cara and Marcia were stuffing napkins and paper plates into a plastic bag. One smudged page of notes almost escaped onto the deck, but Brandy captured it and thrust it back helter skelter into the notebook. Without comment, John turned his eyes upward and shook his head.

MacGill moved to a swivel fishing chair beyond the live well. He drew on his pipe. "And how did you know, lass?"

Brandy smiled. "The simplest solution's usually the best. The scientific method teaches us that. The night I drove the Bullens to the motel in Cedar Key, Frank Bullen complained to me about Allison. Said she ran off to this desolate place and got herself bludgeoned to death in a cheap tourist cabin. Later it dawned on me. I hadn't told him how or where she was killed. Neither had Detective Strong.

"Then I remembered how he'd asked his housekeeper to spy on Allison. The woman was still sneaking around when I was there. The housekeeper said she'd reported Allison's plans to her husband, said once Bullen followed Allison to a party and forced her to come home. Did it make sense he'd ignore her running away? The housekeeper also told me he'd gone on a business trip about that time.

"I re-read the cashier's account. Allison was frightened when she got to Otter Creek. Why? She didn't know anyone in the area. I realized she must have been frightened of being followed. I'd seen the way Bullen controlled people, even his present wife. Maybe he made life intolerable for Allison. Maybe that's why she tried to slip away with friends, why she took to staying in her room. His first wife, Blade's mother, testified he was brutal, but no one believed her."

Cara gazed into the dark water. "And did he follow her?"

"A man like that's jealous. He had to be in complete charge of his wife at all times. He meant to bring her back. When he saw MacGill drive away with her and take her to a cabin…" She shrugged. "He probably jumped to the conclusion that she'd run away to another man. He said as much to me in the car that night."

The Scotsman knitted his brows. "For that, mind, I'm very sorry. God knows, I only meant to help her."

"Bullen would've been furious, anyway, when she refused to go home with him. He probably didn't intend to kill her. Something in that tightly controlled mind must've snapped. He was already insanely jealous of his young wife, and he couldn't stand that she wouldn't obey. When I saw Bullen with his new wife, I remembered Robert Browning's poem 'My Last Duchess.' It's about a wealthy man who murdered his wife because he couldn't control her. I began to think more seriously about Bullen as a suspect."

She stole a cautious look at Cara. "We think he put her body in the truck of his rental car. Probably thought he could dispose of it in the Gulf or bayou. Of course, the storm got worse and he couldn't. Old timers say you couldn't get near the water. When he came back for the child, she was gone. Later he heard she was safe at the school."

Cara rested her chin on her hand. "The better for me," she said.

"Cara knows now that Bullen didn't believe she was really his daughter. He didn't mind leaving her with a woman who wanted her so badly. He couldn't claim her, anyway, without casting suspicion on himself."

"I hope he was right about my real father," Cara said. Her tone turned ironic. "But don't worry. I won't try to find out."

Brandy gave her a wry look and went on. "Allison's aunt received her post card and thought Allison was safe in Cedar Key; they'd agreed not to communicate once she arrived, except in an emergency. Allison was afraid her husband would trace her."

Cara sighed. "Something warned me about Frank Bullen, even before you called. I wouldn't go to New York. I didn't like Mrs. Bullen's superior air. Or her suspicions about me." She glanced at Marcia with a half smile. "But mainly it was Bullen himself. He wanted to plan my whole future, and he practically called Cedar Key a hick town. He thought the hotel work Mr. MacGill gave me was demeaning. He even wanted to dictate what I wear. I saw how he bossed around his wife. I didn't know what control was until I met him."

Marcia frowned. "How can the Sheriff's Office prove he murdered his wife?"

Brandy patted her notebook. "Bullen was extradited from New York two days ago. The State's Attorney has a tight case. Frank Bullen's prints matched the partial on the flashlight. But other evidence pointed to Bullen even before that. An enlarged photograph shows him among the unknowns at the Island Hotel during the hurricane.

"After all, Bullen knew her bus schedule. It would've been simple to rent an unfamiliar car and be at Otter Creek when she got there. The cashier said she heard another car pull out right after MacGill's."

The Scotsman lowered his thick eyebrows in concentration. "If I follow you, lass, he parked behind the hotel like the others and took refuge in the lobby. When it came his turn to lay up sandbags in the basement, he discovered the cistern and dragged the poor woman's body down the back stairs."

The basement always horrified Cara, Brandy knew, and she shuddered, remembering the grim mouth of the cistern, hidden away in a separate room, the fetid smell of its water. But Cara's dark eyes had turned wistful. "You also asked for my mother's wedding portrait."

"The other vital enlargement," Brandy said. "I'd admired the elaborate ring Frank Bullen's present wife wore. Then I realized it looked familiar. It's a dead ringer for the one in Allison's wedding portrait. The insurance company verified that. It's also a dead ringer for the one the cashier described."

MacGill's lower lip came forward. "The murdering sod would splash money around to make a show, but he wouldn't part with an expensive piece of jewelry? You're saying he took it off his dead wife's hand?"

Brandy nodded. "Might've identified the skeleton. Years later he couldn't resist giving it to his new wife."

Marcia dropped her head. "Fact is, we might've known the truth sooner if I hadn't been so foolish. I kept the blue teddy bear all those years, in case I needed to produce it for Cara. Then when the time came, I hadn't the courage to let her go." Her expression turned fierce. "But that man actually meant to pay me for rearing her."

"Frank Bullen was not noted for sensitivity," Brandy said. "But there's even more to the case against him. It's surprising what an eleven-year old sees. Blade may have been a terror, but he was a bright terror. Early on, he figured out what had happened when his stepmother disappeared. Right after his father returned from his business trip, Blade noticed her ring suddenly turned up in his father's dresser drawer. The little cherub was accustomed to rifling through Bullen's things, looking for money.

"When his father asked him to check up on Anthony Rossi, Blade confronted him with the truth. Some friendly blackmail between son and father."

MacGill puffed on his pipe and a wisp of smoke drifted to starboard. "A canny lad, he was, always had an eye for the main chance."

"The housekeeper told me Bullen was disappointed in his son. Now Blade says his father threatened to cut him out of his will, said if Blade let Rossi rake the old murder case up, Blade wouldn't get a cent." Brandy frowned, remembering. "After the son killed poor Rossi, he tried to throw me off the scent, pretended to be my editor telling me to come back to Gainesville. In New York he set a drug dealer after me." She grinned. "Now he's trying to save his own skin by singing like a bird. His testimony should cinch the case."

Cara stood, picked up her tote bag, and stooped to give Meg a final pat. The cream-colored mask lifted beside Brandy's feet, then dropped between her paws with a soft "wuff."

Brandy watched Cara join her foster mother at the metal gate. "In a few months both cases will go to trial."

Cara nodded. "And in a few days I go to the University of Florida. I've got an interview in the Fine Arts Department. I'm also reporting to a Gainesville photography studio. Be taking yearbook pictures part time. The head photographer read about me in Brandy's story and thought I deserved a chance." She linked arms with Marcia. "Before that, Mother and I are going to relax, take a little trip across state to St. Augustine. Unlike Frank Bullen, we like historic places."

With a smile, Marcia turned to MacGill. "We've invited Angus to join us. He deserves a rest. Detective Strong gave him quite a scare."

"And Truck?"

"Truck will have to find someone more his type."

Cara knows her biological identity now, Brandy thought, had faced her terror of storms, had made Marcia understand she meant to live her own life. Perhaps Cara had indeed climbed out of her own private hell and found the simple salvation that had always been before her.

MacGill put out his pipe, tucked it in his pocket, and helped steady Marcia as she stepped off the gently rocking boat onto the dock.

"You'll probably get a lot of Bullen's money eventually," Brandy said. "He's your legal father."

Cara arched her neck. "I don't want anything of his."

Brandy leaned toward her. "Think of the money like this. It should've gone to your mother." She glanced again at her note pad. "According to Strong, we all should agree with the Bible. 'The Lord will abhor the bloody, deceitful man.'"

Cara nodded. "The lowest circle in hell, I remember, was for deceit."

As Marcia's station wagon rattled out into the road and headed for Cedar Key, Brandy laid her bulging notebook on the boat table, studied its frayed edges, and then gazed at her disheveled shirt and jeans. Another memory rankled. She turned her face up to John's. "I suppose Tiffany Moore was tidy."

He drew her against him and tucked her head under his chin. "Tidy and incompetent. True, most architects have a sense of order. But the saying is, opposites attract. You and Strong aren't the only ones who can quote. Do you remember the Robert Herrick poem? 'A sweet disorder' does 'more bewitch me than when Art is too precise in every part.' Somehow, I often think of that line."

She lifted her head and looked into teasing eyes.

"Miss Tiffany Moore wrote her finale with our firm," John said," when she decided to *improve* the blue prints after I'd signed off on them. I'd spent hours trying to drum a few fundamentals into that spacey intern's head."

Brandy closed her eyes and drifted with the river. "There's one thing I never figured out," she said, ruffling one of Meg's golden ears. "Why did Moose suddenly leave the houseboat the night of the hurricane? Cara and I saw him watching the mainland, and then he took the skiff and went ashore. It gave us a chance to get away."

Her gaze followed the opposite riverbank where a dark rim of trees curved toward Little Turkey Island.

"When the marina owner was captured, he explained why you two got away," John said. "Moose believed the cops had nailed him. He thought they were using a spot light to search for his boat. He saw it moving among the trees over on the mainland, a bright, round light. He went ashore to investigate. No one was there."

During the hurricane Brandy remembered asking Cara where the Shell mound ghost was when they needed her light. Maybe she had been there, after all.